Just desserts . . .

The demon's jaws opened wide. He bit off the head of the prisoner he carried in his left hand. His tongue, blue and as furry as the pelt on his back, forked out and cleared his broad lips of debris.

"Come down from there," he said as he chewed. He crooked the index finger of his free hand in the direction of the defiant one without apparent rancor.

The other prisoners huddled on the slope beneath the Preacher, awaiting an outcome that could only be disastrous for them.

The demon tossed away the nub of the prisoner he'd been eating. He burped a gout of blue-white flame as hot as the core of a star.

The jet of fire enveloped the defiant Preacher from knees to bald scalp—dimmed the reflected light of Phlegethon as it flashed through the opening—and glanced upward along the wall of basalt that glowed white and crumbled at the touch.

A thirty-ton chunk fell from the basalt dome, crushing the demon like a fly in a drop-forge. One hand projected from beneath the edge of the fallen rock. The fingers twitched spasmodically.

Mithridates looked from the prisoners stunned by the impact of the falling rock, to the cadre cringing in horror at the top of the ramp.

"Follow me!" he roared, once king and a leader again. He swept his arm toward the ramp and the exit beyond it. "We're getting out of here!"

EXPLORERS IN HELL

David Drake
and
Janet Morris

EXPLORERS IN HELL

This is a work of fiction. All the characters and events portrayed in this book are fictional, and any resemblance to real people or incidents is purely coincidental.

A Baen Books Original

Baen Publishing Enterprises
260 Fifth Avenue
New York, N.Y. 10001

First printing, July 1989

ISBN: 0-671-69813-3

Cover art by David Mattingly

Printed in the United States of America

Distributed by
SIMON & SCHUSTER
1230 Avenue of the Americas
New York, N.Y. 10020

I tell the tale that I was told:
Mithridates, he died old.
—A.E. Houseman

But he had died; and his status here in Hell—

"You fool!" Mithridates cried to the soldier, an Egyptian with a Garand rifle and a cheetah-skin helmet. "Do you know who you're pushing?"

The soldier answered with a vertical butt-stroke.

It was a clumsy blow, because the rifle was almost as long as the soldier using it was tall. Still, the Egyptian had thick wrists, broad shoulders, and a real enthusiasm for his task. The steel butt-cap raked up Mithridates' ribs and struck the left side of his face like a bomb going off.

Mithridates—King of Pontus; Conqueror of Asia; Liberator of Greece; Deputy Ruler of Hell itself—bounced back into the tailgate of the truck toward which he'd been herded. He could see—from his right eye—and his body could certainly still feel pain, but he was barely aware of soldiers' hands gripping him and tossing him into the back of the crowded vehicle as if he were one more sack of rice.

Bodies shifted beneath him. Voices cursed without enthusiasm, the voices of men who knew that having a body flung on top of them was the least of the torments they could expect in the near future.

They were the losers, men the Romans had rounded up from the palace on suspicion of involvement in the failed coup. . . .

Involvement in Mithridates' coup, which had failed.

The interior of the truck stank. The canvas covering was moldly; gasoline had spilled or was leaking back from the tanks in the cab; and the human cargo sweated fear. The tailgate slammed. Chains rattled as the safety hooks were forced into place.

Didn't want prisoners to fall out if the tailgate bounced open, after all.

"Sit the hell up!" somebody growled as he shoved at Mithridates with a cleated boot. Most of the prisoners were as apathetic as fish in a net, wide-eyed and gasping and hopeless.

"Here, steady," said a calmer voice, female, and a hand began to dab a wet cloth against his injured cheek. The truck lurched forward, throwing Mithridates against the tailgate again—but from the inside.

He must have closed his good eye when he hit the floor of the truck, on his back. He opened it now and stared at the ruins of his hopes.

They were pulling out, last of the line of trucks laden with prisoners. An armored car followed them. It ran on three large cleated tires and a fourth tire meant for a much smaller vehicle—but it ran, and the bronze-helmeted Roman glaring from the turret was obviously spoiling for an excuse to use his twin machineguns on a would-be escapee.

The guns might jam; this was Hell, after all.

But there was no real escape from Hell either.

Men, most of them soldiers of one sort or another, milled on the lawn of Augustus' palace. The building beyond looked immaculate, despite the black smoke trailing from several of the upstairs windows to merge with Hell's universally sullen sky.

Someone ran out the front door of the palace, between the pillars that looked so imposing unless you were close enough to see that the contractor had made them of stuccoed wood—and hadn't used a good grade of stucco. The man shouted at the departing convoy, but the truck rumbled too loudly for Mithridates to even guess at his words. He was a Roman soldier, a centurion judging from the fact that his helmet had a transverse crest and he wore his sword-sheath on his right side—

But he was waving the blade in the air, and Mithridates was sure that he recognized the man's face. It was the man who'd run beside him at the battle of Cabira, Mithridates' last chance of defeating the Romans and saving his kingdom from the systematic looting that would otherwise last as long as Rome ruled Pontus.

One of his own bodyguards, armed in Roman fashion, he'd thought as he spurred his horse toward the routed enemy. But he'd looked down as the centurion looked up at him—

And plunged his sword a hand's-breadth deep in the royal thigh.

The real guards had finished the fellow instantly,

but it was too late by then. He'd felt red-shot darkness squeeze the consciousness out of his skull, barely aware that he was slipping from his horse—and that the battle was slipping away when his men saw their leader fall.

Serpent magic had cured the wound in a matter of days, but flight and exile were all that remained in life for the monarch who'd frightened the Romans as no one before in their history.

Mithridates screamed over the muttered curses of his fellow exiles as the truck jounced them toward whatever doom Hell and the Romans had in store.

"Careful," said the female voice; but the truck lurched sideways into a hole that threw it like an axle breaking.

Mithridates' head bounced into one of the stanchions over which the canvas cover was stretched. Red light and darkness closed over his mind.

But through it glared the face of the centurion who'd failed—again—to finish off the enemy he'd died to stop.

Mithridates was dreaming of thunder as the sea crashed onto the coast during a winter storm. He opened his eyes, expecting to smell salt. He smelled sulphur instead.

Of course.

The convoy was driving down a gorge so narrow that the truck beds ticked the rocks, adding a sharper note to the echoing rumble of wheels and exhausts. There were streaks of dull red light on the walls, more like blotches of fungus than the irruptions of lava they probably were.

There was no other illumination. If the armored car still followed the convoy, it was blacked out or hidden by the frequent angles of the zig-zag descent.

Nothing about the present surroundings encouraged thoughts of escape, even if escape in Hell were possible.

Mithridates leaned over the tailgate and looked up, ignoring the warning of the woman who seemed to have attached herself to him. He could see out of both eyes, though clotted blood cracked in tendrils of fire along the nerves of his left cheek when he moved.

There was nothing to see, no matter how high he looked, except more patches of gummy rock breaking sullenly through the walls of the gorge.

He sat back, shocked despite himself.

The woman's arm encircled his shoulders and pulled him firmly away from the stanchion that had knocked him silly once already.

"That won't be necessary," Mithridates said in a calm voice. He'd been King of Kings—and very nearly King of Hell. But now . . .

"You took a bad knock," the woman said. "A couple of them." Though her grip loosened, he could feel the contact still when the truck lurched severely.

Mithridates squinted at her, though it was too dark to make out the woman's features beyond the fact that her hair was shorter than his own. Her arm was slender, though strong.

"I expected to be held under house arrest until things were sorted out," he said. "Given in charge to Romulus, perhaps, in one of the outlying fortresses."

He heard the greater bitterness in his voice as he

went on, "Or even to Pompey. Caesar knows *he'd* keep me close in the hope that if he did a good job, they'd let him crawl back into the power structure. But this . . ."

He stared into the darkness. The pain of failure was so overwhelming that he didn't attempt to massage the merely physical agony out of his face and battered ribs.

"You know where we're being taken, then?" the woman asked. For the first time, she spoke to him with something other than solicitude.

Mithridates didn't recognize her voice. He was certain that he'd never heard it before. So what was she doing in a truck loaded with supporters of his failed coup?

"Who are you, woman?" he demanded sharply.

He felt her shrug. "My name's Earhart," she explained without apparent rancor at his tone, "but call me AE. The Emperor of Xipangu sent me with a message for one of the big-wigs here, Mithridates. I'd just landed—"

"Landed?"

AE snorted. "If I can call it that," she said. "It was an autogyro, and when the wheels touched down on the back lawn of the palace, they fell off. Par for the course, here, I suppose. Better than par."

He'd sent couriers to Xipangu, asking for a troop of samurais to act as his personal bodyguard. He'd wanted men he could trust because they owed nothing to anyone else involved in the Mediterranean squabbles that had been Mithridates' life while he lived—and seemed destined to be his eternity, now that he was dead.

"What did the Emperor say, AE?" he asked, trying to keep from sounding too eager. If the samurais arrived unexpectedly, there was still a chance. A chance to get out of this immediate predicament, at any rate.

Her long leather coat rustled as she shrugged. "No idea," she said. "I was given a sealed dispatch case to deliver. Never been in this place—that place, I mean, the palace. So I walked in and asked somebody who was giving orders where I could find Mithridates."

She snorted, much as she'd done before describing her landing. "Not the right question, I'm afraid. They took the dispatches and hustled me into this truck just before they threw you in."

AE leaned forward, trying to get a look at his injuries. "Are you feeling better?" she asked. "I used to be a nurse. Not that there's much I could do for you, even if we could see. Not here."

"I'm Mithridates," he said. "I'm sorry that you've been dragged into this. And no, I don't know where we are, but I'm afraid I can guess."

Her body made another rustling shrug. "I'll listen," she said simply. The remainder of the truck's cargo seemed to have been jarred to sleep or to their own personal nightmares by the journey thus far.

"The Pentagram has certain secret holding facilities," Mithridates explained. He enunciated precisely, so that he could claim that the words didn't frighten him. "I was aware of this, of course . . . but even I wasn't certain of all the locations. That's because nobody comes back from them."

He paused, swallowing back the bile rising in his throat and threatening to choke him. Caesar couldn't have arranged this; wouldn't *want* to have arranged this. Perhaps the humiliation of being dragged in a formal triumph, followed by decapitation and the hideous agony of the Undertaker's slab. . . . But not this. This was forever.

Asmodaeus must have been very angry indeed.

Or Satan himself was.

Mithridates leaned out of the truck and screamed, "You're not done with me yet!" into the eternal night.

"Shut him the hell up, won't somebody?" a voice muttered in apathetic despair.

Mithridates sagged back.

AE touched his arm. "It's not your fault," she said. "Me being here, I mean. I just wanted to fly. I'd have done the same thing, even if I'd known what would happen when I landed."

Mithridates shook his head, too lost in the depths of his personal disaster to take in the details of what his companion was saying.

"I'd been trying to fly again ever since I got here," AE went on. "It never worked. . . . None of them ever got airborne for me. And then a man would say, 'Step aside, little lady . . . ,' and he'd get in the cockpit—"

"They *need* me in the Administration! Do they think Ramses is even *aware* of half the ongoing projects, much less on top of them? Without me . . ."

"—and go roaring off like a bird, his scarf flapping, and he'd turn and wave. Every time."

The tremor in her voice, the sudden rigidity of her hand on his arm, called Mithridates out of himself. "Pardon?" he said. "I'm sorry, I didn't catch—"

AE's muscles relaxed slightly. Her fingers squeezed his arm in a needless apology for the anger she'd allowed herself to show. "I was just saying," she explained, "that I'd never been able to get a plane airborne since I got here. Until the Emperor gave me the message to take to you. That little autogyro purred, simply purred, as we lifted off."

"You should have known when it worked for a change that something like this would happen on the other end," Mithridates said bitterly. He was going over and over again in his mind the way his coup had failed at the last instant, after he'd planned everything so carefully. . . .

"You don't understand," said AE. "It doesn't matter how things ended. I got to fly again, when I thought I never would."

She and the man who'd been King of Kings—but an exiled failure when he died—looked out at the starless, hopeless night.

And thought of how long "never" could be in the eternity of Hell.

There was light again when the truck grunted to a halt.

Paradise, pitiless and pure, glared down on a cosmos in which everything was foul and pitiable. The convoy was so deep below what passed for Hell's surface that the illumination was only a line as jagged as lightning between walls of black despair.

The truck's human cargo was too numb from the ride's hammering to look out, even when the tailgate screeched down.

"Off and on, you dog turds!" shouted a man in

field-gray coveralls and the cropped helmet of a Nazi paratrooper. He didn't expect a response, because even as he spoke his calloused hands were reaching for the ankles of the two exiles closest to the tailgate.

Mithridates and AE skidded out, onto a surface of basalt broken into chunks large enough to feel like all sharp angles. They staggered to their feet, hunched over from stiffness, and tried to stagger out of the way before the next pair landed on them.

The paratrooper was faster. Two Assyrian soldiers hurtled into the king and the woman, knocking them onto the jagged gravel again before they could get clear.

AE swore like a mule-driver, though under her breath.

"*Move* it, dog-turd!" said an American wearing the Smoky Bear hat of an American drill instructor. He kicked her feet out from under her.

The DI's boots and other leatherwork were a mildewed gray. He scowled to notice them when he glanced at AE. His left thumb rubbed his Sam Browne belt fiercely. The mildew flaked off, but the leather refused to take even a vague polish.

Mithridates helped his companion up. A scarred man wearing a white shirt with lace cuffs and throat gestured them languidly with his sword toward exiles gathered at the mouth of a cave, under the watchful eyes of more armed men. They stumbled in that direction.

Only three of the trucks in the convoy had come this far. Mithridates glanced at the men still being pushed and dragged out of the vehicles that had arrived earlier. He only vaguely recognized most of them. They'd been involved in the coup—most of them, at any rate—but calling them "plotters" would have been to overdignify them.

They were nothing but spear-carriers: Assyrian and Anatolian peasants whose job had been to guard a door or a cross-corridor. Men who were to keep their mouths shut and do exactly as they were told, while their betters accomplished the delicate business of changing a government by force.

Mithridates wasn't their superior any longer.

There were about a dozen guards—cadre—emptying the trucks. That meant the prisoners outnumbered them by at least ten to one, but there was no real risk of a riot now. The men being hauled from the trucks were beaten to jelly by the long ride, mentally as much as physically, and the guards had absolute moral ascendancy over them.

Mithridates looked around and drew himself straighter. His mouth twisted itself into a sneer of contempt.

A man in high boots and a soft gray uniform with STATE POLICE on his shoulder patches sauntered over to Mithridates and Earhart. He was slapping a cattle prod—the side, not the electrified tip—into the palm of his left hand.

It would jab out like a striking snake, Mithridates knew. He held himself very still, a king in soul if not in fact, and waited for the pain.

The state trooper reached out with his left hand and took AE's chin between his thumb and forefinger. "What's this we hev hyar?" he demanded of nobody in particular. "There hain't supposed to be any wimmen hyar."

"We've got what they send us, Dauphin," called the paratrooper as he tossed the last prisoner from the third truck. "Let's get them in the hole and be done with it."

"Wimmen hain't good fer anything but fuckin' en fuckin' up," said the state trooper. "And there hain't no fuckin' here."

"Not a lot left to fuck up, either, Dauphin," said the paratrooper. "Let's—"

AE spat in Dauphin's eye.

The trooper swung his cattle prod at the woman, but Mithridates caught him by the wrist.

"Watch it!" cried a soldier in spatter-camouflage fatigues near the mouth of the cave. He leveled the nozzle of his back-pack flamethrower at Mithridates and began squeezing the two-stage trigger.

The mouth of the cave was about twelve feet high. The blue-furred demon who strode out had to duck to keep from brushing the rock.

"Dauphin, what's going on here?" the demon boomed. The claws of his hands and feet, and the spiked collar around his dangling penis, sparked when they brushed the rocks. The man with the flamethrower jumped aside, obviously afraid that the demon would trample him into the gravel if he didn't move.

"Nothing, suh," said the trooper, jumping back and bracing instinctively to attention. "We-uh jist bringin in the nixt draft, is all."

"Then bring them in!" said the demon, turning back into the cave. A tail from which mange had stripped half the bristles waggled behind him.

"You heard the man!" ordered the paratrooper. "Let's *move* it, dog turds! Double-time!"

Mithridates, Earhart, and the other prisoners shuffled into the cave. They weren't capable of double-timing, but neither did the cadre have to prod them along.

Nobody wanted to see what would happen if the demon stepped out again.

There were three branchings immediately within the cave-mouth. The sound of tools on rock echoing down the central corridor was sharp enough to ring through the human screams.

"This way, this way," called a centurion at the branching, waving his vine-wood swagger stick down the middle way. "Move it up, dog turds. There's a lot of rock to shift before *you* next see daylight!"

He was a Roman. At this juncture, his nationality didn't make him especially hateful to Mithridates; and he *wasn't* the man from Cabira.

"This place doesn't look natural," commented AE. She raised her voice with each syllable as she found the background noise was much louder than it had seemed. It filled everything. . . .

The corridor dropped into a ramp, down into a huge excavation. The fitful lighting came from human bodies, writhing in cages as they burned.

"Come on, get your tools," said a naval petty officer wearing a striped shirt and his hair in a tarred pigtail. He stood behind a wooden counter; the alcove behind him, carved out of the basalt, was filled with rock-breaking tools and wicker baskets.

The Assyrian prisoner at the head of the line, just in front of Mithridates, grunted without comprehension as the sailor thrust the handle of a pick toward him. The sailor's lips pursed and he rammed the shaft into the Assyrian's stomach.

The load of prisoners had been out of the trucks and mobile long enough to have regained some of their spirit. The Assyrian reached over the counter and grabbed the petty officer by the throat.

What he might have done next was interrupted by the demon, who stepped past Mithridates and plucked the Assyrian from the ground with the thumb and forefinger of his right hand. The demon's claws crossed in front of the prisoner's Adam's apple, but the grip wasn't lethal.

Yet.

The demon leaned into the excavation. "Liszt!" he shouted. "Do you need a "—he slackened his grip on the Assyrian's throat. The man began to bleat in terror—"C below middle C?" the demon concluded.

The screaming paused. "Whatever your magnificence wishes, noble sir. I wouldn't dream of making suggestions to one of your supernal genius."

The demon stepped forward, carrying his prisoner with one hand and picking his pointed teeth with his left. The petty officer rubbed his own neck as he watched in fascination at what was about to happen.

Mithridates felt himself jostled from behind. He looked around and found that the whole draft of prisoners was pressing closer to get a good look at the fate of their fellow. The cadre watched with twisted smiles, making no attempt to push the prisoners back.

There were already a hundred or more workers in the excavation, hunched over their tools or weighted down by the baskets of rubble they carried toward an opening on the far side. They watched also; but their arms continued to move in almost a pantomime of working. Their eyes followed the demon to a keyboard in a niche near the entrance.

The man seated at the keyboard had white hair, wild eyes, and a cringing expression. He rubbed his hands in fear as the demon approached him.

A dozen naked men lay on their backs behind the keyboard, strapped to the bottom of a frame. Loops of their intestines were drawn up and over the top of the frame.

The demon held his prisoner up, choosing the location with care, and inserted the tip of a claw just beneath the man's sternum. He jerked his finger down sharply, opening the Assyrian like a trout on a flat stone.

"Oh," AE said, burying her head against Mithridates' shoulder. "Oh."

"One learns to expect these things here," he murmured to her in surprise.

She raised her eyes. "I spent the War," she said, "as a nurse's aide in a military hospital. I've seen horrors that bad and worse."

She paused. "I'm used to seeing pain. But I'll never get used to cruelty. God help me if I do."

The demon spread a place on the frame for the Assyrian; clamped the man's limbs; and drew out coils of intestine, yellow and purplish and slimed with blood.

The man began to scream as soon as the demon released his throat, but the victims already on the frame lay in panting silence beside him.

"Maestro," said the demon with a coy arch of his wrist. "The Mephisto Waltz, please."

Liszt bowed from his stool, turned to the keyboard, and began to play with exaggerated motions of his fingers. The loops of intestine quivered as hammers struck them. The men strapped to the instrument screamed in a ghastly parody of music—

And Liszt screamed also, for a coil of his own guts formed the upper register of his instrument.

The demon laughed, puffing out flashes of blue-white flame. He walked back up the ramp and past the prisoners who gulped as they squeezed aside.

"Take your tools, humans," the demon called over the screams in a bass trill. "Be good little workmen for your master."

Mithridates took the pick the Assyrian had refused.

AE snatched a mattock from the grinning petty officer. When she looked around her hesitantly, the state trooper gestured toward the excavation with his cattle prod and ordered, "Git down they-uh en dig, bitch. Thet's all they-uh is fer you fum now on."

The pick helve burned Mithridates' hands. He tried to put it down, but he couldn't get free of it. It stuck to him like tar, and it seared like burning sulphur.

At the bottom of the ramp, a man wearing the embroidered blue robe of a Chinese mandarin gestured with the hand that didn't hold a basket of broken rock. "Down here, noble sir," he called. "I'll show you what to do."

Mithridates and AE, at the head of a straggling line, walked down the ramp to the floor of the excavation. The cadre threatened and shoved, but for the most part the men behind the one-time king followed because they were used to following.

In the alcove about them, Liszt played and screamed with exultant enthusiasm.

"Good sir," said the Mandarin, bowing as they reached him. "I can see that you're a person of quality. And *madam*," he added, bowing again. "This is truly a surprise."

"My hands hurt," AE said. "This . . ." She twisted the mattock handle to which she stuck as Mithridates did the pick.

"Yes, one of the unpleasantnesses of this situation," the Mandarin said easily. "Just use them, please, madam. Dig. We can still talk."

Both of his listeners swung their tools at the rock beneath them. The blows were half-hearted—Mithridates chipped a handful of gravel from the refractory basalt, while the mattock's broader blade accomplished even less—but the pain in their hands lessened measurably. They looked up at the Mandarin in surprise.

"Yes," he said, shifting his own basket. "The same with me, I'm afraid. But one learns."

His slanted eyes narrowed. "But you're Mithridates, are you not, good sir? Late King of Kings?"

"I was," Mithridates agreed. He swung his pick again, because the pain returned with redoubled force when he stood idle. "My companion is AE, a person who flies. And you?"

The Mandarin shrugged gracefully.

"A dabbler in hidden knowledge at one time," he said. "More of the knowledge was hidden than I realized until too late. Since then, various other matters, until some . . . of my superiors decided I might be better out of their way. Here."

Mithridates looked around him. The prisoners who'd arrived with him—because of him—milled in confusion and growing pain. They were trying vainly to drop the tools that hurt them, but it hadn't occurred to any of them that work was the way out of their pain.

They were soldiers, after all.

"All of you, listen!" Mithridates called. His own palms were beginning to ache with the strain of not swinging his pick. "Dig!"

He suited his action to his words, bringing the tool around the down with a clang and another slight spit of gravel. AE set her mattock blade in a crack and levered at it experimentally.

"This is the way to stop the pain!" Mithridates went on, raising his pick again. "Dig!"

A few, then more, of the new draft began digging at the rock. They were obeying Mithridates rather than hopeful for the result—but it did work, well enough for Hell, and their fellows joined in. The sound of tools redoubled, and more dust filled the air.

"They would have figured it out in time, you know," said the Mandarin. "That sort aren't worth your concern."

He bent at the waist and began gingerly to toss bits of rock into his basket. He'd had long fingernails at one time. The nails were broken now, and the skin of his fingers was raw.

Mithridates drew his head back. "What do you mean, 'not worth my concern'? They're my retainers."

"*Why* are we digging here?" said AE in an obvious attempt to prevent trouble. "Is it just, you know, make-work because we're being punished?"

"Madam," said the Mandarin as he straightened, "I would answer you if I knew. It is said that everything here proceeds according to Satan's intent—"

"That's nonsense," interjected Mithridates, finding that he could lean for a moment on his pick helve without unbearable pain. "Nothing happens here according to *anyone's* intent. Not even his."

"Of course, noble sir," said the Mandarin, bowing in false obsequiousness. "But the intent remains nonetheless . . . and it is certain from what I have heard the guards say among themselves that there are other groups nearby, digging as we are . . . for Satan knows what reason."

"Or God," AE murmured.

"I suspect, madam," said the Mandarin, "that Satan hopes his adversary does *not* know what he's doing down here."

Mithridates struck at the rock. There was an art to it. You had to choose the angle where the point would strike as carefully as you aimed an arrow. The pick, though heavy and awkward, was capable of precision . . .

"The Greek gods I worshiped in youth were false to me," he said aloud. "There is no true lord but the Fire my forebears worshiped on the throne of Persia."

It struck Mithridates that disaster had at least brought him the benefit of companionship. He had no need to hide his plans or worry that those nearest to him were plotting his downfall. Being condemned without hope meant that he was also without fear.

"Speaking of fire," AE said, "what are . . . those?"

She gestured with her mattock at one of the baskets hanging on a chain from the twenty-foot ceiling. The pain on her face as she looked up wasn't because the tool urged her to greater efforts.

The men looked up also. The sex of the victim in even the nearest basket was doubtful, since all the hair had burned off and the body was black except where yellow flames wrapped it. It had probably been coated with tar before being ignited, but the fire continued fitfully long after both the tar and the body fats should have been consumed.

The body was still alive. Its mouth opened and closed—the lips had been burned off, along with the eyes and nose—and its charred hands brushed the metal cage as feebly as the flames licked its writhing body.

"Oh, those were early Christians who chose martyrdom," said the Mandarin as he resumed his desultory job of putting rubble in his basket. Presumably, when his load was complete, he'd carry it to the hole in the wall across the cavern and tip it in, the way other basket-carriers were doing. But as slowly as the Mandarin and the rest of the crew in the excavation worked, the job would take—

Mithridates froze at the thought. The job might take all eternity. That was within acceptable parameters.

"And they're *here*?" AE cried in the grip of an emotion as strong as that which drove her to spit in Dauphin's eye. "That's, that's—bestial!"

"Pardon, madam. I was too brief," explained the Mandarin as he shuffled forward in his stoop, scraping his load along behind him. "I don't mean those who accepted martyrdom. I mean those who *chose* it, when the authorities would just as soon have looked the other way. Surprisingly few people really *like* to torture and kill other people, you know."

He looked up at the cadre, gathered at the top of the ramp. The SS pioneer in spatter camouflage rubbed the nozzle of his flamethrower like a giant penis, hoping for the prisoners to rush up the gravel slope.

"Though there are always enough, of course," the Mandarin concluded.

"They *wanted* to be burned like that?" Mithridates asked in puzzlement. He thought he heard moans coming from the burning cage, but it must have been his imagination. Nothing so soft could have been heard over the sound of tools on rock—and Liszt at the keyboard.

"Yes," the Mandarin agreed, "though I don't suppose they realized precisely what they were wishing for."

He met Mithridates' eyes. "There's a lot of that here, you know. People getting what they said they wanted. What did *you* want, King of Kings?"

"Who are you to question me?" Mithridates retorted angrily. He began to chop at the irregular rock, squinting against the flakes of rock that his blows threw toward his eyes.

Though it was an easy enough question to answer. He'd wanted power, and he'd gotten it. The power to lose *everything* through a misjudgment so slight that he still didn't see how his coup could have failed and brought him . . . here.

Here.

Mithridates straightened and looked at the Mandarin. "I want to get out of here," he said in the same tone of flat certainty as he had the afternoon he'd ordered the massacre of eighty thousand Roman civilians. "Where does that opening lead?"

He nodded to the hole to which basket-carriers staggered to dump their burdens.

"To a glass-edged drop down to a river of fire," the Mandarin answered calmly. "The heat, even for the moment it takes to tip in the rubble, is a pain more intense than anything I've felt since the Undertaker was finished with me. There is no way out."

"There *is*," Mithridates said harshly, glaring around the black walls of the excavation. If he had to dig at a slant all the way to the surface, he *would* get out of this. In despite of Caesar, in despite of Asmodaeus—

In despite of Satan himself. He was Mithridates, King of—

"Brothers in torment!" called a cracked voice loud enough to echo throughout the excavation. "Sinners! Throw down your tools!"

Mithridates glanced around the excavation. Dust, bad light, and the echoes hid the speaker for a moment. A man stood at the hole into which baskets were emptied. He was silhouetted by the faint glow that reminded Mithridates that there was a river of fire below.

"Who's that?" AE asked, nudging the Mandarin to get his attention and nodding in the direction of the silhouetted man.

"Evil damned souls that we are, yet this evil we prepare is worse than our past sins by as much as those sins cringe beneath the loving purity of God, my brothers!"

The Mandarin shrugged. "John, I've heard, but that means little enough. He's called the Preacher here—down here. He does this occasionally."

The Mandarin's face lost its impassivity for a moment. "It makes a break of sorts, you see."

"We are *damned*, brothers in sin," cried the Preacher's cracked voice. "We are lost utterly and absolutely, without hope of redemption. But they *shall* not ask us to rouse the Old Serpent!"

"He's on the basket detail," the Mandarin went on, fingering his own burden and absently reaching for flakes of stone to add, slaking his pain for the moment. "It isn't good for some people. The fire beneath gets to their brains."

"We are sinners, but Satan is the greatest sinner of all, and it is his sin of pride that will destroy him and destroy us all, my brothers. Blast into smoke and memory—him and us and this Hell that was made for our sins!"

"Though from the way he talks sometimes about the sun glancing from the rocks of the Isle of Patmos," the Mandarin added, "it may be that the damage was done long before he came to be sent here."

"Throw *down* your tools, my brothers, because no torment of Hell can equal the torments of God's tears should we succeed in our mad enterprise!"

"The poor man," whispered AE. "There were so many like that. Especially the ones who'd been gassed . . ."

"Pipe down over there!" called one of the cadre from the entrance. His voice, unlike the Preacher's, was almost lost in the volume of the excavation. "Get back to your work!"

"In his pride and anger, Satan would loose that which he cannot control. Brothers in sin, brothers in degradation, we must no longer be fooled into thinking that the surcease we gain by working is not to be paid for with a terror and destruction worse than even the mad pride of Satan can imagine!"

"Pipe down!" called half a dozen of the cadre in unison. Their linked voices didn't have the authority of the Preacher's cracked demands.

The madman—the Preacher *must* be mad, though Mithridates found his eyes turning uneasily toward the rubble-strewn floor beneath his feet. What was it down there, the thing they were digging for?

But the madman blocked access to the disposal area. Other basket-carriers paused on the slope left in the rock as the diggers ground their way down. Usually the carriers staggered to the top of the ramp; dumped their loads; rested for a moment, out of the glare reflected from the river beneath; and trudged back down for more rock as the pain in the hands gripping their empty baskets became unbearable.

They were clumping now before the Preacher, like sheep huddled at the feet of their shepherd. On the floor of the excavation, some of the diggers had ceased work also.

The Preacher's voice was a whiplash, but its very harshness made the prodding ache of the tools endurable.

"He's never done *this* before," the Mandarin muttered. "How can he stand like that? The heat is agony, pure agony. . . ."

The Preacher wrung his hands together, gripping the handles of his empty basket. Mithridates knew from the burning throb in his own hands that the pain must be hideous, but the Preacher wore an expression of beatific joy.

"There is bliss immeasurable in resisting sin, my brothers!" the Preacher cried.

He was mad, but his words had power; hellish power in these depths of Hell. "God's eternal mercy has given us the chance not of forgiveness—for we have sunk too low to ever be forgiven—but of not sinking lower yet into punishment!"

Dauphin, the state trooper, had drawn the nickel-plated revolver from his holster. He crouched with his legs spread and both hands on the weapon's rosewood grips.

"Oh, no . . . ," AE whispered.

A long shot for a handgun, Mithridates thought. Certainly too far for compressed air to lob the flamethrower's dollops of blazing gasoline. The cadre wasn't armed to fight; only to brutalize. . . .

"Better that we should hurl ourselves into Phlegethon!" the Preacher cried, gesturing into the blazing hole behind him.

"His flesh should shrivel," whispered the Mandarin, staring at his own bleeding fingers. He rubbed them together, his eyes opening wider in speculation.

Dauphin pulled the trigger six times. The *tsk-clack!* of the revolver's lockwork was audible in a ghostly way, because none of the diggers' tools were striking the rock. Orange light glinted on the cylinder as it turned, turned again, again—rotating all the way around to its original position.

None of the cartridges fired when the hammer struck them.

"Lead us, Preacher!" someone shouted from the excavation floor.

The paratrooper and the fencing master took three strides together down the ramp to the excavation floor. A full-bearded Assyrian with the shoulders of an ox turned to face them, raising his mattock high. Half a dozen of his fellow prisoners stepped up beside him like a phalanx in close order.

The paratrooper looked at his scarred knuckles; the fencing master at the deliberately blunted edge of his weapon. Their eyes met and they backed quickly to the entrance level again, making sure that they stood behind the combat engineer pointing his flamethrower.

"But *far* better, brothers in sin, that we take ourselves out of this pit and through the caves into what will seem the green lands of Paradise compared to the devastation we would release by continuing on this mad path!"

"Dauphin!" thundered the blue-furred demon. "What's going on here?"

Even the Preacher fell silent for a moment while the trooper babbled to the demon scowling down at him. Dauphin's words were inaudible to the prisoners, but the glitter of the revolver as he waved it made his excuse obvious.

And obviously vain. The demon gripped Dauphin by the throat with one hand, lifted him, and with an artist's delicacy slit the state police uniform and the man's belly with a claw.

Dauphin was able to scream when the demon tossed him underhand in the direction of Liszt's keyboard, still holding a loop of intestine hooked on the point of his claw. The demon dropped the guts and sauntered down the ramp without bothering to clamp the trooper properly into the frame.

Dauphin bawled like an infant as he tried to stuff himself back into his torn body cavity. His guts jerked along the ground as he pulled them hand over hand, picking up grit and flakes of sharp rock.

The other members of the cadre looked at the victim—and looked away, watching the demon uneasily as he walked across the excavation toward the Preacher.

The Assyrian phalanx disintegrated as soon as the demon appeared. They'd been soldiers who'd prepared for death many times—and met death in the end, as even pacifists must. But the shambling, grinning demon was beyond the willingness of anyone to face, even the bravest or stupidest of men.

Mithridates turned slightly, offering to meet the demon's eyes from a distance . . . but the demon had another focus now.

"Even you, thing of evil and child of evil!" the Preacher cried against the backdrop of lambent Hell.

A prisoner with a pickaxe waited until the demon sauntered past him, then turned and planted his tool in the middle of the blue-furred back. The cavern rang as though he'd chopped at an anvil.

The demon reached back one of his gangling arms without bothering to look for his victim. His clawed fingers closed on the prisoner's shoulder and jerked him forward. The pick dropped to the floor, chipping the rock slightly.

That was more effect than it'd had on the demon.

"You cannot repent, thing of darkness," bawled the Preacher, pointing a long, bony finger at the demon who strolled toward him. "But self-interest alone should prevent you from aiding in this doomed enterprise. Come with us! Join us as we seek the mercy that can never be offered you!"

The demon's jaws opened wide. He bit off the head of the prisoner he carried in his left hand. His tongue, blue and as furry as the pelt on his back, forked out and cleared his broad lips of debris.

"Come down from there," he said as he chewed. He crooked the index finger of his free hand without apparent rancor.

Tall as the demon was, the Preacher loomed above him with the advantage of the ledge on which he stood. The clawed blue arms might *possibly* reach the Preacher's ankles. More likely, the demon would have to walk up the slope cut into the side of the excavation, just as the humans did with their loads of rubble.

The other basket-carriers huddled on the slope beneath the Preacher, awaiting an outcome that could only be disastrous for them.

The demon took another bite of the prisoner, like a shepherd boy munching on a scallion. The blue jaws could open amazingly wide. One of the prisoner's arms flopped to the ground as the shoulder to which it had been attached vanished into the demon's maw.

"Brothers in sin, creature of darkness! We have denied Satan. Now all that remains is for us to leave this place of greater damnation—"

The demon set his arms akimbo and began to laugh, drowning out even the Preacher's cracked ravings. The raucous bellows echoed from the curving walls and the rock ceiling vaulted high above, filling the chamber like bubbles in slime.

The Preacher waited in silence, glaring down into the demon's foul hilarity.

The demon tossed away the nub of the prisoner he'd been eating. He burped a gout of blue-white flame as hot as the core of a star.

The jet of fire enveloped the Preacher from knees to bald scalp—dimmed the reflected light of Phlegethon as it flashed through the opening—and glanced upward along the wall of basalt that glowed white and crumbled at the touch.

The Preacher's scrawny calves stood upright for a moment, sheared off at the angle at which the flame had spurted from the demon's mouth. Swirling flecks of carbon and calcium were all that remained of the parts of the body wrapped in the momentary blaze.

The right leg toppled over. The left continued to stand, mummified by the intense heat. The demon began to laugh.

A thirty-ton chunk fell from the basalt dome, crushing the demon like a fly in a drop-forge. One hand projected from beneath the edge of the fallen rock. The fingers twitched spasmodically.

Mithridates looked from the prisoners stunned by the impact of the falling rock to the cadre cringing in horror at the top of the ramp.

"Follow me!" he roared, once king and a leader again. He swept his arm toward the ramp and the exit beyond it. "We're getting out of here!"

As he strode for the ramp, his silken trousers flapping at his ankles, Mithridates didn't have time to be surprised that AE was the first of his fellow prisoners to fall in step with him. The woman was quicker on the uptake than the heavy-muscled peasants, swinging tools as they once had swung swords—

And she was at least as brave.

Prisoners fell in behind them, drawn as much by the movement as by the orders he'd shouted. The Mandarin looked at Mithridates, then up at the head of the ramp where the cadre bunched together like sheep behind the bellwether.

The SS pioneer was at the head of the group, kneeling behind his flamethrower.

The Mandarin stepped aside, letting ex-soldiers rush past him in the mad hope of becoming ex-prisoners.

"Look, we can drop them now," said AE; and did, tossing aside her mattock to clang and dance as it hit the ground.

Mithridates' hands didn't throb as they had, even when he stood transfixed by the Preacher's voice. Whoever the man was, he'd had a power over his listeners.

Enough power to damn himself to Hell, at any rate. If Mithridates had still been in the Administration, he'd have checked to see where the fellow was reassigned.

But for now—

"Get back!" shouted the guard with the flamethrower.

The state trooper, Dauphin, was crawling toward the group of his fellows. He was trying to keep his intestines in with his left hand as he crept forward on the other three limbs, but the tear in his belly was too long. Loops slipped out above and below his hand, tangling with his knees.

Mithridates dropped his tool. The muzzle of the flamethrower was only twenty feet up the slope from his chest now. The pick would have made a dangerous weapon under the proper circumstances, but it was useless here. He'd win not by some physical act, but rather by regal majesty—

Such as remained in this hidden basement of Hell.

"One more step and I'll crisp the lot of you!" the pioneer shouted. "Nothing's different for you, dog turds!"

But a great deal was different for the cadre. They were terrified: by what had happened to Dauphin; by what had happened to the demon . . . and by what might happen to them, now that things were changing in a place where nothing changed for the better.

Mithridates waved the woman back with a quick flick of his hand. This was for him to handle alone, using his personal authority.

"It's over for you," he said forcefully, taking a step forward—though a short one. "Put that down. The Flame is my god. The Flame will stand by me."

Mithridates stepped closer, remembering the sounds at Cabira—rending metal and the screams of horses dying.

The guard looked beyond the ex-king to the dark mass of prisoners, hulking and lethal. He turned his head away, as if his mind were separate in intention from the nozzle in his hands.

"Pollux, let's go!" cried another member of the cadre in sudden panic—spinning on the heel of one hobnailed boot, headed for the exit.

The pioneer squeezed the double triggers of his weapon.

The hose connection separated from the fuel bottle. Black napalm squirmed out like a beast-catcher's lasso.

A pool of orange flame exploded, engulfing the group around the flamethrower.

Mithridates leaped back, startled by the flash and slap of heat. Members of the cadre bolted in all directions, like ants from a stirred-up nest. In the center of where they'd bunched, the pioneer was dancing in a growing rope of flame that stripped his clothes and flesh as he screamed vainly.

"Get 'em!" cried an Assyrian, lunging past Mithridates. He'd kept his shovel and used its broad blade as a spear by thrusting under the rib cage of the fencing master, who stumbled in his direction. He pitched his victim sideways off the ramp; certainly a mercy, since the guard's face was melting in its wrapper of napalm.

Like a wedge bursting a hostile shield-wall, the released prisoners swept past the king—and the woman—who'd led them to that point. The cadre provided no opposition. Most of the one-time guards were afire, and they'd always governed the prisoners by moral superiority rather than direct force.

When their pretense of superiority vanished, there

was nothing left to oppose the picks and bloodlust of the men they'd dominated.

The flames themselves should have slowed the onrush, but the leading prisoners ignored the pools of gasoline. After the first scores of booted feet had tramped through and scattered the napalm, there was nothing left but smoky trails on the rock—

And sputtering flames to mark the mangled bodies of the guards.

Liszt continued to play. Mithridates glanced at the keyboard; but there was nothing he could do for the men there, and they were no responsibility of his.

The ex-prisoners, by virtue of the fact they had followed his lead, *were* his royal responsibility now. He hadn't the faintest notion of what he could do for them—or for himself.

"Did you know that was going to happen?" someone asked, AE asked, from beside him. "Can you really control fire?"

The woman was so tall that when he turned, their eyes were on a level. For a moment Mithridates considered alternatives: boastful agreement; regal disdain for a personal question asked by a commoner—and a female besides; or—

"In life, my god never offered me such a sign of approval," he said. "None of my gods. Here—well, prayer fails even more often than tools do, weapons . . ."

He glanced across the excavation at the Preacher's legs. Both had fallen over. "What I thought," he said, "was that I could face them down, the guards."

"You almost did."

"Yes. And I almost became Ruler of Hell."

The Mandarin was approaching with a bland smile. His arms were crossed, and his hands were tucked into the opposite sleeves to hide their injuries. Mithridates gave him a wintry smile, though he'd been an old man himself before he decided that it was a king's business to *lead* his armies.

"Have you decided what you will do now, noble sir?" asked the Mandarin with a hint of superiority in his voice.

His careful gaze around the milling prisoners was a gesture of its own.

"Of course," Mithridates said. "We'll go back up the canyon the way we were brought here."

He knew that was a hopeless plan; but he knew also that by stating it with assurance, he prevented the Mandarin from turning his special knowledge into control of the situation.

For the Mandarin obviously *had* special knowledge.

The regal certainty took the Mandarin aback, as it was intended to do. "Why, surely, noble sir," he protested, "you realize that there will be more convoys coming this way before we could possibly reach the surface. Even if an alarm hasn't already summoned an armed force that will restore us to captivity."

AE looked from one man to the other. Her eyes were noticeably cooler when they rested on the Mandarin.

Mithridates shrugged, as if he hadn't come to the same conclusion about the only escape route he could imagine. "Alarms don't work here," he said in idle disregard. "And as for more prisoners—we'll take over all the convoys we meet. We'll *ride* back with a real army."

It would be impossible to turn trucks around between the walls of rock, and Bellerophon himself couldn't edge the vehicles up the narrow switchbacks with their steerable axles in back.

Mithridates turned as if to call an order to his milling "army." He glanced over his shoulder at the stricken Easterner. "Why?" he asked. "Do you have another idea?"

"Indeed, noble sir," the Mandarin gasped in relief. "To put ourselves under the protection of the mighty Zahhaq, whom we can reach through the caves themselves. I . . . have had the honor to present myself to the magnificent Zahhaq several times in the past, and I've been impressed each time by his nobility and the splendor in which he keeps his retainers."

"You've been *here* before?" AE demanded sharply. "And escaped?"

"Madam, I misspoke," the Mandarin said with a deep bow. The flash of fear that marred his impassive visage proved that he had misspoken indeed. . . .

"It was because of my endeavors on behalf of Zahhaq—and on the behalf of other unfortunates whom I led to his protection—that I was imprisoned here myself," he continued, calm again. "Personages as high as Satan himself fear Zahhaq and his ability to protect the weak from their oppressors."

"He's a god?" Mithridates pressed. "Imprisoned here by other gods?"

"He is . . ." the Mandarin said, pausing to look over his shoulder. The claws of his fear tore momentarily at his placid expression. "Zahhaq is, I think, a man, noble sir. but here"— he shrugged—"labels matter little. He can protect you, as he's protected others. And I can lead you to his palace through these caves."

An Assyrian—Mithridates recognized the man by his bloody shovel, though he didn't know the fellow's name—shouldered the Mandarin aside, then braced to attention facing Mithridates.

"Sir!" he said in the clipped shout of a veteran non-com. "Section Leader Kalhu reporting for orders!" He wore a scar that traced its way from his forehead to his chin, where it appeared as a white streak in the full beard.

"Fall the men in, Section Leader," Mithridates ordered crisply. "We'll be leaving at once, through the caves." He nodded toward the Mandarin. "We have a local guide."

Kalhu saluted. "Very good, sir!" he said in obvious relief that he had somebody to give him orders again.

"I'll lead, then, noble sir," the Mandarin said. He too was relieved. "I'm glad that—"

"Column of fours, you misbegotton whoresons!" Kalhu bawled. "Get your thumbs out of your butts and fall in!"

"With your permission, noble sir," said the Mandarin after an instant of lost composure. He bowed, then scurried to the head of the column forming at the entrance.

AE watched in mild amazement at the speed with which the freed prisoners did the thing old soldiers know best how to do—form lines and wait for further orders. She glanced at Mithridates. "Do you trust him?" she said quietly, though the Mandarin was well out of earshot.

"The Easterner?" Mithridates replied. How many times had the King of Pontus ordered an army to fall in? And how many of the men who'd obeyed his orders had lived to fall in the next time?

"Of course not," he said. "But—"

He met the woman's eyes squarely. "Asmodaeus was very angry when he sent me here. Now that . . . this has happened . . . Satan himself will be equally angry. I don't know what the Mandarin has planned, but I'm sure that it can't be as bad as what we'll find if we wait for Satan to react."

He grinned coldly to rob his next words of the cold truth they stated. "Besides, I was always one to take a chance."

"Sir! Section ready!"

"Then move them out, Section Leader!"

Whatever it really was, Mithridates thought as he watched the column step off on its right foot—a trifle ragged, but they were a scratch formation; they'd settle in . . .

Whatever it really was, it felt like escape at the moment.

For the first mile—

Perhaps a mile. Distances in Hell were deceptive when they weren't utterly false, and this Underworld of the Underworld was certainly no more regular than the higher levels.

For the first perhaps-a-mile, the column straggled along in what would have passed for a natural cave—though Mithridates had never in life seen a cave through stone as refractory as basalt. Kalhu or one of the other leaders had thought to make torches of rags dipped in napalm and carried on the heads of picks.

At the end of the column, the only guide was the stomach-wrenching odor of gasoline, naphtha, and the soap used to jelly the mixture. Mithridates and AE closed the line, urging on stragglers because there was no one else to do the job.

There were no chasms, nor did the rock suddenly narrow into a wormhole through which a man fit with difficulty. Even so, many men found it terrifying to march through absolute darkness; and here, in the bowels of Hell, terror was the logical response to *any* event.

AE's soothing voice and obvious concern got more of the frozen stragglers moving again than did the king's crisp orders; but Mithridates had to slap one burly mattock-wielder and drag him a few steps blubbering before the soldier was able to continue the rest of the way on his own.

Before long, even the smell of the torches vanished. Men gripped the belts of the men ahead of them, stumbling and cursing and increasingly frightened. "I wonder how Kalhu and the Mandarin are managing," said AE, voicing the question that Mithridates had already formed in his mind.

He grimaced, peering vainly into the darkness—

And realized with a wrench of his guts that he could see the men ahead of him waving against a dim ambiance. There was light again. Of a sort.

"I'm going forward to talk with the Mandarin," said Mithridates in a carefully emotionless voice. "Can you handle things here?"

He wasn't sure how the woman had become his

second-in-command. But then, he wasn't sure how he'd come to lead this assemblage of victims himself. . . . Someone had to do it, he supposed.

"Hey! I can see!" bawled a soldier whose Anatolian accent was thickened by relief.

"Yes, of course," she agreed with a nod. Her hair was in tight waves, but the bangs over her forehead bobbed to emphasize the gesture.

"Pass me through," Mithridates ordered, putting his hand on the biceps of the man immediately in front of him before stepping by. "Pass me through," he repeated as he gripped the next bearded Assyrian firmly, watching for the swing of the pickaxe on the fellow's shoulder.

He continued up the line in the same fashion, moving in stages like an inchworm instead of jogging through the men at the rate his worry wanted to drive him.

Racing ahead would be fatal. Hell's equivalent of fatal, at any rate: the excruciating pain of the Undertaker's slab, followed by whatever Satan thought was a proper response to the events that had just transpired in the excavation.

The armed soldiers were a lot like mules. They couldn't see out of the back of their heads. Anything from behind which seemed to be—*could* be—a threat or a challenge was likely to be battered into the middle of next week. By telling each man what was happening, rather than rushing up as a bump and a glimpse in the corner of the eye, Mithridates made sure that he'd be treated as the leader instead of an attacker.

There had been leaders who would have signed

their own death warrants had they appeared in the middle of their troops; but not Mithridates, King of Kings. Even in his last days, the troops who'd mutinied against his orders would rather have taken him alive than killed him. . . .

"Sir, where's the light coming from?" somebody called from behind the king. He ignored the question, since he had neither time nor an answer.

The illumination came from flecks of light in the walls; quivering, shimmering glows of short duration and uncertain color. Sometimes they arrowed past the straggling line, headed in the direction of travel.

The walls weren't normal rock any more.

Now they had translucent depth. To sight alone, there was nothing material between the men and eternity. Those who stretched out an arm to the side felt something cold and enveloping—pressure rather than contact.

They didn't reach out again. The invisible walls drew the line straighter than it had been when spreading out meant your head or elbow clipped the basalt.

An ex-prisoner further up the line—a stranger in a ragged blue uniform, not one of the men who'd been arrested at the coup's failure—heard the question and turned. "Yeah, what's going on now? Sir?"

There was challenge in the man's attitude—but it came from nervousness, not real anger. Still, a panicked army could stampede faster than a herd of cows.

"Steady on," Mithridates said, patting the questioner reassuringly and drawing him back into motion as his leader stepped past. "I'll learn precisely what's going on in a moment. For now, I'm just thankful that *my* guts aren't being stretched to the ceiling."

"Um!" the man grunted in agreement.

"Pass me through," the king said calmly to the next man in line.

It was good that the men were nervous and needed reassurance. If it hadn't been for that, Mithridates knew that his own body would be tense and shuddering uncontrollably. But a king couldn't be frightened in front of his subjects.

Mithridates was a king again.

He felt his stride lengthening as he neared the front of the line. It was as if he were on a horse striding downhill, though he wasn't passing other escapees any faster than before and the gaps between men weren't growing wider.

The ex-prisoners marched onward with worried glances to either side. They didn't let their eyes catch those of their fellows. Subconsciously everyone was sure that the column was on the edge of panic which would surely occur if individuals let their fears build on those of the men around them.

And there was nowhere to run in panic. Probably not even back, to the excavation and its endless round of pain, because the lighted passage they were in was no longer a cave. The walls were *of* light, now; bright, glowing rings of mauve and magenta and chartreuse separated by bands of shadow in whose blankness lurked faces.

The only direction was forward. They were falling down a well that only *seemed* to be horizontal.

They should have been warned.

The Mandarin should have warned him.

"Mandarin!" Mithridates snarled as he saw the blue silk robe shimmering in the tunnel's light at the front of the column.

Kalhu was a step behind and a step to the right, carrying his bloody shovel at port arms and ready for anything that came through the pastel ambiance.

"Mandarin, damn you! S—" "*Stop,*" Mithridates meant to say, but he wasn't sure they could stop or that they wanted to, not here in this light-wrapped no-place.

"Explain yourself!" he demanded instead as the bland Chinese face turned to meet his angry glare.

"There is no need for concern, noble sir," the Mandarin said. There may have been an undertone of superiority in the first syllables, but that melted into obsequiousness when his Chinese eyes caught the way Kalhu was measuring him for a shovel-stroke at the king's slightest hint.

The men stepped along together, legs flexing forward and back; but they were dust-motes in a windstorm, their motion wholly controlled by the unseen current that whirled them onward. The bands of pastel light snapped by so quickly now that they merged, blurring into a dirty olive color like that worn on the military uniforms of so many of the New Dead.

There was no lack of soldiers in Hell.

"How are we moving?" Mithridates said. "Where is it that we're being taken?"

"We are on the way to Zahhaq," the Mandarin replied, bowing slightly toward the king in token of subordination. "We will come to no harm, noble sir.

My presence with you is proof of my faithfulness to your interests."

He bowed again. The walls of sickly, saturated light raced by.

"But *how* is it happening?" Kalhu interjected suddenly. The stiffness of the squat soldier's voice was proof that he was keeping himself from panic only by iron control.

The Mandarin felt safe enough to give him a sardonic nod. "I cannot tell you the mechanism, soldier," he said. "Only that it is safe. We will reach a way station soon—the same, no matter from which direction we arrive. And then we will go on to Zahhaq."

Mithridates stared at the Easterner. He felt that he was viewing a figure painted on a thousand transparent layers. The visible surface certainly wasn't the reality . . . but what was beneath if you peeled the top off was no more real than what had covered it.

Each layer glittered with knowledge, intelligence, and truth of a sort . . . a limited sort. But when you got to the bottom of the Mandarin's personality, there would be nothing at all.

Men who had no bottom were useful. They could always be swayed to the will of a Mithridates—or a Caesar: those whose certainty of purpose and emotion anchored them against the tides of fate.

Empty men were very dangerous as well.

"Section Leader Kalhu," Mithridates said, the decision waiting until the words announcing it were on their way off his tongue. "You will proceed to the end of the column, telling each of the men that the situation is under control and that we will shortly be arriving at a way station."

The Mandarin had said nothing about *when* they'd arrive. "Understood?"

"Yes sir," Kalhu said crisply.

Mithridates gripped the Assyrian's shoulder. "I'm depending on you, Section Leader," he said calmly. "We'll regroup when we bivouac at the way station."

"Yes *sir*!"

Kalhu marched back down the column, swaggering with the king's confidence in him. The section leader's cheerful arrogance was the best tonic the men could possibly be offered. His attitude was much more important than *what* he was saying to them as he clapped their shoulders and thumbed them onward.

The Assyrian's body wavered as his legs drove him against the current. All Kalhu's stocky strength sufficed only to hold him steady against the rush of events driving onward.

Mithridates thought of the woman at the end of the column, comforting stragglers in the darkness that preceded this light-bounded fury. Then he looked at the Mandarin and smiled.

Mithridates had been raised to believe that a king did not himself carry the weapons of war. He'd trained himself away from that exalted pinnacle when he learned that warriors better obeyed a leader who *led* them; but for the moment, he was unarmed.

If the Mandarin had played them false, Mithridates would throttle him bare-handed.

The feel of the ground underfoot changed before Mithridates noticed that in the distance there was light *in* the tunnel rather than simply of the tunnel.

His boots were scuffing on rock again; and someone waved a lantern to guide the column as the walls flickered down to the blank darkness of unlit stone.

"Halloo the tunnel!" echoed a voice. "Who goes there?"

"Let me handle this," the Mandarin murmured with another quick bow to Mithridates.

The Mandarin trotted ahead before the king could stop him. The blue robe of honor hid his shuffling feet and gave him the look of a toy drawn forward swiftly on a string.

Mithridates followed, taking full strides but not trying to catch the Easterner. That would be undignified.

There was a metallic sound from down the tunnel; a gunlock, or perhaps a ballista, being cranked to full cock. The king paused, raising a hand to halt the column behind him.

"I am known to your masters," the Mandarin was saying to the blotch of lantern light. His hands were hidden within the opposite sleeves. "I have the honor on this occasion to guide the noble Mithridates and some two hundred of his servants."

The lantern wobbled closer, illuminating the silk-and-metal threads of the Mandarin's garments and the horse-faced man who'd challenged them. The guard wore a drab uniform with puttees and carried a long bolt-action rifle in his right hand.

He nodded to the Mandarin and stepped aside. "Reckon you'll do," he said. "Let 'em pass, boys."

The Mandarin bowed to him, then waited while the king and the remainder of the column strode up.

A metal-shod door, strapped to the cave wall with

hinges suitable for the gates of a fortress, creaked open. Beyond was a ten-man squad, outfitted like the first guard—and a plaza open to the gloomy red sky of Hell.

They'd made it. They were free again.

Free to walk the surface of Hell, at any rate.

"Where will we find Sir John?" the Mandarin asked the tow-haired youth marked as an officer by the fact he carried a holstered revolver instead of a rifle.

"He'll be in the Mess with Paullus and General Burnside at this hour, sir," the officer replied. He started to gesture, but the Mandarin was already looking toward the low building across the square plaza. Two-story barracks flanked the field.

"Say," asked one of the guards. "Y'all the reinforcements they say we's to git?"

The tunnel from which Mithridates' men were issuing after him was one of several hundred in a sheer cliff face. Even as the king watched, an alarm clanged from behind another door half a mile away.

The officer saluted the Mandarin and muttered, "It never rains but it pours. Pardon, sir, but we need to check this out. Barracks Five for your troops, I think."

He turned to his men. "All right, men. Double-time!"

"We 'uns could *use* some reinforcements!" the talkative enlisted man called over his shoulder as the squad jogged away in the direction of the new alarm.

"Column of fours, you scuts!" Kalhu was bellowing. "Fall in!"

The line-of-march converted itself to column of fours with a minimum of fuss, even though there hadn't been time yet to organize the "army" in a formal way. By the time they'd gotten here—by the time they'd been damned to Hell—many soldiers had held a little rank themselves.

Quite a lot of them had made non-com a dozen times—and been busted back to the ranks—before they died.

"Barracks Five is that one, noble sir," the Mandarin said smoothly to Mithridates.

With his hands still in his sleeves, he nodded to indicate one of the buildings to the right of the square. The barracks were frame structures painted dull yellow with dark brown trim; not prepossessing, but certainly the neatest building the king had seen yet in the Underworld.

There were even sign-boards in front of each, black with the barracks number indicated by a gilt Roman numeral.

"But I think you and I should report to Field Marshal French," the Mandarin continued. "As a matter of courtesy, and to work out the details of our further passage."

Mithridates looked at the Mandarin sharply.

As AE approached through the column, burly, bearded men stepped aside for her. She looked willowy, but she was as tall as most of the soldiers even though they outweighed her by a half.

Her eyes caught the tension between Mithridates and the Mandarin as she neared them. Her face set, but she showed no other form of concern. "Yes?"

"Our friend here says we need to arrange our further passage," the king said coolly.

AE nodded. "Then we'd better do that," she said. "The little building?"

"Section Leader Kalhu!" Mithridates ordered. "March the men to the barracks marked 'Vee' and arrange for billeting." The Assyrian was at least as competent to handle that sort of administrative chore as the king himself was. "I'll join you shortly with further orders."

"Yes *sir*. Section, forward—*march*!"

"Shall we go, Mandarin?" Mithridates continued over the crash of boots stamping in unison.

The Mandarin smiled, and the three of them set off for the Mess.

Through the gaps between the buildings, Mithridates saw that except for the cliff behind them, the facility was surrounded by swamp. The parade square over which they were walking was artificial—a gravel surface packed and rolled, several feet above normal ground level. Dark patches showed that water still wicked its way upward, but it was a very professional—and successful—piece of engineering.

Something hooted in the swamp.

"What's out there?" asked AE.

The Mandarin shrugged. "A swamp, as you see," he said. "A river."

"The river leads to Zahhaq?"

"It may indeed lead to Zahhaq, noble lady," said the Mandarin with sarcastic emphasis. "There *is* a river which Zahhaq has led to encircle his city. But we of course will take the practical route, through the tunnels beneath this way station."

"I'm not so sure," the woman said in apparent calm, "that the swamp route wouldn't be preferable."

The Mandarin *tsk*ed with his tongue and looked to Mithridates for support against female foolishness.

Mithridates met his eyes, but there was only appraisal in the regal glare.

The Mess Building was on posts, three steps above the gravel. The windows and front door were covered with screens of copper wire.

Something lanced Mithridates through the light fabric of his trousers. He looked down and saw a huge mosquito struggle airborne again with a load of royal blood. A dozen more had landed and were raising their heads to stab down.

After all, one couldn't expect a swamp in Hell to be *better* than one in the upper world.

"There's usually a guard," said the Mandarin with a hint of concern as he paused on the top step. "Still, they're probably just short-handed at the moment." He drew the door open against its twanging spring.

"Ah!" called someone from within the room. "Mandarin! Very good. We were just wondering when you'd turn up again."

Mithridates and AE followed their guide into a room awkwardly balanced between gaudiness and simplicity. Three men stood there holding glasses: all of them portly; none of them young—and otherwise as different as they could be.

Against one wall stood a walnut hutch holding a massive silver-service. Across from it was an ornate mahogany sideboard racked with bottles and decanters. And directly opposite the door was a marble shrine on which were displayed wax death-masks whose visages resembled that of the ruddy-faced Roman wearing a tunic and bronze body armor.

Mithridates stiffened. If this whole operation had been a trick of Caesar's . . .

"Sir John French," said the Mandarin, "allow me to present Mithridates, late King of Pontus. He's in command of a unit of two hundred and three souls. Exclusive of his companion, of course."

AE stepped forward unbidden and stuck out her hand to the field marshal to shake. "Amelia Earhart, Sir John. I presume that since I'm here, I have a soul also."

"Oh, but of course, my good lady," said the moustached, white-haired Englishman. "I'm sure our celestial colleague meant no disrespect. But it wouldn't do to count you on the ration strength, you see."

"Ambrose Burnside, sir," said the man in a blue uniform who stepped forward, transferring his glass to his left hand in order to offer his right to Mithridates. "Do you prefer 'your highness'? We don't stand much on rank in this Mess, but we try to adapt our ways to those of our guests."

"A drink, perhaps?" said the third man, the Roman. "Wine? Whiskey? Perhaps a dash of brandy for the lady, to restore her from what must have been a very difficult journey?"

"I don't use stimulants," AE said crisply. Almost to herself, she added, "I had my father to show me what comes of that course."

"Introduce me to your friend," Mithridates said, holding Burnside's hand but glaring at the Roman beside him. "I'd like to know what he's doing here."

The Roman raised his eyebrows. "Have we met?" he asked coolly. "If there was some problem between us in the, in the past, I assure you that I've long forgotten it."

"Can't imagine that it was anything of the sort, old boy," French said. "Besides, bygones are bygones, not so? King Mithridates, permit me to introduce Lucius Aemillius Paullus. Had the little contretemps with Hannibal, don't you know?"

"Cannae," Mithridates said, feeling his body relax. "Long before—" He paused, thinking of how to recast the question. "You're not connected with Julius Caesar, then?"

Paullus shrugged. "Probably a relative, old boy," he said. "Knew some of his great-greats, of course. Good pedigree, but I never thought any of them would come to a fart in a wind-storm. Begging your pardon, madam." He bowed to AE.

Burnside swirled his glass and snorted. "Stretching it a bit to call it a stimulant, I must say," he noted. "They call it whiskey, so I drink it as whiskey, but that's about as far as it goes. Here." He looked morose, and his bushy side-whiskers seemed to droop.

"Well, it's important for all of us to keep up the side," boomed Sir John. "And if for Mistress Earhart that means avoiding drink, why, it's all the more for the rest of us. Eh what?"

"You've gone over the arrangements with our guests, then, Mandarin?" Paullus said the corners of his eyes glittering as the pupils angled toward Mithridates.

"What arrangements?" the king asked. He edged back and twisted, so that as nearly as possible all four of his potential enemies were in front of him.

Sir John looked up from his glass of port. Propriety

stiffened him to attention in his bemedaled khaki uniform.

"Your highness," he said, punctuating the address with something between a nod and a formal bow. "We're badly in need of reinforcements. We're happy to open our facilities to those needing passage, but we must require a draft of six men per centum of those arriving."

He bowed again to AE. "Healthy males only, of course, Mistress Earhart."

"Five percent was the figure arrived at, I believe, Sir John," said the Mandarin. His voice ranged through a narrower band of tone than it normally did.

"Sorry about that, Mandarin," Burnside said, turning back from the sideboard where he was pouring himself another glass of whiskey. "That was the arrangement in the past, yes. But we badly need the men, I'm afraid."

"We can carry over the excess to the next draft through," Paullus offered. "Rather than rounding in our favor."

"That's only three men, Lucius," Sir John noted. "I scarcely think we'd have justification for demanding another recruit on that basis anyway."

"Oh," said the Roman. "We wouldn't? Sorry, I was never very good at figures."

"Quite all right, old man."

"What do you mean, 'recruits'?" demanded AE in a voice of deadly calm. "Sir John French, I *know* the morass you made of France and Belgium—"

"Hold hard, old girl," Burnside objected. "Scarcely Sir John alone, you know."

"No, no, Ambrose, she has every right to be upset," the British field marshal said. He shook his head sadly. "Wasn't prepared for it. Made mistakes."

He raised his eyes and stiffened the chin beneath his fine white beard. "Made *only* mistakes, some said at the time; and I'll not deny it now. But I've learned."

"We've all learned," Paullus interjected.

"Men were living in *mud*!" AE said. "Their feet rotted! They couldn't get dry! Their rations were a scandal! They were surrounded by the dead who couldn't be buried or who were dug up again by shells or further *damnable* entrenching!"

Her voice was an octave higher at the end of the diatribe than it had been when she began. Her face was flushed.

"Mistress Earhart," Sir John said quietly. "Everything you say is true. And more. I can only apologize—and beg you to believe that I've learned from my past mistakes."

The Mandarin leaned his head close to Mithridates and murmured, "Do you have any control over the female, noble sir? After all, we have no choice but to agree to the terms they offer for the use of their facilities."

"I have the choice to refuse *any* arrangement regarding men who've given me their allegiance!" Mithridates blazed.

All eyes in the room switched to the new disagreement.

"I don't recall any such ceremony," the Mandarin rejoined. "I think you're being rather too nice in your concerns, noble sir.'

"Oh, come now," interjected Sir John. "Play fair, Mandarin. Formal ceremony or not, if they were willing to follow the king through the tunnels to get here, they've offered their allegiance in the most telling way."

"Your highness," said the Mandarin, blandness coating his exasperation. "What alternative do you see? If we attempt to reach Zahhaq on foot, the swamp"—he removed a hand from his sleeve and gestured toward a window with one broken nail—"will drink us all."

"I will not by my will—"

"A moment!" Burnside said, loudly enough to focus attention on him.

Sweat beaded Burnside's bald forehead. He mopped it with his sleeve and continued in the pause the others allowed him, "King Mithridates, your concern for your troops does you great credit. I believe, however, that if you'll allow us to take you around the facilities, your concerns will be answered."

"Your reasonable concerns," Paullus said. "None of us would deny it. But we've learned."

"There, what could be more fair?" the Mandarin said, spreading his hands out toward Mithridates.

"Easterner," Mithridates said distinctly. "If you attempt to patronize me again, I will have you disemboweled." He nodded toward Sir John. "Off your premises, if you gentlemen would prefer."

Paullus chuckled appreciatively and said, "We don't prescribe codes of behavior for our guests among themselves. Feel free."

The Mandarin bowed impassively. "Forgive me, noble sir. But I assure you, I have only our combined best interests at heart."

Mithridates ignored him. "Ambrose," he said, "gentlemen. I accept your offer to show me the site. I can't claim that my own prospects are so marvelous that any of those poor beggars would be punished to be separated from me."

"Jolly good!" Sir John said, opening the screen door and gesturing the group onward.

"I think you'll be amazed at the progress we've made in the, in the time we've been learning," Paullus murmured confidentially in Mithridates' ear. "And not to put too fine a point on it, old fellow, but . . . the swamp out there is fairly grim."

"We know," Burnside added from the king's other shoulder, "because that's all *we* had to start with."

Sir John paused ten paces from the Mess Building and tapped the ground with his high cavalryman's boot. "Gravel fill," he explained. "Thirty-seven thousand cubic yards of it."

"What?" said AE in amazement.

"Every bit of it," Burnside agreed, stamping his own boot for emphasis. "We refused—absolutely refused—to run the facility unless the Administration provided us with the proper support."

"Took forever to get them to believe we were serious," Paullus said reflectively. "Very unpleasant time that was for us. . . ."

"Worth it, though," Sir John said. "We got the fill at last. Worth it for the men under our charge. And worth it for us not to have repeated the mistakes we made, that is to say, before."

"Other generals lost battles," muttered Burnside as he stared down at the ground. Where his heel had dug, water raised by osmosis was darkening the gravel.

He scuffed the indentation smooth again. "What

they really hated me for," he continued, "was marching the survivors through the mud afterwards. And they were right to hate me."

"Steady on, old boy," Sir John said, patting his colleague on the shoulder. "We've all learned better since."

"But we're not perfect," said Paullus. "Not yet."

"Still," said Sir John, "our guests don't want to know our problems. They want to see how we've dealt with them. To the barracks, I think?"

"Your men are in Five?" Burnside asked. "I believe that was the next one open in the rotation?"

"Yes, that's—" Mithridates said. A mosquito the size of a small bee settled on his cheekbone, blurring in his peripheral vision. He slapped it. "That's right."

"Deuced sorry about these," Sir John said as he led the group toward Barracks Five. His back was straight, and the military precision of his strides was unaffected by the cloud of mosquitoes descending on him as well as on the others. "There's no way to drain the swamps, obviously."

"We've put through a request for a *helicopter*," Paullus said, enunciating carefully. "It's a machine that flies. Do you know anything about them? Some of our latter-day recruits say they're very useful for spraying insects to death."

"Not a lot you can do here with hand pumps, you can imagine," added Burnside. He slapped himself, leaving three long streaks of blood across his bare scalp. "Until then, I'm afraid we all have to suffer."

"They *did* send us horses for this operation, though,"

Paullus noted. "It's been ages since we've had cavalry, despite all our requests."

"It's our duty to make do with what we have," Sir John said, "so long as it doesn't affect the welfare of our troops. But speaking as an old cavalryman myself, I'll admit to a sense of pleasure at *that* news."

The barracks door flew open with a bang as Burnside. in the lead, reached for the handle.

"You the guys with the weapons?" demanded an Assyrian with enough scar tissue to imply he'd fought his way to some rank during life. He caught sight of Mithridates on the step behind the blue-coated Burnside. Ducking back into the barracks, he roared, "Atten-*shun*!"

Definitely a non-com.

"What's this about weapons, Sir John?" Mithridates murmured to French as the two men stepped side by side into the single room that comprised the building's ground floor. The center of the room was empty. Men straightened to attention in the groups where they stood talking or jumped down from the bunks lining the two long walls.

"We thought we'd equip your unit," the field marshal explained. "All of them, not just the recruits we take."

"Arms," said Paullus with a bitter twist to his full, red lips. "That's the one thing the Administration doesn't try to short us on."

"We need more fill," Burnside said.

"We'll get more, Ambrose," Sir John replied with a touch of exasperation. "But at the moment, we're showing the facilities to our guests."

Mithridates could imagine how many times *that*

exchange had occurred in this side-pocket of Hell. Aloud he called, "As you were!" to the troops stiffened to attention.

Kalhu trotted toward them from the opposite end of the barracks, stepping to the outside of the bunk row rather than cutting across the cleared space. The floor was hardwood, scrubbed smooth though unwaxed.

"Your highness," Sir John said with an anticipatory smile, "why don't you ask your sergeant-major here how he finds the accommodations?"

"Sir, it's a palace!" Kalhu burbled before Mithridates had time to relay the question. "It's all made of wood, and I don't remember when I've seen a bivouac so clean."

He batted at his neck, crushing one of the mosquitoes that had entered before Paullus slammed the screen door. With unslaked enthusiasm he continued, "We're to be issued arms and rations as soon as all the bedding's distributed upstairs."

AE walked over to the nearest bunk bed and examined it while the soldier who'd appropriated the location watched her. A woolen blanket was drawn over a pair of sheets, coarse but clean. Beneath them was a straw tick and a ten-slatted bed-frame.

Paullus frowned and measured the gap between slats with the fingers of one hand. "That can't be comfortable," he said. "Are we this short of frames? Perhaps we could rob some from one of the barracks which aren't in use at the moment?"

"Sir?" said the soldier whose bed it was. He wore a uniform like Burnside's: one of the contingent in the excavation before Mithridates arrived. "This is jest fine. Haven't had it so good since they bunked us down in the Capitol Building before things rightly got started."

"This is . . . ," AE said, watching Sir John French out of the corners of her eyes. "This is very good."

"What do you mean by rations?" Mithridates asked sharply.

A man in khaki and puttees, like the guards at the cave mouth, trotted down the stairs from the upper floor. He threw something between a wave and a salute to the command group before plunging out the back door on some hasty errand.

"That was Simpson," Sir John said, as if the words explained anything. "You'll be able to judge soon enough."

"We can't claim anything for it," said Paullus glumly, "except that we provide the food for those who use it here."

"It ranges from bland to worse, I'm afraid," Burnside agreed. "We can't make it more palatable, but at least we can share it with the men."

"*That's* a mistake we haven't repeated," Sir John agreed. "Aloofness, disregard for the poor beggars under our charge."

Another khaki-uniformed soldier opened the front door and shouted, "All right, you lot!" The command group turned to face him. "Oops. Sir?"

"Carry on, Dennis," Sir John said. "We're merely here to observe."

The soldier nodded, then resumed where he'd left off: "Fall in on the drill field for weapons issue!"

The screen door didn't have time to close before the first of Mithridates' men obeyed the summons. The barracks emptied, second floor mingling with the first. The men moved with the enthusiasm of living soldiers looting a wine shop.

Unlike liquor, weapons worked more often than not here in Hell.

"I wonder what it would take to get *me* this excited," Mithridates murmured to AE as the troops jostled past them. But his heart was stirring. . . . He too found excitement in the notion of arming himself properly. He'd always had a bow and quiver beside him, even at meals. . . .

"After you, your highness," Sir John said as the last of the common soldiers disappeared onto the gravel square. Nodding, Mithridates followed them.

Three soldiers in khaki stood by a chuffing, massively overloaded truck. A gasogene cylinder was welded to the vehicle's front bumper, cooking charcoal to get flammable gas which in turn powered the engine.

Barely. It was remarkable that a gasogene could drive a truck sagging as deep as this one did on its springs.

"*In* ranks, frog-spawn!" Kalhu bellowed. "*You* know your places!"

The troops had formed up initially, but a pause in control and the excitement of seeing men in khaki unloading bundles of spears made the stiff ranks tremble like jelly in the sun. Under the section leader's watchful eye, the men stepped forward one by one, to be handed their equipment from the back of the truck.

"As a rule, we supply the arms that were familiar to the men in life," Paullus said.

"That's how we equip our own troops," Burnside

added. "Though of course we can make other arrangements if you like, your highness."

"I don't see that that will be necessary," Mithridates said, because he had to say something. This was all too good to be true. . . .

"I don't see that they need weapons at all," said AE with unexpected vehemence. "We aren't, we aren't *attacking* anybody, we're trying to escape." She fixed Mithridates with a hot glare. "Isn't that so?"

The king drew himself up. "I don't imagine that you're really that naive," he said. He stepped around the formation, walking toward the men who'd already received their weapons.

"Want to see them, sir?" volunteered the nearest Assyrian proudly. He held out the spear he'd just been issued, a diamond-shaped iron head socketed onto a sturdy shaft of about the man's own height. His conical bronze helmet with ear-flaps fit without adjustment.

Mithridates took the spear and pinged the head with a fingernail. It rang cleanly.

"First rate," he said as he returned the weapon to the man who'd used the moment to sling the baldric that supported his new sword.

"Look at *this*!" insisted the next man in line, one of the newer lot. His face shown as brightly as the brass receiver of the rifle he displayed to the king.

"It's a Henry!" he explained with enthusiasm. "Evan Worth in my company found one at Sharpsburg, but we couldn't git no bullets fer it. But look!"

He thumbed open the flap of the pasteboard box he held in the other hand. Inside, flat lead bullets alternated with the glittering bases of brass cartridges. "Ten boxes of 'em!" the soldier crowed. "I could fight the hull Yankee *army* with these!"

Mithridates smiled in feigned appreciation. This man—all his men—were so happy. What did their leader have to make *him* bubble with enthusiasm?

"Sir?" called Dennis, the soldier distributing weapons. "Your highness?"

Mithridates looked around.

"Would you like one of these?"

Dennis was holding up a bow and quiver. The bow's horn reinforcements were dyed red, the tips were ivory, and the baldric and tassels hanging from the quiver were gold.

The king wasn't aware of speaking as he stepped forward, but the murmured, "Oh . . ." he heard could have come from his throat as well as from those of the other men who saw the beautiful weapon.

It was unstrung, of course. He tried the tension between his two hands and felt the smooth, strong action of the perfectly formed composite.

"Yes, I would like this," Mithridates' lips said, while his hands slung the quiver over his left shoulder and his mind lost itself in the beauty of the bow.

As the king returned to the command group, Dennis smiled; or perhaps smirked.

"Well," Sir John said, "shall we adjourn to the Mess again, your highness? Or would you care to see the other units billeted here at the moment?"

"We just got in a draft of Chinks, Mandarin," Burnside volunteered. "They're dossed down in Two. Want to go see if there's any friends of yours among them?"

The Mandarin fixed Burnside with his eyes. "In life," the Easterner said with metallic clarity, "I had no friends, noble sir. I very much doubt that I've formed any friendships here."

"Sorry," Burnside muttered, wiping his scalp again. "Misspoke. Try to do better."

"The cadre's mostly from the Western Front at the moment," Sir John said. "We rotate them, of course."

"And there's the Celtic cavalry in Barracks Seven," Paullus offered.

"French, old boy," Sir John corrected. "They're told off for the operation this afternoon, your highness," he went on with a brisk diffidence. "Better not to disturb them now, don't you know? Might make them think the brass is concerned about their performance."

"A splendid lot of men," Burnside said. "And their mounts as well. Very unusual luck to get anything of the sort, particularly as a formed unit."

Sir John slapped another mosquito. "No need to stand here and be eaten alive," he said. "We can discuss it over rations and port in the Mess.

"And," he added with a sidelong glance at Mithridates as they tramped across the gravel, "we can discuss the draft of men you'll be supplying us."

Mithridates murmured something noncommittal. He was only vaguely aware of Sir John's words or the sounds of the last of his troops being armed.

His hands slid slowly over the polished perfection of his bow.

"You understand that with your unit and the Chinese draft arriving together—" said Paullus as he distributed waxed cardboard packages of canned rations.

"Wouldn't you know it?" grumbled Burnside.

"—we have to fend for ourselves at dinner?"

"Wouldn't have thought of it, once," Sir John said, gingerly unfolding the tiny can-opener that came in the ration packet. "Do without *my* batman so that some Cockney oick could sleep on clean sheets?"

He snorted. "I had a lot to learn. But we'll get it right yet."

"Allow me, mistress," Burnside said, leaning over AE and taking the opener from her unpracticed fingers. He levered the sharp, concave blade up and down, nibbling the lid jaggedly open.

"Now, be very careful," Paullus warned. "We don't want our guests hurting themselves."

"*Very* good, Mistress Earhart," Sir John added enthusiastically. "Beanie-weenie. Sometimes we've gone for months with nothing but scrambled eggs."

"Occasionally we get rations that are freeze-dried," said Paullus. "But we try to save those for units that are going on an operation shortly."

Mithridates had watched Burnside open AE's can and did the same with his own. The interior was a sickly yellow-white, with nondescript flecks.

Sir John peered over. "Oh, bad luck, old boy," he said. "Ham and eggs."

"Though it all tastes the same, really," Paullus noted as he raised a forkful of a similar mixture.

Mithridates took a careful bite of his reprocessed eggs. "It's edible," he said in amazement. Had the tunnel taken them somehow out of Hell?

"We insist that it be edible," said Burnside as he

finished opening his own can—and grimaced. "The Administration won't go any farther than that—"

"No Cordon Bleu cooking here," Sir John interjected with a chuckle.

"We made a minimum standard on the food a condition for our serving," Paullus said, continuing Burnside's line. "And by choosing cases at random for ourselves, we can keep pretty close tabs on what the troops get."

Sir John gestured toward the king with a forkful of something nondescript. "They need our expertise," he said forcefully. "They can punish us, but they can't *use* us without our cooperation."

"And we won't cooperate unless they make it possible for us to avoid our past mistakes," Burnside said. "Which, by God, we're going to do."

"We're going to get it right, you know," Sir John said, leaning toward Mithridates and AE across the table from him. He went on in a conspiratorial whisper, "I shouldn't say, I know, but—I think this afternoon's operation will be the one."

"Since we've finally gotten cavalry, you see," Paullus said. He took a deep swallow of his wine, apparently without thinking, because his ruddy features scrunched up when the sourness hit him.

"The magnetism of the charge," Burnside said as solemnly as a priest speaking of his god. "Drawing all with it—"

"Sweeping away every hesitation and impediment," Paullus continued.

"And bringing success," Sir John concluded. He stood and lifted his glass. "Gentlemen. To success!"

Burnside and Paullus jumped to their feet. The

three of them drank the toast with their eyes raised to an imagined future.

Mithridates looked at AE in puzzlement, hopeful that the woman's New Dead viewpoint permitted her to make sense out of what their hosts were saying. She met his glance but sucked in her cheeks in a moue of equal incomprehension.

The Mandarin sat beside Sir John French. He continued to pick at his food. His face was impassive, but his *being* radiated an aura of disdain for all those around him.

Outside the Mess Building, a trumpet called imperiously.

"Dash it, they're early!" Sir John blurted. He coughed, spilling part of his drink and spraying more of it from his nostrils.

Burnside stamped over to the window, tugging a watch from his pocket. He hurled it to the floor, springing the case. "Damned thing is never right!" he shouted.

"Nothing is right here," agreed Paullus, joining him at the window.

The implications of what they'd just said drew the two men's eyes together in horrified surmise; then their gazes clicked back to what was happening on the parade square.

Mithridates and AE moved to the door and looked out through the screen. Behind them they heard Sir John muttering as he caught his breath, "No, no. It will be all right. This time everything will go according to plan."

A unit of cavalry, something over a hundred men, was mounting in response to the bugle call. They were gorgeously outfitted, but it was not the blue jackets with red, white, and gold accents that drew a gasp of admiration from Mithridates.

The horsemen wore steel helmets and steel-plate armor over their backs and breasts.

Mithridates hadn't been one of those whose punishment in Hell involved trying to deny the objects and techniques of the ages that followed their death. Computers kept better records than scribes—when they worked, and neither scribes nor computers worked very well here. Horses, boats, and helicopters were all means of transportation. A gun in the hands of a trained man was as effective as a bow in Mithridates' own hands, and that—he squeezed the ivory handgrip of his new weapon—was high praise indeed.

But armor was armor; and steel plate was an infinitely better material for armor than the best possible in the king's own day—cast bronze, or rings of iron wire. He was momentarily entranced by the thought of what he could have accomplished with horsemen like *those*.

The trumpeter—he wore a green coat with no cuirass, and the plume on his helmet was white rather than red like the others—lifted his horn again and blew a piercing signal. The unit wheeled right in two ranks and set off toward the far end of the parade square at a measured walk.

"Napoleon's Cuirassiers of the Guard," Sir John said approvingly, his voice back to normal. "The finest cavalry ever to take the field."

"Even the Secessionists giving themselves airs would admit that," Burnside agreed. He seemed to have gotten over the problem with his watch. "We're damned lucky to get them."

"They're certainly prettier than Moors bareback on ponies," Paullus said with an unsuspected dry wit. "But equipment isn't everything, as I learned to my cost."

"Gentlemen," Sir John said, putting a hand on one shoulder of each of the men at the window. "The testing is over. We've finally gotten it right."

Burnside raised his eyes toward Paradise, though the pain of its unforgiving light drove his face down again at once. "And then we can leave . . . ," he whispered.

"Leave?" AE repeated sharply. She gripped Burnside's other shoulder and said, "Do you know of a way out of here?"

The trumpet called from the far end of the square.

"We need to go," Burnside muttered, turning his head.

"What did you mean?" demanded Mithridates in the voice he'd used to his mother after her plot to murder him had failed.

"You shouldn't talk about that," Paullus said to his fellow.

"*What*?"

"It's our belief—" said Sir John.

"Understanding," said Paullus.

"Agreement!"

"—that the Administration will release us to, to the . . ."

"Other side," Paullus offered.

"Upper levels," Sir John amended.

"To Heaven, dammit!" said Burnside. His face and scalp were red with the vehemence of his belief.

"Whatever," Sir John continued, pressing his lips tightly against the anger that wanted to burst out. "In any case, that we will be released from our duties here when we prove by our success that we've learned from past mistakes."

He took a deep breath. "And now," he said, "we really do have to go to see whether . . ."

"Finally," one or the other of his fellows whispered.

"Whether we've achieved the success we hope. Would you care to come with us, sir and madam?"

With the assumption of agreement—or perhaps because they didn't really care what their guests did now—the three generals strode toward a door that the king assumed opened onto a closet.

The Mandarin had remained seated at the table while the other diners jumped up to watch the cavalry. Now he rose with an unreadable expression, gestured Mithridates—and ΛE, by extension—to follow their hosts, and fell in behind them.

The bugle called in the distance. Mithridates thought, but couldn't be sure, that he felt the building begin to tremble with the impact of many hoofs trotting in unison.

The first thing the king noticed when Sir John opened the door was the light. It was pale, pastel, and stuck to the back of his eyes.

The light of the tunnel by which they had entered this place.

He stepped forward without obvious hesitation. He held his bow; it would be the work of an instant for his practiced fingers to draw and nock an arrow.

A helical staircase of wrought iron led down from the doorway. There was a tubular railing on both sides of the narrow risers, but the whole construction was skeletonized and looked very flimsy.

It swayed with every step the men and woman took.

"There ought to be supports to the ceiling . . . ," AE murmured, drawing Mithridates' eyes upward.

There were no supports because there was no ceiling. Only the blur of light which had no particular color. . . .

Mithridates glanced over his shoulder. AE's expression was calm, though the flare of her nostrils suggested that it was a matter of control rather than ignorance of the possibilities.

Beyond her, in profile because of the way the staircase twisted, was the Mandarin. He'd closed the door behind him when he stepped onto the stairs.

If the Mandarin had followed, they could be sure the situation was safe.

Within the parameters of Hell.

The stairs ended at a platform thirteen steps below the entrance. Wherever they were, it wasn't beneath the physical foundations of the Mess Building. The platform was of welded iron strips with a tubular railing, much like the stairs; and the staircase was the only connection it had to anything solid.

The base of the platform, undulating with the weight of six adults, hung a dozen feet in the air above a featureless plain.

"Where are we?" Mithridates demanded.

"This is the operational area," Burnside said

distractedly, thinking he'd given an explanation. "The charge will be coming from"—he pointed—"there."

"They don't see us," Paullus added.

"There" was up the gentle slope to the right. Rocks showed, but for the main it was grassy sod with a scattering of bushes that wouldn't come up to the knee of a man on foot. The foliage quivered in a breeze that those on the platform couldn't feel.

All the leaves were the color of pale fungus: deadman's fingers crooking up through damp soil.

A bugle blew the harsh, ringing notes that summoned cavalry to the charge in every place and time.

Something touched Mithridates' sleeve; the Mandarin, pointing further down the slope beyond the hovering platform. The ground—if any of it was really ground—became fuzzier in that direction. The grass lost definition, and there were no more shrubs and outcrops to highlight its drab expanse.

"That's the way we'll go out of here," the Mandarin said. "The path of Zahhaq."

There must have been something in Mithridates' expression that he would prefer to have hidden, because the Mandarin added with the ghost of a smile, "Don't worry. It's perfectly safe. I've done it many times."

"They're coming," said AE.

"They're coming . . . ," one of the generals echoed, and, "Soon. . . ."

Sir John French, with his hands on the shoulders of his fellows, said prayerfully, "*This* time we'll show them that we've learned."

A crop of sword edges grew with glittering suddenness atop the hill to the right, as though Jason had been there to sow his dragon's teeth again. The strange ground undulated, and the squadron of cavalry was pounding up the reverse slope with sabers drawn.

The blades rose and sank with the choppy motion of the trotting horses beneath them. Gauntleted hands gripping the brass hilts; the red helmet plumes and all at once, the polished helmets and the set-faced troopers beneath the steel.

The first rank surged over the hilltop. Instead of reining back their mounts on the downslope, the riders bent forward as one. The strides lengthened, the quick-footed hammering of the trot flattening into a canter: swifter, smoother; controlled but with an onrush like that of a seabird stooping on its prey.

The second rank grew ragged as the quickened pace increased the instinct of the following horses to turn the disciplined charge into a race.

"It's beautiful . . . ," someone said. The words were so close to Mithridates' thought that he might have spoken them himself.

One of the riders rose in his stirrups and bellowed, "Vive le Impereur!" He sat again, cutting his saber forward as part of the same motion. All the front-rank blades came down in kaleidoscopic synchrony, and the green-jacketed trumpeter managed to put his instrument to his lips.

Directly beneath the observation platform, in a line parallel of that of the charge, overlapping disks five feet in diameter slanted up from the soil. They were buzz saw blades, and they were already spinning as they rose.

Air shrieked between the kerfed teeth. Then the front rank of horsemen hit the blades.

"*This* time," said Paullus, and to be heard over the carnage he must have been shouting at the top of his voice.

The saw blades slowed with angry howls as fifteen-hundred-pound loads of a horse and rider—flesh, bone, and accoutrements—slammed into the whirling teeth and tried to stall them out.

Whatever drove the saws was equal to the task. Bits flew free—a stirrup; an arm; a bright chestnut foreleg whose shoe was a shining omega as it cut an arc in the sky.

AE's fists were clenched and stuffed into her mouth to keep her from crying out. It wouldn't have mattered. A human can't scream as loud as a horse, and there were sixty horses shrieking in mortal agony before the second rank hit the blades.

There was no way through the wall of spinning steel and no way around at the speed at which the squadron was charging downhill. Several of the riders used their momentum to try jumping their mounts over the sudden barrier of thrashing body parts and the buzz saws that had dismembered the front rank.

That possibility had been allowed for by whoever had arranged the trap. The blades continued to rise even after they left their concealment.

A dappled gray gelding came the closest to success, but he curvetted in the air as the whirling saw chewed off both his hind legs in a spray of blood. His rider pitched backward, over the crupper. He fell on a saw blade that sectioned his shining cuirass with a shower of sparks and a howl like that of a damned soul.

A howl like that of King Mithridates, watching the destruction of men and horses as splendid as any he'd ever commanded.

Burnside began to pound the railing with one meaty hand. The platform swayed. "No!" he shouted. "*No!*"

Sir John turned his back on the carnage. He stood straight, with his arms crossed behind him. His face could have been cast from concrete. Paullus looked as though he were being carried to the execution block, but his pig-narrow eyes gazed back up the hill.

Following the surviving horse and rider.

A bay mare—Mithridates thought she'd been in the leading rank, though that seemed unlikely—had somehow managed to stop short of the whirling blades. Her rider slid forward, focused on the charge and not his riding until the charge disintegrated in blood.

The cuirassier tried to wrap his arms around the horse's neck and save himself, but his instinctive priorities were still wrong: he couldn't cling with the saber filling his right hand, and reflex made him grip the useless weapon tighter instead of hurling it away. He went over the mare's left shoulder as she pivoted uphill to the right.

The rider's chinstrap broke when he hit the ground, his left leg still caught in the stirrup and twisted leathers. The helmet bounded away, meeting a saw blade and sundering into one large chunk and a dozen bits of whirring shrapnel.

The mare bolted back the way she'd come, lurching against the cuirassier's dragging weight. Foam flecked her jaws and breast. The man's right hand continued to grip the saber as he bounced—back, side, breast, and side again, uphill and out of sight.

His left hand held nothing. He'd flung it wide as he fell. It lay with the other wreckage of blood, limbs, and bone chips. Some of the pieces thrashed; some moaned. A few even tried to crawl back uphill.

The buzz saws settled back into concealment with contented purrs.

"So *close*," said Sir John, combing his fingers absently through his short beard.

He lowered his hand and looked at it. His face wrinkled in utter distaste as he realized that he'd been spattered with dollops of blood and brains.

AE turned and began climbing the steps.

"We only missed one," Burnside was saying. "Surely that's close enough?"

But his voice showed that he knew it wasn't.

AE began to run, taking the narrow steps by pairs. The whole platform jounced. Mithridates started after her.

"I still think blazing naphtha holds the greatest hope for the future," Paullus said as the generals followed their guests. "I'm sure that we can solve the problem of ignition timing."

Mithridates tried to bang the stairwell door behind him. The Mandarin's ivory-yellow hand caught it. The men's eyes met. Mithridates turned and followed AE out of the Mess Building.

Mithridates caught up with the woman in the middle of the parade square, now empty. It didn't seem right that he, a king and anyway a man, should run after a female, but her stride was as long as his and left him no choice if he wanted to join her.

AE continued to walk. The only sound she made was the scrunch of her rubber-soled boots on the gravel.

Mithridates swallowed and said, "The horses are always the worst. They scream much louder than the men can, and their voices have the same timbre."

"I don't want to talk about it," said the woman.

She'd worn a silk neck-scarf. As she walked along, she was dabbing with it at the bits of matter that had splashed her on the platform.

The Mandarin wheezed up beside them. Mithridates rotated his torso, drawing an arrow from the quiver with his right hand while his left arm raised and extended the bow—

AE put her hand on his. "No," she said.

Mithridates let the arrow slide back. "Go away from me," he said distinctly to the Easterner.

"This was not my doing," the Mandarin said.

The others walked on, toward Barracks Five in default of a better destination. It was dark as only the sky of Hell could be. Lamplight through the barracks' windows provided a beacon. Grimacing, the Mandarin caught up with the king again.

"You knew what was going to happen," AE said bitterly. "You didn't try to stop it."

"No one could stop it!" the Mandarin protested. "It was their duty. They're *generals.*"

"It isn't a general's duty to arrange the slaughter of his troops!" the king blazed, his hand twitching again toward the waiting arrows.

"It was the only thing *those* three were any good

at," the Mandarin replied. "They're being given the opportunity to perfect their technique—and," he added, "perhaps to escape this . . . place."

"You can't truly believe that they'll ever be released from here for doing . . . ," said the woman. "For doing *that*."

"In life," said the Mandarin blandly, "I thought I knew everything of importance. I was wrong, and that led me to here." He paused. "I cannot prove that our hosts' belief is unfounded. They deserve the opportunity to pursue their chosen means of salvation."

"Not with *my* retainers!"

"Only a few of them," the Mandarin said. "And it's generally very quick. Nothing that that lot"—he gestured toward the barracks—"hasn't undergone many times already, I'm sure."

"You revolt me," whispered AE, speaking for the king as well.

"The situation may revolt you," the Mandarin retorted. "But if you are revolted by reason, then you are mad."

"We'll go through the swamps," Mithridates decided abruptly. "Mandarin, you said that we can reach your Zahhaq by following the river?"

"That isn't a paved thoroughfare out there!" the Mandarin said with a contemptuous gesture. "There's a thousand meandering dead ends, a thousand dangers. We'll all die if you do that—instead of only a few!"

"Listen to me carefully, Mandarin," the king said, "or you will die now whatever our companion wishes. I will not *choose* my retainers for death to save myself or to save a situation. We will risk the swamp."

"You can't—" the Mandarin began.

The barracks' door opened in a flood of yellow light. They'd reached the building without noticing the fact in their argument.

"Got a problem you'd like me to take care of, sir?" Kalhu asked in a hopeful voice. Wearing armor of iron scales, he was almost broad enough to fill the doorway. Light quivered along the blade of his bare sword.

Mithridates smiled. "Thank you, Section Leader," he said, "but our discussion was over. I think our guide realizes that. No?"

"I'm not a guide for the swamp," the Mandarin said desperately. "We'll all be—"

There was enough light now for him to see the faces of AE and the king. He took a deep breath and made a distracted swipe at the mosquitoes, which were settling on their victims again. "Perhaps," the Mandarin said carefully, folding his hands into his sleeves again, "there is a way to reach our destination without meeting the generals' terms. At night, the Mess Building is deserted except perhaps for a guard—"

"Them?" asked AE. "Won't Sir John and the others be there?"

"They quarter themselves with the men," the Mandarin said. "Usually with the next unit to be readied for an operation. They say they've learned not to be aloof."

"*They* don't die!" the woman said.

"No, but they live," Mithridates answered softly, thinking of the endless cycle of failure in intention compounded by failure in execution. And they weren't mad, not really; no more than they had been in life when they started themselves on this course that Satan would never quite let them complete.

"*I'll* beat him!" Mithridates snarled. He looked up in embarrassment at the trio of incomprehending faces watching him.

"That is," he said calmly, "we'll beat them. Section Leader, ready the men with weapons and rations. Quietly, mind. We're going to break into the Mess Building as soon as everyone's left it."

"Everyone but the guards," the Mandarin corrected. "But there may only be one or two. Our hosts are always short-handed. . . ."

An hour later, the only sound in the encampment was an occasional scrunch of boots near the Mess Building.

"There's only the one man outside," Mithridates said, squinting across the darkness.

"There may be more inside the building, though," the Mandarin noted cautiously.

"Don't guess anybody can sneak up over this gravel," Kalhu offered, "but we can rush him easy, sir."

"There are lights on in the other barracks," said AE. She spoke with a pilot's precision and a personal unwillingness to state the conclusion that the data made obvious.

"Mandarin?" the king said. He knew the sort of man their guide was: trustworthy only insofar as that suited his own expedience.

For the moment, that was enough.

"The barracks to the west," the Mandarin said,

"houses British and American soldiers, mostly from the early years of the twentieth century. No doubt they're being readied for the next operation, since they formed the cadre when we arrived. They will have machineguns and repeating rifles."

AE and the three men squatted in front of Barracks Five, using the building's bulk to conceal their outlines in case something flashed in the sky or the swamp. The rest of the men, armed to the teeth, were waiting within—restively silent.

"The new arrivals in Barracks One," the Mandarin continued coolly, "are an anti-tank company of Chinese militia, from the end of the same century. In the event of the alarm, I would expect at least one of them to run to the middle of the fighting and detonate the satchel charge strapped to her back."

"Um," said Kalhu.

"More likely," the Mandarin went on, "all two hundred of them would do that. That's how they came to arrive here together, after all."

"The generals may get their perfect operation after all," the woman said emotionlessly.

Mithridates looked at her. "No," he said in a similar tone. "One of the bombs won't go off. They're playing by Satan's rules, while *we* are circumventing him."

"Well, maybe I *can* crawl up and scrag him," Kalhu said. "Or one of the boys . . . since there's some scouts."

Mithridates raised himself halfway, then sank back into a crouch. He didn't speak.

He didn't have to. The stresses of his shifting

weight made the gravel crunch audibly, even though his feet weren't actually moving.

"I presume it was designed this way," he offered in the silence.

Though he doubted that it was part of the generals' plan. *They* were only pawns. . . .

"While none of us would be able to approach the guard without being heard," the Mandarin offered in the distant voice that he substituted for diffidence now that he and the king were on terms of armed neutrality, "I believe that a female could . . . immobilize him without an alarm being given."

It was too dark for the four of them to see one another, but the whisper of harness hinted that the men were all turning toward AE.

"I see," she said in a voice that proved she did see—and that she wasn't going to answer the implied question until she was ready to.

"*She's* going to cut his throat?" Kalhu said in a tone of disappointment.

"No, she is not," AE responded while Mithridates' mouth was opening to form his own reply.

"Madam—" the Mandarin began.

"I'll try to hold him," AE continued. "I'll try to take his gun away. But he's not to be harmed, do you understand?"

"Madam, if the guard gives the alarm, we will all be massacred—unless"—the Mandarin's suggestion was more musing aloud than sarcasm—"our leader manages to strike a bargain with our hosts after all. I doubt the rate for passage will be as reasonable as the six percent they offered initially."

"You can't choke a guy silent," Kalhu said flatly. "Maybe cut his throat, yeah."

"I'm not being unreasonable," AE said, unaffected by the low-voiced hostility from both the men who were arguing with her. "Two of you can get to the corners of the building by going through the swamp. It's the last few yards from there to the man that are the problem, and . . ."

She shrugged with a creak of leather. "And I'll undertake to hold his attention."

"That's absurd!" snapped the Mandarin. "You have no conception of what the swamp—"

"I still say—" said Kalhu.

"All right," said Mithridates. "That's what we'll do. I'll position myself around the corner. And, Section Leader? I'll want a trustworthy man to accompany me."

"You *can't* mean—" the Mandarin said. He stopped, because even as he articulated the words, he knew that the king meant whatever he said.

"I'll go myself, sir," Kalhu replied promptly.

"No. I need you here to bring the men across when we've dealt with the guard. Pick someone steady."

"It won't be ladylike," the woman said musingly. She took off her leather helmet and fluffed her hair, then carefully folded the headgear and buttoned it into one of the pockets of the flying suit.

"I don't suppose he'll be able to see me properly," she said. "But I'll know."

"We'll need time to get into position," Mithridates warned. "I don't suppose there's any safe way to signal, so wait as long as you can. Before dawn."

He thought of Burnside's watch. If only time were more regular here. . . .

AE laid her hand on the king's. "Wait," she said quietly. "You have to promise that the guard won't be hurt."

Kalhu snorted.

Mithridates was silent for a moment. Then he said, "All right, I accept your condition."

"What do you think *his* word's worth, you fool?" the Mandarin said, his anger getting the better of his intellect.

"Perhaps it's worth your life, Mandarin," Mithridates said softly.

He tapped their guide in the ribs with the end of his bow. "Oh," he said, "and one other thing. You'll go with me. I want to be sure of where you are when we overpower the guard."

Kalhu went inside the barracks to pick a soldier. He was still chuckling at the Mandarin's horrified gasp.

The swamp was as bad as the Mandarin insisted it would be.

Barracks Three was empty, so they could safely walk around it on the gravel. The lights were on in One, the barracks nearest the Mess Building on the east side of the square. Someone was reading a harangue about duty, interrupted frequently by hundreds of girlish voices chanting, "Die for the memory of Premier Chiang!"

Mithridates shook his head in amazement as he stepped over the edge of the graveled square, into the swamp. He didn't want *that* lot noticing him.

And he couldn't imagine any leader being willing to form a unit like that, in itself an admission of failure. Battle wasn't a matter of hurting the enemy, it was about *winning*.

The way Mithridates was going to win. Again. At last.

He swore by Fire and Darkness as the ooze tried to engulf him.

The parade square was built within a retaining wall of cypress pilings set closely against vertical sheets of corrugated iron. The piles were eight inches in diameter and must have plunged at least twenty feet down into the muck.

Despite that, the wall quivered when the king and the two men following him used it to pull themselves along. The whole facility was an island of gravel, floating by the will of whatever power chose to order Hell.

The Mandarin whispered, "I told you—"

There wasn't a true bottom, just the network of roots, dead leaves, and the dust that had settled onto them and now was mud. Mithridates found that if he stepped carefully, the mat spread beneath his feet like a wet sponge and he sank only to his ankles.

If he weren't perfectly careful—and perfectly lucky—his leg stabbed through like a spear into a melon.

No one in Hell was perfectly lucky. And after five or six consecutive disasters, not even an erstwhile King of Kings found the spirit to be careful.

"—so," the Mandarin completed bitterly as he dragged himself up from the hole his foot had dug for him.

Mithridates considered threatening to drown the Easterner if he didn't shut up. The third member of the group was an Assyrian named Shamwas who insisted on wearing his newly issued mail shirt on the expedition. He leaned close to the Mandarin from behind and muttered, "Open your mouth again, buddy, and I'll stand on you till it don't open no more."

Mithridates slurped waist-deep in the swamp. He was still smiling when he drew himself upright again. He'd always looked for subordinates willing to use their initiative.

The three of them made considerable noise—but there were other things sloshing through the swamp. The generals—and their guard at the Mess Building—seemed to accept those sounds with equanimity.

Which was more than Mithridates could do, half-sunken and doubtful that he could clear an arrow from his mired quiver even if he had warning before jaws closed on his legs.

A fetid breeze blew toward them past the Mess Building, further cloaking their sounds. Mithridates could hear the guard when he neared the east end of the building; walking . . . whistling. The tune was familiar. "Yankee Doodle."

But only the first verse, and that off-key no matter *what* mode or scale the guard thought he was using.

Other footsteps sounded on the gravel.

The Mess Building had been set against the retaining wall. Mithridates could almost touch it now. He took a chance, the necessary chance, and dragged himself back up on the gravel.

It was a harder job than he'd expected. The fill

was neck-high on him when he started; the swamp held him like the mouth of a giant grouper, sucking him back to devour him; and the cypress pilings trembled as if he were gripping a juggler's stilts, threatening to topple over on him.

If they did, the whole building would follow. That would suit Satan's sense of humor very well. . . .

Clear at last, Mithridates sprawled on firm ground. He opened his mouth as wide as he could, to minimize the sound of his gasping.

"Who's that?" the sentry called. He strung "that" out into two syllables, "they-it," on a rising inflection.

Mithridates rose and picked his way toward the front corner of the building. He hoped that the noise he and the men behind him made would be hidden by the sidewall, or that the sentry's attention focused elsewhere.

"Who goes there?" the sentry demanded with death and panic in his tone.

His safety clicked. He already had a round chambered.

"Just a lonely friend, soldier," AE called softly. "You're American too, aren't you?"

"Ma'am?" said the sentry.

Mithridates risked a glance around the corner. Light from Barracks One gleamed on the rifle, angled up instead of being pointed at the intruder. The sentry was in front of the door, ten feet away.

Easy to rush him, grab him.

But a shot in the air would be as complete a disaster as one aimed straight at the king's own heart. Trying to break through to the tunnel entrance in the certain crossfire would send them all back to the Undertaker's slab—

And Satan's whim, unless *this* were Satan's whim.

"Who're you?" the sentry asked. Before AE could answer, he added, "You're a *woman*?"

"Oh yes, I'm that," AE said. There was a whisper of bitterness in her tone; but there was nostalgia as well, and soft memories. "My name's Amelia. What's yours?"

"Burton," said the sentry shyly. "Burton Atwater." Then, "I didn't know there was women here."

AE's face was a soft blur, shaped into features only by the sound of her soothing voice. She was taking short steps, easing her way toward the soldier's left side without seeming to threaten him. Even so, Burton edged away from her—which brought him that much nearer the trio at the edge of the building.

"Only me, Burton," AE said. "That's why I'm so lonely."

"Ma'm, I don't think—"

"Were you in the European War, Burton?" AE went on quickly, cutting short the boy's nervous attempt to return to his Orders of the Day.

"Europe, ma'm?" "You-rope" in his twanging accent. "No ma'm. I'd never been beyond Red Oak till I went to Cuba."

The rifle's lockwork and the long bayonet fixed to its muzzle gleamed as Burton straightened to Attention—heels together, back stiff, and his right hand beneath the rifle butt, holding the weapon vertical. If they rushed him now—

"We took San Juan Hill, ma'm," Burton said

proudly. "That's in Cuba." In a wondering voice, he added, "I was shot there. In the leg."

"They charged straight uphill into entrenched riflemen," the Mandarin whispered. His voice startled and infuriated Mithridates, though because of wind direction and the angle of the building, there was little risk that the sentry would hear them.

"Completely unnecessary," the Mandarin continued despite Mithridates' frantic attempts to shush him without making a greater commotion. "Their commander should be here with Sir John."

"Oh, you poor boy," AE said. Her concern was only partly play-acting. "Were you . . . were you all right afterwards?"

"I don't rightly know, ma'm," Burton admitted. His rifle wavered as he looked down at the gravel. The king jerked his head back around the corner.

"I was real poorly for two days, maybe three . . . And I don't seem to remember much after that."

"Oh, you poor boy," AE repeated softly as she walked closer to the sentry; close enough to touch him.

"Ma'm, you've got to get away from here!" Burton said sharply, bringing his rifle down again. The woman was already too close for him to keep her beyond the muzzle. He backed a step.

Someone tugged gently at Mithridates' elbow. Shamwas had moved up alongside the king. The Assyrian gestured his willingness to leap onto the sentry.

Mithridates shook his head.

"Burton, what's the matter?" AE murmured. "I'm just so lonely." She was edging closer again. "I just want somebody to hold me. Won't *you* hold me, Burton?"

The sentry stood, trembling but transfixed, as though he were a rabbit in a serpent's hypnotic stare. The woman's pale hand stretched out toward his cheek.

"Hold me, Bur—"

"Jezebel!" the sentry screamed. His rifle filled the night with its blast and blinding red flash. "My mother warned—"

Mithridates swung the sentry against the side of the building. The fellow's head hit the wood; he collapsed like a stuffed doll, his rifle making an additional clatter against the gravel.

"There's still time!" the Mandarin shouted, tugging Mithridates toward the steps by his sleeve.

The king slapped him away absently with a backhanded sweep of his bow. "AE!" he shouted. "Are you—"

"I'm all right!" the woman cried. They were both shouting—and both half deaf from the muzzle blast. "He wasn't aiming. Just frightened . . ."

A signal rocket shot off from the steps of the cadre barracks. Its trail kinked at a crazy angle and it zipped across the parade square, shedding sparks. A second rocket performed properly, punching three hundred feet up before dissolving in a cluster of white stars.

"Sir?" demanded Shamwas.

"Back to the barracks," Mithridates ordered. He grabbed the Mandarin with his free hand. "Fast! Forget the swamp!"

The door and windows of Barracks One smashed

outward with the enthusiasm of the anti-tank company to join the action.

The king and his companions bolted past the singsong babble of human bombs. The girls were stumbling and objecting to the darkness, since their eyes were adapted to the lamplight inside. Their instructor tried angrily to restore order.

The quivering signal cluster was light enough to guide Mithridates, but the falling-trashcan *thump*! of a mortar behind the cadre barracks warned that an illuminating flare was on its way.

"Halt!" shouted Burton. He began to fire across the empty parade square as fast as he could work the bolt of his Krag-Jorgensen.

"*Attack!*" screamed the Chinese instructor. It was hard to tell whether the response from the two hundred throats of her charges was a word or simply the mindless squeals of so many excited lemmings.

"Sir, what's going on?" Kalhu demanded.

The flare burst high overhead, throwing down pitiless magnesium shadows. Mithridates' men were formed in eight kneeling rows in front of the barracks, waiting for orders with anxious eyes.

A satchel charge went off. It was louder even than the screams that preceded it. The night shook.

"Into the swamp," Mithridates ordered. "We're going to Zahhaq by the river. Everyone hold the spear of the man ahead so we won't get separated until we're clear—"

More satchel charges went off—perhaps a dozen, simultaneously. Most of the Mess Building's metal roof sailed up on a bubble of white light.

"—of this mess and can get organized."

"We can't—" the Mandarin began.

Mithridates had been dragging the Easterner by the wrist. Kalhu grabbed him by the throat instead as he sprinted for the swamp, bawling, "Follow me!"

Behind them, machinegun fire was punctuating the intervals between bomb blasts.

Phelps, the Confederate soldier who'd been so proud of his Henry rifle, looked around at what the light of Paradise displayed. He spoke for most of the men when he said, "I never *seen* so Christ-bitten a stretch of land before!"

Certainly he spoke for Mithridates; though the king would have phrased his assessment differently.

They'd struggled their way to firm ground—what passed for firm ground—in the darkness. The island on which they squatted was crowned with a grove of thorny acacia trees. Water—covered with bright green tufts of floating cabbage—lapped the mud at a few points, but for the most part the land was extended by mats of papyrus like those surrounding the way station.

Men were missing. Mithridates couldn't even guess how many had disappeared in the night, but he'd certainly lost more than the generals demanded as payment for passage through their tunnel.

"If you give in to . . . evil," said AE with a pause before she spoke that particularly absolute word. "Then you feed it. You were right to take the risk."

Mithridates grunted, pretending to concentrate on clearing the leeches from his ankles with the head of an arrow.

But he hadn't had any choice. They were his

retainers, and he *couldn't* have decreed their deliberate slaughter.

"Anyway," said AE, "everyone may be all right. Just not here."

"Yes," said the Mandarin in a voice almost too bland for sarcasm. "Whatever could give one the impression that this swamp is a place of death and desolation?"

A young heron fluttered on the edge of a nest above them, then slipped. Its squawk of fear ended on the spikes of the next branch below. Feathers fluttered, then all was still. Legs, wings, and the long black neck hung down from thorns. The startled eyes were already glazing.

All the acacia branches were decorated with similar rags of feathers.

An adult bird clattered back to its nest. Its left wing was a frame of bone and desiccated cartilage from which only a few flight feathers dangled. The right wing was more nearly whole, but the bird's rib bones were visible and its skull was bare. Its mate croaked interrogatively through a beak whose lower half had fallen away, while a bright-eyed chick watched in mingled fear and hunger.

Mithridates stood and eyed the acacias, wondering if there were any way to climb for a better view. Not without falling like the heron chicks, he supposed.

A man might not be killed instantly by the long acacia spikes. Instead, the wounds could fester and eat away his flesh for days. . . .

"The way station is in that direction," the Mandarin said, pointing past an inlet of cabbage-covered water toward the north of the island. "If there's anything left after last night."

"We've escaped from the way station," said AE forcefully. "We don't want to go back there."

"And that's the *only* guidance I can give you in this swamp," the Mandarin continued as though the woman hadn't spoken.

"Which way does the river flow from here to Zahhaq's city?" Mithridates asked abruptly. "Are we upstream or downstream, here?"

"What an interesting question . . . ," the Mandarin said.

"Then answer it!" Mithridates snapped in a tone that brought Kalhu to his feet with a hand on the pommel of his short-sword.

"Downstream, I should think," the Mandarin said. *But* . . . his eyes hinted.

"Where is Zahhaq's city?" AE asked. "What . . . what does it appear to be?"

"Madam, I'd rather not get into speculations of that—" the Mandarin began in the assumption that he could be supercilious to the female.

"Lady asked you a question, gook," said Kalhu, taking the Mandarin's ear between the thumb and finger of his left hand. He lifted the Easterner's throat to lay the cool blade of his sword across it.

"Then Babylon, your graciousness, and will you kindly take your sword away before an accident—"

Mithridates waved the Assyrian back with exasperation, though he could understand how Kalhu felt. "All right," he decided aloud. "We'll build rafts of the wood here—"

"There isn't enough!"

He looked at the Mandarin. The sword had irritated the Easterner, but Mithridates' eyes—

The Mandarin bowed without irony.

"We will build rafts, gathering enough trees from this and surrounding islands," Mithridates continued. "We will pole our way upstream until we reach . . . Babylon. We will—"

"Cap'n, what'll we do fer vittles?" Phelps interrupted. "I been on short rations before, but thet don't mean I learnt to like it."

"There will very likely be villages along the shores as we go along," the king said crisply.

"I don't know that," whispered the Mandarin, his face close to the mud.

The great, barbeled head of a catfish rose through the layer of cabbage. It burped stale air before gulping down a fresh bladderful and disappearing.

"And we may be able to catch fish and game as we go along," Mithridates continued. "In any case, we don't know how far we have to go. The food you were issued at the way station may be sufficient."

The Mandarin straightened. He kept his face calm, but the mocking sneer in his eyes couldn't be hidden.

And the king couldn't bring himself to anger, because he too knew how absurd the hope he'd just articulated was.

"If it warn't fer bad luck," Phelps said morosely, speaking for everybody in this *place*, "I'd have no luck a'tall."

"There's a ship!" shouted one of the Assyrians, pointing down the channel through the papyrus. "But it's on fire!"

"Glory hallelujah!" cried Phelps. "A steamboat's comin' to take us offen here!"

"If only he's right," murmured AE; and the king echoed the words in his mind.

The vessel, a little stern-wheel paddleboat, was lurching its way along on a course which reed banks separated from the escapees' island except at narrow intervals. The boat was within a hundred yards of them, but in another few minutes all of the vessel save the flaring baskets atop her smokestacks would disappear from sight forever.

Mithridates could see black crewmen on the vessel's deck. None of them looked to the side, and the chuffing engine overwhelmed the shouts of the men on the island.

One of the Americans in Mithridates' entourage pointed his muzzle-loading rifle skyward and squeezed the trigger. The hammer clacked loudly against the cap; the gun didn't fire.

"Dang," said the man, lowering his weapon.

"Some of you wave your shirts," AE ordered. "They can't possibly come this close and still miss us."

The rifle banged, recoiling out of the hands of the man who was examining it to see why it hadn't gone off. The Minie ball splashed a crewman's brains against the paddleboat's deckhouse. The dead man and the billet of firewood he'd been carrying hung in the air for a moment while the echoes of the shot died away.

Both objects toppled over the boat's side. A white man wearing a black coat and bowler hat leaned from the deckhouse and bellowed, "What the devil do you mean, sir!" over the shriek of vented steam.

The boat continued to coast forward, but the

captain had disengaged his paddlewheel preparatory to reversing down the cross-channel to Mithridates' island. He called something angrily to his surviving crewmen, all of whom were lying with their faces pressed against the deck and their arms crossed over their heads.

"Dang," the rifleman repeated, this time with a cheerful inflection. He began to reload.

Mithridates smiled broadly. "Do you see, Mandarin?" he said. "The first thing that's necessary for success is the willingness to take risks. We'll reach Babylon with no help from those butchering generals of yours!"

He couldn't imagine why AE was hiding her face in her hands. After all, if the captain wasn't overly concerned about the accident to his crewman, why should they be?

Mithridates fluffed out his mud-stiffened trousers, wishing that he could greet their rescuer in better state.

The captain, a ruddy-faced man whose beard and moustache were bleached almost orange by exposure, strode to the bow when his vessel grounded six feet short of the island's baking mud. He jumped with less hesitation than Mithridates would have shown in like circumstances, splashing muck in every direction and sinking above the ankles of his knee-high boots.

He strode out of the water, kicking cabbages ahead of him, and stamped his boots. Instead of cleaning them somewhat, they sank again to the uppers in a shore that was little firmer than the channel.

"Baker," the man said, extending his hand to the king. He was a squat, muscular fellow, and he radiated an air of ill-suppressed violence that contrasted with the strict formality of his bowler and dark suit. "Sir Samuel Baker, at your service."

Mithridates shook the man's hand. "Mithridates," he said, wondering precisely how he should identify himself. "Late of the Administration," he continued after an imperceptible pause.

"Why, really?" Baker said with dawning enthusiasm. "Sextus Mithridates, King of Pontus, Enemy of Rome, and all that?"

"Why, ah, yes," the king said. It wasn't a reaction he'd expected from one of the New Dead.

"Read about you in school," Baker explained. "And I've spent a good deal of time in your old stamping grounds besides."

"You're a Cappadocian?" Mithridates said in puzzlement. Though the fellow could be a descendant of the Celtic bandits who'd settled to the southeast of Pontus—

"Good Lord, *no*!" Baker spluttered. "I'm British, of course. But I've potted moufflon sheep in the Taurus, and a proper challenge it is, too."

Mollified by the memory, he eyed Mithridates' bow and said, "You're a sportsman as well, aren't you? Have you ever brought a stag to bay and finished him yourself with a knife-thrust to the heart?"

Mithridates stiffened. "I've taken my share of boar on foot with a spear," he said sharply.

"Commendable, very commendable," Baker agreed. He lifted his hat and scratched his scalp. "I'll have to try that myself one day."

Sweat and the hat's protection left the hair on his head several shades darker than his whiskers.

He turned and nodded toward AE. "And is the lady your, ah—one of your wives?" he asked.

"My name's Earhart," said AE, offering her hand with no sign of being disconcerted. "Amelia, but I prefer AE.

"And," she added, cutting through the small-talk in a way neither of the men had managed, "at the moment, we're trying to get up the river. To Babylon."

Baker looked startled again. "Surely not Babylon?" he said.

Mithridates looked at the Mandarin, who bowed and said, "Noble sirs, I have stated my belief—but I can claim no more for it than belief." There was a spiteful glint in his eyes as he raised them again to the king. "You chose not to attempt the route I was sure would lead to my lord Zahhaq."

"Well, that would be a change from expectation," Baker said, shaking his head. "Although—"

He looked around. "Although frankly, my expectation was that I'd never reach the headwaters. Be permitted to reach them, you see."

The other men on the island were crowding about the leaders with anxious expressions. None of them dared break into the discussion, but they made a loud background of clanking harness and "What'd he say . . . ?" repeated scores of times in whispers.

Mithridates nodded agreement with his own deepest fear, the one he was afraid to form even in his mind. All of this, the escapes, the seeming rescue, might be a plot of Satan's. . . .

Or a plot of the Power who toyed with Satan as well.

"You see," Baker explained, "I have the boat, but I'm fearfully short-handed. At the moment, I've only four boys to cut fuel." He remembered something. "Three, that is."

"Terribly sorry about that," Mithridates offered sincerely, a leader apologizing for injury to the property of another leader. "It was an accident, of course."

Baker shrugged. "I quite understand," he said. "No other way to get my attention. Believe me, I would have been far the greater loser had I missed you and steamed on. *Now* I've got enough crew to cut my way properly through the Sudd instead of prodding at it again and again in hope of finding a channel clear all the way to the source."

Baker stared backward in his mind's eye. "As I thought," he mumbled, "I'd have to do for all eternity."

"If we're going to attempt this," said the Mandarin, "then the sooner we begin . . ."

"Yes, yes, of course," Mithridates said. "Kalhu, start getting the men aboard."

He pursed his lips as he estimated the paddleboat's capacity mentally. "It'll be tight, but not as tight as a warship with all her oar-benches full. We'll manage."

"Not so fast, old boy," said Baker brusquely enough that the king's eyebrows rose in expectation of a challenge. "First—"

"Off and on, you scuts!" Kalhu bellowed, delighted to have orders and a plan of action. "Column of twos!"

"—we need fuel, all the fuel we can get. Any axes in your lot?"

"Perhaps a few," Mithridates said, glancing around his troops. He relaxed again to realize that Baker's concerns were purely practical ones.

"No matter," the Briton said. "The swords will do well enough, I'm sure. And they'll do splendidly to hack our way through the Sudd, yes. . . ."

Baker's ruddy face looked like that of a saint permitted a vision of his god.

Mithridates found the expression disconcerting. It reminded him of Sir John French talking about perfect success . . . and he was more than a little afraid that his own face looked the same way when he let himself think about defeating Satan.

"Kalhu," the king ordered, "we'll need these trees—all of them—for firewood. Tell off a sufficient number of men and cut the timber up in one-cubit lengths."

"Yessir," agreed the section leader. "The rest to board?"

"Of course, of course," Baker interrupted. "Board them at once and I'll start teaching them their new duties tending the boilers."

Mithridates gave a tight nod that Baker could ignore if he chose to do so. The fellow didn't offer the deference to which a King of Kings—or the Deputy Ruler of Hell—became accustomed, but he seemed utterly determined to accomplish his goal.

And so long as his goal was the same as the king's, Mithridates didn't feel pressed to adjust the situation.

The paddlewheel churned a full circuit against the clinging mud before Baker's vessel got under way.

Florence was the name on the vessel's deckhouse and perhaps originally on the bow, though all her hull paint had been worn away by slogging into the massed vegetation.

Baker handled his rudder cautiously. Controlling the flat-bottomed, shallow draft boat was more like guiding a ball across smooth stone than it was to driving a chariot. Inertia turned fractionally skewed control inputs into groundings—bucking along the side of the cross-channel as the paddle tried to ingest papyrus, then squelching inexorably broadside into a mud bank from which it took three hours to extricate them.

"They'll learn," said Baker, still jovial with the turn of his fortunes. "We'll ground a dozen times a day, and your chaps will get the business of clearing us down pat."

"There isn't *time* to ground a dozen times a day," said AE tartly.

Her tone startled Mithridates. Then he realized she was finding a sane source of frustration on which to let out the anger she felt over the slave's death. At least she knew that everyone around her was confused by the degree that the accident had bothered her.

"Oh, don't worry, madam," Baker said cheerfully. "Soon they'll have us off in a matter of minutes. Well, an—"

The boat grounded again, fiercely enough to throw everyone forward. Men shouted and cursed one another as they sorted themselves out.

"—hour or less," Baker completed. Braced by the control wheel, he was still standing upright. He backed off the steam and strode to the bow, with the king and AE in tow. The Mandarin flaked dried mud from his robe as he followed at a slightly greater distance.

The *Florence* had run a dozen feet up onto a carpet of reeds. The vegetation bobbed and rippled to either side and in front of them.

"It looked like we were all right," Kalhu said as he glowered at the reeds that had waited around an almost imperceptible angle of the waterway.

"Go on, probe it," Baker ordered. "One of you lot use your spears."

A black who'd been part of the *Florence*'s original crew tried to take a spear from one of the Assyrians—who knocked him down without even wondering what the crewman had in mind.

Kalhu, with a glance at Mithridates for approval, lay flat on the deck and thrust his spear down into the reeds. "Nothing," he called. "Nothing solid." His shoulders heaved down a final hand's breadth, then withdrew.

"There's less at the bottom than at the top," the section leader said as he rolled to his feet again. He peered at his spearhead. There was no trace of mud on it. "Nothing but water and roots." He frowned. "Is that possible, sir?"

"It certainly is!" Baker said. He either didn't know or didn't care that Kalhu had spoken to the king. "And now that I've got the crew, we'll treat it as it should be treated. Twenty of the men will cut, and we'll put the rest on drag ropes until we break through."

He beamed out over the papyrus. Many of the bracts at the top were bursting open with an abundance of seeds. "The Sudd won't defeat us now," he promised Fate aloud.

"You don't . . ." wheezed Mithridates as he set his weight against the drag rope. His right leg drove a hole through the roots, doing nothing whatever to pull the boat forward.

The same thing happened to at least nine tenths of the other men on the ropes paired to either side of the channel their fellows had hacked into the choked, floating mass Baker called the Sudd.

"Have to be here," the king said, completing the sentence as he mechanically lifted his leg and tried to find a firmer purchase for it.

Fresh leeches humped their way toward his boot tops. Mosquitoes buzzed them briefly, then rose to find other flesh to probe. Professional courtesy in Hell.

"You don't have to be pulling a rope," said AE calmly. Even without a portion of the boat's weight to burden her, the woman sank more often than she managed not to.

"Pull!" bellowed Kalhu at the head of the starboard rope.

"It looks better if I—" Mithridates said, and pulled, and sank, both legs this time, the left that took the thrust and the right that tried to lift the other clear again. AE put her arm around the king's shoulders and gave him the minuscule support that was enough to let him fight free again.

"Water!" someone cried.

To Mithridates, sunk to the knees and soaked to the waist, it sounded like a bad joke. But AE turned and looked, her face brightening in hope. "It's Baker," she said. "He's got a better view than we—"

"Pull!" ordered Kalhu enthusiastically.

They all pulled, even though half the team was staggering and off-balance from their latest surge against the drag ropes. The *Florence*'s twin stacks burped black smoke as the engine torqued the little vessel forward to the best of her ability.

The channeling crew cheered. Each of them clung to the next man's belt with one hand while chopping and sawing the reed mats with his sword—stoop labor of the worst variety.

But a man in the center of the line had lurched forward because there was nothing more solid than floating cabbage beyond his last cut, and then the men to either side of him were kicking and cursing in the water beside him, damning the rest of the crew for not dragging them out faster.

"We're through!" AE cried, and so many throats took up the call that it was almost a minute before any of those on the drag lines realized that the men in the water were screaming and clambering back onto the mattress of Sudd while blood spread in the sudden current that bobbled the cabbages.

Mithridates found his footing.

A man on the *Florence*'s deck fired over the bow, a bang and a gush of white smoke. Baker was running forward with a double-barreled weapon of his own, while Assyrians still aboard the vessel snatched up their bows or spears.

The Minie ball kicked up a vertical feather of spray eight or ten feet ahead of where the man had disappeared in a gush of blood. A huge crocodile surfaced in the middle of the plume, unharmed by the shot.

When the man in the beast's jaws screamed, blood bubbled from his mouth and nostrils.

Mithridates had an arrow nocked and ready for the smooth, practiced motion that drew the arrow to its razor-sharp barbed head. The bowstring would break, or the laminations of the bow itself would separate. . . . The weapon had gotten wet as he trudged forward with the rope, and anyway, this was Hell.

But he'd been the foremost archer of his day as well as the greatest king, and his skill at archery was beyond any boorish Roman general to take from him.

The string held; the bow held—

And the arrow disappeared to the fletching in the throat scales of the crocodile.

The beast's head tossed, flinging the man away jeweled with blood. He hit the water and sank as air whistled through the punctured lungs and body cavity.

Bullets, arrows, and a few thrown spears struck the crocodile and bounced off its armored back as it arched in a dive. Baker fired a charge of shot that spattered in a wide oval over the surface. Several of the pellets could be seen glancing away in shimmering arcs.

Mithridates nocked a second arrow, but he held his bow in a rest position.

Kalhu was making angry attempts to halt the stampede of men toward the boat, trampling one another and splashing with cries into the newly cut channel. The king ignored the commotion.

"Did you hit it?" AE asked.

They were alone beside the hawser, which scores

of men had been drawing a moment before. Arrows and an occasional musket were being fired over half a circle from the deck—with no target except the surging reed mat.

"I killed it," the king replied with the pride of exemplary accomplishment.

"Watch it," AE said. The two of them hopped over the rope looping forward like a hungry python as the *Florence* bulled her way unaided through the new-cut channel. Baker had returned to the deckhouse.

"Section Leader!" Mithridates ordered. "Get these ropes taken in or they'll foul the paddle!"

The clear, ringing order quelled panic as no amount of Kalhu's bellowing would have been able to do. Men paused, helping their fellows out of the water and grasping the hawsers even before Kalhu had time to organize the operation.

"I wish the man could have been saved," said AE as they walked back to the vessel themselves. "But with wounds like that, nothing could have been done."

"Of course," said Mithridates. His hands and face were black with the mosquitoes settling to feast, but his mind was on the perfection of the shot he'd made. He was smiling.

"Of course," AE murmured as hands reached down from the *Florence*'s deck to help them across the ribbon of open water, "none of us can be saved, can we?"

If the king heard her, he gave no sign of it.

The *Florence* was loaded heavily with over a hundred armed men aboard her, but the water above the barrier of Sudd was glass-smooth except for ripples left by wading birds and hippos.

The marshy banks and the shallows were alive with birds in gay plumage. Ibis with yellow beaks and brilliantly red legs and masks squabbled with the gold-purple-scarlet splendor of crowned cranes. Spoonbills, storks, and perhaps a hundred other species patrolled the reeds and mud flats in stunning profusion.

Mithridates felt his hands begin to itch with anticipation.

"Keep her steady," Baker said and handed the wheel to one of his black assistants. He took one of the double-barreled shotguns beside him in the deckhouse, a fine weapon with silver mountings.

He looked at Mithridates and said, "Shall we see, then, old boy?"

The king smiled agreement.

Together, the leaders walked toward the bows of the vessel. The other two surviving blacks followed, each of them holding a gun and reloading equipment. They were too familiar with the drill to require orders.

"What's going on?" AE asked the Mandarin, trying to keep the concern out of her voice. She hadn't heard the discussion that led to this, because it had been conducted in the leaders' eyes at the moment Baker and Mithridates met.

"A man once said to me," the Mandarin answered cryptically, " 'Things don't work here the way they're supposed to.' He was right, of course. I think that's because we keep attempting to do the same things we did—above."

AE looked at the Mandarin, then started for the bow.

"And of course," the Mandarin continued to himself, "those are most likely the reasons that we're here. . . ."

Baker fired both barrels. The charges of heavy shot ripped through the massed birds in an explosion of feathers. Victims flapped and hopped at crazy angles, like dice bouncing on a hard table. Uninjured specimens at the fringes of the carnage launched themselves into the air.

Mithridates began to shoot with the speed of a machine.

The wings of a royal ibis froze in mid-beat. Its head hung limply from the point the arrow pierced its spine and long russet neck. Two crested cranes fluttered down together, pinned by a single shaft. A pelican tumbled, its neck held in a curve by the arrow that snapped through its body and into the back of its skull. A—

Baker fired his second shotgun. Birds only a little distance from the lead-cut swathes looked around at the gunshots they hadn't learned to associate with danger. Baker lifted the third gun from the hands of the black ready to load the second.

A rain of arrows splashed the mud banks, spiking an occasional bird to the ooze—usually without killing the victim instantly. Wings and long, splayed legs thrashed against the ground in frenetic death-dances. Riflemen joined the action, cloaking the *Florence* in tatters of white smoke as she steamed slowly through the humid air. Sometimes the bullets missed or clipped limbs, but when a two-ounce ball hit a big bird squarely, it flung the body like a feather pillow through the mass of other targets.

Phelps, near the leaders in the bow, fired into the water at a knotted limb or the nostrils of a hippopotamus. Whatever it was disappeared before his third shot, but he continued firing with grinning enthusiasm until he emptied the fourteen-round magazine of his repeater.

There was a pause while gunmen reloaded and the archers massaged their string-scraped fingertips. Baker hefted the reloaded shotgun he'd just been handed by his first assistant, then lowered it regretfully.

The sky to port was black as birds panicked by the commotion escaped to the other side of the river, but the only targets nearby were those thrashing in their death throes.

"Put in to the bank," he ordered the helmsman. "We'll retrieve our arrows, what?"

Mithridates nodded. He hoped the Briton had noticed not only that the royal arrows had all struck targets, but also that they'd been aimed for particular effect rather than simply to bring down single birds with hits in the center of mass.

"Who knows?" said the Mandarin with his hands in his sleeves. "There may even be a few edible varieties among them."

AE looked at the Easterner without expression. She sympathized fully with the ironic disdain in the words; and it disturbed her to agree with the Mandarin in anything.

"M'Tchiki . . . ," Baker said, looking at his second assistant. His full moustache fluffed as he thoughtfully pursed his lips. "Load your piece with solid ball, I think. In case we have other visitors."

He and Mithridates grinned tightly at one another.

AE scowled at both of them and walked to the vessel's port rail, staring across to the far shore while men tumbled over the starboard side to pick up arrows and trophies of their handiwork.

The river was unguessably wide, here. Although the *Florence* seemed to be resting on the mainland, the land immediately to port was a muddy island. The knobs and sprawling green humps farther into the stream were islands as well, for as far as AE could see across the hazy water.

Nothing was stirring on them, in the water, or in the air. The huge flock of birds had vanished like a jellyfish in the noon sun. The light of Paradise had taken on an amber cast in the last minutes, as though it were shining through a flask of urine.

AE glanced around. The Mandarin stood close to her, blandly smiling. She stepped past him, tight-lipped. Her boots rapped quickly on the deck as she walked to the far rail.

"Mithridates!" she called.

The immediate margin of the river was mud, but grass grew on the firmer ground just beyond and alternated with thornbush and acacia within twenty feet of the shore. Hooves and paws of many types had trampled the mud, though for many yards those tracks were being obliterated by men sightseeing through the carnage of moments before.

The king—splendid in purple and gold above the waist, khaki with dried mud below—waved back. He was a hundred yards from the *Florence*, accompanied by half a dozen Assyrian soldiers carrying trophies spitted by gold-banded royal arrows.

"Come back!" AE shouted. "Something's wrong. Come back!"

The king said something inaudible to Kalhu at his side.

"All right, everybody back aboard!" the section leader bellowed.

Baker and his black gunbearers were between AE and the king. He looked up, tilting his bowler against the glare. "What's this?" he called to her angrily.

The Assyrians—even the Americans, though they were Baker's close contemporaries—began to move without argument. Some glanced back at the king in disappointment; some, from the way they hunched together and quickened their pace, either sensed *wrongness* as AE did, or were willing to accept anybody's fears as justified.

"Now just a minute!" Baker said as men streamed past him; voices stilled, eyes darting from the ship to the landscape to their companions . . . hands tugging arrows free and dropping the bloody trophies in which they'd been imbedded. "There's no need to—"

His assistants tensed. Their posture made it clear they would bolt for the ship in a moment, whether or not their master released them.

Mithridates stepped close to his British colleague and murmured something into his ear. Baker grimaced but relaxed enough to wave the blacks on ahead of him. The king gave Baker a comradely pat with his free hand.

Mithridates was smiling, but his left hand held his bow with an arrow nocked. He'd readied the weapon since AE called, and his friendly glances to see how the men were reacting swept back and again across their surroundings.

AE felt a surge of warmth to realize that the king wasn't merely humoring her: he'd taken the warning seriously.

Though she herself couldn't tell *what* was wrong.

The *Florence* rocked on her bed of mud as the men piled aboard her. The three blacks were getting up steam. Baker's assistants had bolted back so quickly that they'd seemed on the verge of throwing down the guns on the way.

"Most of you lot shift astern!" Baker ordered grumpily as he stamped aboard the vessel. "And you, young lady—"

The rush to the stern was general and violent. The *Florence*'s bow rose from her mud cradle with a sucking noise and a whiff of sulphur from vegetation decomposing in an absence of oxygen. The boat slipped back into the channel even before one of the crewmen engaged the paddlewheel without being ordered to do so.

Mithridates, the last of the men on shore, blurted, "By the cleansing Fire!" as the bow rail rose, lifting him by the one hand with which he'd managed to grip it before the boat moved.

Without hesitation or calling for help, AE caught the king beneath the left shoulder and crooked left knee that wobbled for a purchase. He swung aboard, holding his bow high so as neither to damage it nor to spike anyone with the arrow held across the grip between his middle and index fingers.

The king's body and the woman's were similar:

rangy, with scarcely enough muscle to cover the bones beneath—until those muscles contracted and showed how they'd been trained by the stresses of a hundred-pound bow or the mechanical controls of a large aircraft.

"Not all of you, dammit!" Baker shouted. "Do you want to sink us?"

He waded into the mass of men, jerking them forcibly toward the bow again. The third one he seized was Kalhu.

Briton and Assyrian stared at one another for a moment. The men were already moving apart, lessening the boat's dangerously stern-heavy condition; the black at the wheel seemed to have matters well under control.

"Fine, that's the way it should be," said Baker, releasing the section leader—who hadn't budged. Baker stamped over to Mithridates and AE, resuming where he'd left off: "Now, young lady, what's—"

A pair of huge skeletons, arsinotheres from thirty million years before Man, trampled snorting through the brush screen. One of them smashed the lower branches of an acacia, though there was plenty of room to have stepped aside and avoided the thorns.

Their skulls turned, as if they were viewing the *Florence* with their empty eye-sockets.

"Rhinoceroses?" Mithridates suggested as his left hand twitched upward and back, instinctively bringing his bow into position before lowering it as useless.

The skeletons began to trot along the shore, angling in the *Florence*'s direction. Their shoulders were as high as a man was tall. As they approached, the creatures lifted their skulls. Huge, paired horns swept forward over their snouts, and smaller, vertical horns sprouted from just above the eye-sockets.

"Farther to port!" Mithridates shouted. "You at the helm! Take us out into the stream more."

"Not rhinos," Baker said, cocking the external hammers of his musket and raising the butt to his shoulder. "Horns are wrong. But—"

AE put a hand under the weapon's fore-end and lifted until the muzzles were pointing into the yellow sky. Baker glared at her in speechless fury.

"Don't be absurd," the woman said.

Baker looked at Mithridates, then followed the king's somber gaze back to the shore. One of the arsinotheres blatted loudly, though the skeleton had no lungs to drive the sound nor nostril flaps to break it into sharp, angry segments.

"Yes," said the Briton softly. "Yes, of course."

The *Florence* began to draw away from the arsinotheres. They halted and slashed sideways in a play of slaughter, sweeping fountains of mud from the shore. In minutes, the skeletal creatures were out of sight from the vessel's deck.

But the sky was still a purulent yellow, and there was no animal life to be seen from the *Florence* for the next week.

The water was mirror-smooth and, like a mirror, doubled the heat and glare that Paradise hurled down on the paddleboat. One of the Americans used his ramrod to dangle a fish-hook over the side. The line was one he'd unraveled from a stocking, and another scrap of cloth acted as a lure.

He'd used an ibis feather for bait earlier, but

somebody'd eaten the plume during the past night. It didn't seem to matter. None of the fish had been interested in the feather, either.

A pair of vultures circled overhead. Like the arsinotheres, they were skeletal. Occasionally they swept low over the *Florence*, wafting with them a stench of decay.

"This has to end," Baker mumbled to Mithridates. "This never happened until I took you aboard."

The king looked at him, then looked away. Mithridates' jaws worked slowly on a scrap of harness that Kalhu had offered him. His own clothing didn't include any leather items. . . .

"Shut up, you fool," said the section leader—as big as Baker and, like Baker, driven to the edge of madness by his hunger. "You'd never have gotten out of the reeds if it weren't for our king."

"Would that I hadn't . . . ," Baker said. But he didn't mean that, and the truth of Kalhu's comment was too obvious to bring a more violent rejoinder.

AE could have borrowed a hat with a brim, but instead she shaded her eyes with both hands as she peered over the bow. Alone of the folk aboard the *Florence*, she kept up a level of interest in what she was doing instead of simply going through the motions.

Mithridates let his eyes follow the line of the woman's. He tried to imagine that there was—that there could be—something interesting in the changeless vista of sere vegetation, mud-yellowed water, and jaundiced sky.

"There," AE said. She pointed. Lack of food had sharpened her features to the fineness of a mummy covered with parchment skin.

"There what?" said Baker.

"Sticks in the water?" said Mithridates.

"By God, a fish-trap!" said Baker.

A pair of reed fences V-ed into a narrow throat downstream, then opened into a circular pen to hold the fish that had been routed into it. Baker understood its significance—as soon as AE called the fish-trap to his attention.

"George!" he called to the man standing blank-eyed at the wheel. "Put into shore at once. There's a village here, and they'll feed us."

"They may be starving too," AE protested.

"By *God* they'll feed us!" Baker repeated. When his hands opened and clenched, light shone from the bristles on the backs of his fingers.

One of the scouts stepped back into view on the hilltop and waved down to the main force with his blue forage cap.

Kalhu glanced over at Mithridates, who nodded.

"Move out!" the section leader ordered. The loosely ordered double line of troops—riflemen in the front rank, except for the trio who acted as scouts—began to straggle up the hill.

"You're planning an attack," said AE, tight-lipped. She didn't look at the king as she spoke.

"An attack may be necessary," Mithridates replied. "That's less likely if we overawe the natives to begin with. No village existing around here will want to try conclusions with *my* force."

Acacias and flaking basalt boulders were the only variety in a landscape of yellow grass. The fish weir had been empty, but there was a dusty trail leading from it over the hill. The village couldn't be far.

"It's going to be dark soon," AE said.

"You can stay with the boat," Mithridates said.

"And pretend nothing was happening?" AE replied. "I suppose I could try. But I've never been one for staying at home."

A squad of ten Assyrians and two of the black crewmen—M'Tchiki followed Baker with an extra gun—guarded the *Florence*. Mithridates looked around him, considering what it would be like if the boat were lost and they had to trek the rest of the way to—Babylon, Zahhaq, wherever—on foot.

He'd led armies through wastes this grim before.

"A penny for your thoughts," AE said.

The king smiled at her. "Planning," he said. " 'If this goes wrong, what then?' It served me well in life."

He paused. The smile faded. "Of course, things *did* go wrong. At the end, everything went wrong—even the poison I took to prevent my mutinous soldiers from handing me over to the Romans."

AE's grin was friendly and her tone softer than her words as she gibed, "Then Hell hasn't been much of a change for you."

"They're in sight!" Baker called.

Below, near an outcrop of particularly large boulders, nestled a village of circular, thatch-roofed mud huts. Walls, roofs, and rocks were a medley of deepening shades of gray. There were about twenty dwellings in the complex—each consisting of five or six separate huts built around a central courtyard.

The settlement was half a mile distant, and for a

moment Mithridates thought they might be able to slip all the way up to the walls unnoticed by using the available cover. Then a black carrying a trumpet hollowed from an elephant tusk leaped onto one of the boulders and blew a warning that echoed with plangent clarity across the wide valley.

"Double-time!" Kalhu shouted, anticipating the order the king was about to give. Mithridates' tiny army jogged toward the village, its spears and rifles slanting sideways but ready for use at a moment's notice.

The king looked over at AE. She wouldn't meet his eyes, but she was jogging with the rest of them, determined to be up with the leading men when they reached the circling huts.

The trumpeter had disappeared within a compound, but his ivory horn sounded again. Shadows fluttered on the gray walls as frames covered with thornbush were dragged across hut openings. Here and there, light glinted when a spear was lifted.

"Kalhu," Mithridates called, "hold up fifty—" panting as he ran "—yards from the walls," spitting out another phrase each time his right sandal touched the ground.

"No!" shouted Baker, "No! All the way! Storm the walls! Before they get organized!"

"Sec-*shun*!" Kalhu bellowed. "Halt!"

An arrow wobbled out of the village, aimed through the interstices of a brushwood gate, but lofted over the top in a high arc. In all likelihood, the arrow was meant only as a warning. It didn't reach the men—the lines had merged as the section jogged forward—crouching down as they caught their breath.

"What are you doing?" Baker demanded. The run had reddened his face still further, but he wasn't breathing any harder than Mithridates himself.

"Give me your neckerchief," the king said to AE.

He handed her his bow in exchange for the square of white silk that kept her neck from being chafed by the collar of the flight suit she still wore. Waving the kerchief from the tip of an arrow, Mithridates walked slowly toward the village.

After a moment's hesitation, Baker joined him. The Briton still carried his double-barreled musket.

Though the individual dwelling complexes appeared to be randomly placed, there was only one gate into each—and a single gate into the village as a whole. Capturing the place against determined opposition would be a matter of battling to control one strongpoint after another—with no final victory until every individual hut had been bloodily taken.

"We come in peace," Mithridates called fifty feet from the gate.

Another arrow sailed over the wall. This one struck between the leaders and their waiting troops. "Go away!" someone called through the gate in an old man's voice.

"We can't jeopardize our purpose simply to coddle savages," Baker said. He was as little affected by the arrow as Mithridates tried to appear. "We need the food—"

"We come in peace!" Mithridates repeated forcefully. "We're travelers and we need food to continue our journey."

He and Baker continued walking forward at a measured pace.

At the corners of his eyes, the king could see his men preparing to try conclusions with the villagers. The Assyrian bowmen were as scornful of the local archers' quality as the riflemen; but the troops hadn't considered what it would be like to crawl through narrow alleys in which a spear was better than a gun, and the natives knew every trap and turning.

"We have no food here," the voice from the village quavered. "The Nyam-Nyam raided us last week and took everything."

"The end justifies the means," muttered Baker. "I've got a double charge of shot in each barrel. I can clear the gateway, and then we rush—"

Mithridates stepped in front of his companion to forestall the plan he'd just offered. "Wait here," he said/ordered.

Mithridates was within twenty feet of the gate. He continued to walk forward. "Come out and talk with me," he coaxed. "We can't bargain when we can't see each other."

"We can see you," the voice insisted. "Now go away. We haven't got any food."

"If you won't come out . . . ," the king said after a moment's hesitation. "Then let me come in. We have to see each other to talk."

He heard a voice, then several voices merging in a rising argument within the screen of thorns. He turned to Baker and called, "Sir Samuel? Go back to the men. I'm going inside for a moment."

The argument within was becoming very heated.

"I don't think it'll be necessary to destroy this place after all," Mithridates said, loudly enough to be heard by the troops—and by those on the other side of the mud wall.

The argument ceased. "All right," said the original voice grudgingly. "But we won't give you any food."

The spiky gate slid a few inches to the side. "Farther," Mithridates demanded. It slid another inch.

"*Farther*," he repeated.

"Then just go away," responded the voice.

Pursing his lips, the king squirmed through the half opening. His baggy tunic caught twice on thorns. He cleared it with care each time before continuing.

The courtyard was crowded with villagers. They were as much an obstacle to entering as the thorns had been. One of the men carried a long reed bow. It was amazing that he'd found enough room to draw it, even for the wobbly warning shots that were all the situation required—for the moment.

Most of the men carried spears. Their points were wafer-thin and long enough to slide all the way through a chest cavity. Unadorned, the natives' skin was reddish-black; but the males were painting their skin and tight, woolly hair gray with handfuls of wood-ash.

"Why have you come here?" demanded an old man with rings of hammered wire in his left earlobe and nostril.

"We're passing through," Mithridates said. He attempted a conciliatory gesture, spreading his arms wide, but he bumped a hut with his left hand, and a pubescent girl—lathe-slim and clad in a belt of two strands of coral beads—with his right. "All we ask is a little food and we'll trouble you no more."

The interior walls were decorated with moldings

and with geometric patterns of ash and ochre. Quite attractive, in their way.

More to the point, the walls were up to a foot thick. Straw-cored adobe would be marginally—only marginally—easier to batter through than concrete of the same thickness.

"The Nyam-Nyam took everything we had," the old man said bluntly. "Anyway, we didn't ask you to come here. Just get out and leave us."

"Perhaps we can help you fight the Nyam-Nyam," the king offered. "Where do they live?"

"We don't need your help," said a man with a pattern of stipples on his cheeks and random knife-scars on his chest and shoulders.

"Oh, they're terrible people," cried a woman with stippled tattoos and gold jewelry, but otherwise no more clothing than the girl.

"Three days' journey up the river," said the old man who'd been sole spokesman before Mithridates entered the village. "So far, but still they come to prey on us."

"This lot can't hurt us," said the scarred warrior. He drew the knife he wore in a sheathe held by a bracelet above his left elbow. "We'll kill him and throw his body over the wall as a warning to the rest."

Coolly, Mithridates plucked a pinch of straw from the eaves of the hut beside him and said, "With all this dry thatch, the Nyam-Nyam will be able to see your village burning themselves. They'll know there's nobody left alive here to raid."

The warrior froze in mid-step, and the chorus of agreement with his plan stilled in horror. He turned his body so that Mithridates wouldn't see him awkwardly re-sheathing his knife.

"Put him out," a woman suggested. "Let them go their way."

"With three days' rations," said Mithridates. "Then we're the Nyam-Nyam's problem. Otherwise, we'll have to stay here and . . ."

He let his voice trail off. His smile was crueler than any words he could have spoken.

"If you burn us," quavered the spokesman, "you burn all our food." He grinned with the unanswerable logic of his point.

"We like our meat cooked," Mithridates said. "We'll be able to salvage enough for three days' rations, I'm sure."

He pinched the girl beside him, checking the layer of fat over her ribs. She screamed and jumped away, colliding with the gate and pushing fiercely at it even though she must have felt the pain of the thorns.

"Let them go to the Nyam-Nyam," said the old man, closing his eyes. He opened them. "Go out to your other devils, stranger," he said. "We'll give you grain for your journey."

"Over the walls," added the scarred man. "We'll throw the bags out."

His face hardened. "Now leave," he said, and he didn't have to fondle his dagger hilt for Mithridates to understand the alternatives.

The king edged his way past the barbs of the gate again. It was a long process. By the time he'd started to walk calmly back to his companions, the villagers had managed to lever the first sack of maize over the wall.

* * *

"Treacherous devils," Baker muttered in remembered anger. "Slipping us a sack of dirt along with the maize. If I had their chief here . . ."

But he wasn't so much serious as seeking an outlet for the fear they all felt as the *Florence* chugged through the territory of the Nyam-Nyam. There was no sign of occupation, but every night they'd heard message drums.

Certainly the inhabitants of the first village thought their neighbors were to be feared.

"We got an adequacy of food," Mithridates said equably—Baker's reaction to fear was anger; Mithridates' was false calm. "We took no losses. It would have been expensive to capture the place by force."

"This appears to be a healthier location," observed the Mandarin. "There's green vegetation, and the birds are back."

He shrugged. "Of course, it's still Hell."

"You know," said Mithridates, eyeing the shore speculatively, "we could get get in some shooting. For food as well as sport. . . ."

"Not until we've dealt with the natives," Baker said bluntly, giving the thought no more consideration than it deserved.

"*Dealing* with the natives doesn't mean we need to slaughter them," AE said, turning from the rail to her companions with a hard look in her eyes. "You feel—even *he* does"—she gestured dismissively toward the Mandarin—"how different things are here. Even the light."

She glanced at Mithridates in appeal. "Don't you

think," she said, "that if we can avoid doing"—hard again—"awful things, that we'll reach Babylon safely?"

"The headwaters," Baker corrected without rancor.

"I've always preferred to avoid open conflict," Mithridates said with a humoring smile. "But that isn't always possible, and the Nyam-Nyam—"

"There's the place!" Phelps called from the bow. "Lots of houses, and niggers all over them!"

The shore around the river bend was bright with fabrics as women washed clothing and hung it on bushes to dry. The village proper was just beyond. Thatched roof-cones poked a dozen feet in the air, clearly visible over the reed fences surrounding them.

Kalhu slid a little closer to his king and murmured, "Don't look as solid as the last place."

"Which means they don't think they need protection from attackers," Mithridates said, expanding the observation by its corollary.

Kalhu nodded glum agreement. "And there's a mother-huge lot of 'em," he added.

The women saw the *Florence* and shouted. They began to gather up their washing with haste and giggles. There was no sign of panic at the puffing, chuffing shipload of armed men.

The male villagers who trotted in handfuls from the huts to the shore weren't panicked either. They carried boat-shaped shields of crocodile hide and lances whose slim shafts were as much as ten feet long.

The iron lance-heads added as much as two feet to the total length. Light from their needle points pricked the attention of those watching from the *Florence*.

Most of the men wore linen shifts, often supplemented with a swatch of leopard or lion pelt. Those who shouldered their way to the front were a royal guard of some sort, dressed in short-sleeved cotton outfits dyed a vivid scarlet. Their lances seemed to average a little longer than those of their fellows, but the difference would be academic to anyone gasping his life out on the blades.

The crowd began to cheer, both men and the women who, having rescued their wash from threat of being trampled, stood with armloads of bright cloth near the shore. There were at least a thousand of the natives. As Kalhu'd said, a mother-huge lot.

Too many for Mithridates' present force to attack, certainly.

"They've got canoes," said Baker, adjusting the percussion caps under the half-cocked hammers of the gun in his hands. "They may come after us if we try to pass them by."

"They appear to be friendly," AE said tartly. "They're prepared for trouble; but for *that* you can scarcely blame them."

"We'll put in to shore," Mithridates decided abruptly, noting that Baker was implicitly bowing to his judgment here. "We need supplies, and after all, they appear to be friendly."

The king smiled at AE. "But we'll be prepared for trouble," he added. "No one can blame us for that."

Mithridates thought he'd made a mistake—a fatal mistake, within the limits of Hell's fatality—when the crowd surged up to the *Florence* on three sides as she squelched her bluff prow into the mud. Men—

even women with bundles of washing—splashed waist deep to reach the boat and try to scramble aboard.

They weren't hostile, even though the rush had the appearance of a concerted attack to Mithridates and the others who feared just that.

"Stop them!" Baker roared.

"*Don't* kill!" Mithridates cried. "But stop them coming aboard!"

There was a struggle all along the front half of the deck rail as those aboard the vessel tried to keep the natives off. The Assyrians were particularly effective with their heavy armor and crossed spears—sometimes spear-butts, but they were veterans who had no desire to try lethal conclusions with ten times their numbers.

Three men trotted from the village carrying a log drum and crossed poles to support it with one end high. A fourth man, heavy and smiling, wearing a red beret and an off-the-shoulder garment that was either silk or polished cotton, followed the drummers.

They set up the equipment. One of them with an ostrich plume in his hair began to hammer out a rhythm with a stick and the palm of his left hand.

The crowd fell back, laughing and excited—even those who were bruised by the enthusiasm of Mithridates' men. The people formed an aisle back to the heavy man waiting in royal state, jostled self-importantly by the men in scarlet. The drummer hammered a crescendo, breaking it abruptly to collapse in smiling exhaustion.

The heavyset man raised his arms and called, "Munza, Chief of the Nyam-Nyam and Greatest Chief of All Chiefs, greets his stranger brothers in iron coats!"

"I told you," AE said smugly to Baker. "Friendly."

"Well, it's certainly not their reputation, is it?" the Briton retorted angrily; but he raised the muzzles of his gun, proving that he agreed.

"I am Mithridates, King of Pontus, King of Kings," Mithridates replied, raising his right foot onto the deck rail to increase the impression that he was talking down to underlings. He held his bow in his left hand, but his gut impression was the same as AE's: the Nyam-Nyam were friendly, improbable though that seemed.

"I come in peace as a traveler," Mithridates continued, well aware that Munza made a more royal figure than he did in his muddy rags and skin covered with insect bites that had festered since his party broke out of the Sudd. "We ask nothing of you and your people except supplies. For which we are willing to pay."

If they could come up with some medium of exchange . . . but that was a bridge to be crossed later.

The crowd dissolved in good-natured laughter. Munza raised his hands again for silence and said, "We are a rich people, Mithridates-Who-Is-Also-A-Chief, but we have few brothers in this place. Welcome, brothers. Feast on our bounty. Go on if you must, but stay with us if you wish and teach us to wear iron coats also."

Mithridates took a deep breath. "Section Leader," he ordered Kalhu formally, "for the time being, you'll guard the vessel with half the men as you choose. I and the remainder will try Nyam-Nyam hospitality."

The crowd of natives cheered when they heard the order. The faces of Mithridates' own men were subdued. They ranged from hopeful to very worried indeed.

"In my house," said Munza, "we'll have beer and you'll tell me about your travels, brother Mithridates."

The chief wore two necklaces. One, of coral beads, supported half a dozen polished seeds. The other was of silver coins, punched through the centers and strung tightly, flat to flat, so that Mithridates couldn't guess where they'd been minted.

Not around here, certainly. Unless . . .

Unless Babylon were just up the river after all.

"Is there a great city around here?" asked AE. "With stone walls, perhaps?"

Munza looked behind them at the woman. "Is that one yours?" he asked. "She's an interesting color. I'll trade you as many wives as you like for her. Eh?"

"No," Mithridates replied. "I keep her for her wisdom. But thank you for the offer."

He hoped that would end the discussion.

He'd thought of trying to keep the force with him together, but that plan seemed neither possible nor useful in this sea of natives tugging soldiers to one side or the other to entertain them. If the Nyam-Nyam were determined to have a massacre after all, fifty men would be overwhelmed as quickly as parties of two or three together.

"There are no peoples in the world as great as the Nyam-Nyam," Munza said pompously, returning to the question now that he'd let it wait long enough that they could pretend it hadn't been asked by a female. "No one lives in stone houses anywhere, though I have heard . . ."

The chief's thick lips pursed, though it was doubtful whether he was considering the answer—or simply whether he *would* answer. "I have heard," he continued, "that there might be such a place very far away."

He waved vaguely, up the river—but that might have been chance. "Only there are no people in it. If there were people, they would be subject to the Nyam-Nyam, as all peoples are, my brother."

"I have heard—" Mithridates began.

"Here, my brother," Munza interrupted. "Enter and refresh yourself."

Munza had led them to a huge arched hall, open at both ends for light and air but stretching more than a hundred feet on a side. Thirty-foot pillars supported the ridge pole, and a row of lesser pillars—each a tree bole, as straight and well-polished as an arrow shaft—buttressed the lower curves.

Hundreds of people were already present. They cheered the chief and his visitors.

A chair with a slanting back-post and a low wicker seat supported by brass legs shaped like hourglasses faced inward, shielded from the sun by the roof overhang. Munza seated himself on it and gestured Mithridates to the edge of the seat beside him. There was no other piece of furniture in the hall.

"Ah . . . ," said the king. "Perhaps a stool for my—"

But as he turned, he saw AE was no longer with them. The tall woman had turned away when she saw the arrangements.

She waved when she caught Mithridates' eyes, calling, "I had enough of formal levees when I was alive. I think I'll sightsee on my own."

"No," the king called. "I want—"

Want what? Her to protect him? To be able to protect *her*, in the midst of this armed crowd?

In any case, it didn't matter. AE had already disappeared, ignoring the king's peremptory order and whatever he might choose to add to it.

Sighing; uncertain of how he felt about a woman who acted like a man and a king's equal—

Not that he was a king. Not that he was a *man* in this place that was as Satan made it.

—Mithridates relaxed as much as he could on the bench. Munza took the center with the back-post, and the wicker sagged so that the two men's thighs were in contact.

Munza began what was clearly going to be a long harangue to his people, explaining that his brother Mithridates, chief of the folk with iron coats and almost as great a man as Munza himself, was visiting to offer homage to the Nyam-Nyam. . . .

There were hundreds of people lining the sides of the royal hall—the center, between the columns of shorter pillars, was kept empty—but the Nyam-Nyam village was so populous that life went on unaffected throughout many parts of it.

Initially AE was jostled as she walked against the natives still crowding into the hall, but that traffic soon thinned and she was left to wander the dirt streets at her leisure. The village stank—

But Hell stank, and the glare of Paradise was no

more painful here than through the cracked walls of the Palace of Augustus.

"Wah!" called a surprised voice as AE walked past the open gate of a dwelling compound. She paused and looked in. Two women with hair as tight as skullcaps peered from the doorway of the grass hut facing the gate. They ducked back out of sight with a giggle.

AE pursed her lips, then stepped into the compound.

Six huts—one of them much bigger than the others—were arranged in a rough circle whose interstices were closed by a grass fence. AE walked gingerly across the courtyard, expecting to be challenged.

One of the women poked her head out momentarily and blurted "Wah!" again, but there were no other signs of life.

"May I talk with you?" AE called as she put a hand on the doorjamb and looked inside.

"Why would you want to talk with us?" one of the women—there were only the two of them—asked coquettishly. She wore small gold rings in her left nostril and lower lip, as well as a G-string from which a tuft of lion's mane hung to cover her hairless pubic wedge.

"Are you alone?" AE asked. Hollowed gourds and wickerwork sifters hung from the walls of the hut. The women's hands were white with the flour they were grinding on a large, vaguely concave stone in the center of the hut.

"All the rest went to hear the chief," said the second woman. Her cheeks were scarred in a pattern of three parallel lines and, though she didn't wear rings, her headband was made of small gold conchos.

"Who wants to hear *him* again?" said the first woman with a haughty sniff. "*We're* grinding corn for the feast tonight."

She emphasized her words by stroking the rounded stone in her hands across the flour and unground grain.

"They'll beat us if we don't have it done," explained the other woman, who didn't feel a need to put a better face on the situation. Shyly—she acted like a little girl, though she was older than her fellow and had stretch marks as well as ritual scarring on her belly—she reached out with one of her white-dusted hands and touched AE's wind-roughened cheek in wonder.

"Well, I . . . ," AE said.

She was suddenly embarrassed to be intruding. Both women resumed their work in a tentative way, but their eyes remained fixed on the light-skinned stranger as they slid their mortars forward and back.

This people, for all its spears and threatened beatings, was as close to an idyllic society as she'd seen in life—much less in Hell. She had no business here. Their whole gang of armed ruffians—Mithridates' gang and Baker's gang, but hers as well (she couldn't escape her partnership)—had to leave as soon as they received the Nyam-Nyam's offer of provisions.

Otherwise they'd repay the natives' generosity by corrupting them. She *knew* the sort of men she was among. Baker—who should have been the best of them—and Mithridates, who perhaps *was* the best, the most decent—had been the ones to lead the slaughter as they steamed through the flocks of birds along the riverbanks.

"I must go," she blurted, turning quickly and striding out of the compound before her tears could flow and embarrass her further among these simple folk.

"Good-by, lady," the women called in unison behind her. Then one of them giggled again.

AE walked briskly between further hut complexes, letting the hot air dry her eyes. She hadn't expected to be reminded of simple goodness in a village of black savages. No doubt the Almighty—in whom she had never believed until she found herself here, where His being could be conjectured only from its total absence—had His reasons for condemning the Nyam-Nyam too. . . .

But for the moment, AE could only wonder whether existence in Hell would not be more bearable if she had a black skin.

Though that meant she never again would fly.

AE heard music through a nearby fence. For a moment she hesitated; then she swung open the gate and called, "Hello, may I come in?" as she entered.

"Oh, look," said the woman chopping vegetables at a long table in the shade. "Her face is pink!"

The children helping—half a dozen of them, both boys and girls—giggled appreciatively. "Where's your iron coat, lady?" asked the oldest of them, a girl of perhaps ten. Abashed at her effrontery, she ducked as though the spindly cane legs of the table could hide her from AE's smile.

The naked baby on the mat beside the table was crying softly. Paradise had sunk enough in the red sky to blaze directly onto the infant, and his newborn limbs were too uncoordinated for him to turn or to shield his eyes with his pudgy hands.

The bald-shaven man sitting cross-legged in a hut doorway plucked an arpeggio from his five-string lute, then launched into the seductively simple tune he'd been playing as AE passed the compound. He smiled at the American, but he neither spoke nor got up to acknowledge her presence. He'd hung a pair of leather squares from a twist of red yarn around his neck.

The native woman sliced a gourd with quick draw-strokes of her knife until she reached the neck, which she flung onto the dirt of the courtyard. "Do you like gourds, lady?" she asked. "Do you like yams?"

The oldest girl scooped the gourd slices into a shallow wooden bowl. A young boy gripped the bowl carefully with both hands, then trotted past AE with it and out of the compound.

"I like gourds, certainly," AE said. "Will they be boiled?"

"Oh, yes, boiled," one of the girls chirped. "How else would you eat gourds, lady?"

The man began to sing, using his voice for the burden of the music while his fingers plucked counterpoints from the lyre. He had a dreamy expression.

"Pardon me," AE said, her own face trembling between a friendly smile and a frown, "but is the baby yours? I'm sure he can't be comfortable in the sun like that, can he?"

The man broke his song with a great guffaw. "*Your* baby, Alburkah. *Your* baby!"

"No, no, it's from a slave," the woman said in obvious amazement. "Meri, bring it here. It's crying."

The oldest girl ducked under the table and scooped the infant up off the mat. The boy with the bowl, now empty, slipped back into the compound past AE.

"Lady, would you like a drink?" Alburkah asked as she accepted the baby and laid it on the table in front of her. "Meri, get the lady a calabash of water."

"Thank you," AE began, wondering whether the Nyam-Nyam were so blessed—or un-cursed—in their simplicity that water here would be refreshing. "I—"

Alburkah held the infant by the ankles and cut its throat with the knife she'd been using for the gourds. The tiny arms thrashed as blood spurted over the ground and vegetable scraps. Meri was dipping a calabash into a large-mouthed pottery jar shaded under a separate grass screen.

AE stuck her hands over her mouth as she ran from the compound. She wasn't going to scream, but she was afraid she might vomit.

The dwelling compounds were all identical, and the streets merely the portions of the village that weren't fenced apart from one another, but AE's sense of direction took her back to the royal hall by a route more direct than the one by which she'd wandered to her disillusionment.

Occasionally she met natives as she ran through their streets. When she did, her lips curled into an expression of loathing that would have shocked her if she could have seen it.

Munza was standing when AE reached the hall, concluding a period with, "—to my greatness!"

Mithridates had more room on the seat, but his posture had sagged during the oration into a reminder that physical pain was not the only possible torment.

"Ee, Munza, ee!" screamed the crowd of squatting villagers. "Ee, Munza, ee!"

AE shook the king roughly by the shoulder. Mithridates snapped around, raising the bow that he hadn't let slip even in his somnolence.

"We have to go at once," the woman said curtly. "They're cannibals."

"Who is there so great as I, who rule all this place from rise to set of the sun?" Munza resumed, ignoring or not noticing the discussion behind him.

"But they're so friendly . . . ," Mithridates said in amazement. He glanced at the chief and the assembly, judging their reactions if he—

"*Come,*" insisted AE, tugging the king's sleeve.

"All right," he agreed, rising from the royal seat and striding from the hall without a backward glance that might draw pursuit.

"Don't run," he added as they slipped past a fenced compound that hid them from the royal hall. "And don't look furtive. When we reach the boat, we'll organize parties to gather in the men still in the village—"

The *Florence*'s steam whistle began to scream.

"I'll have his *heart* for—" Mithridates started to say. His face blanked as he realized the context of what he was blurting in anger.

Villagers and men from the *Florence* piled out of dwellings. Many of Mithridates' men were stumbling as they tried to pull up their trousers or don their mail shirts again without putting down the weapons they'd snatched when the alarm sounded.

From the looks on the men's faces, their frustration at the whistle's summons was no greater than the frustrations they'd been experiencing in their attempts at pleasure until then. The sweaty native women who followed the strangers into the street were sullen. They'd hoped that with the newcomers it would be different. . . .

But Hell was Hell. A statuesque woman stood straddle-legged, glaring at the pair of Assyrians who'd just left her compound. She manipulated herself for a moment, then flounced back into a hut with tears of disappointment glittering in her eyes.

Mithridates didn't notice the woman. He was too concerned at the uproar behind them, suggesting that Munza was leading his audience with him toward the source of the alarm. That *damnable* whistle continued to scream.

Beside the king, AE's face was set over a complex of emotions. She could all too easily see herself in the village woman's fury of sexual frustration.

But after watching a baby slaughtered for dinner—for *her* dinner—she was willing to exist in Hell, so long as the Nyam-Nyam were here too.

Baker was ready with a double-barreled gun in the bow of the *Florence* when Mithridates reached it. The shallows were being sloshed to muck by returning men unwilling to wait for their fellows to climb aboard where the prow was grounded firmly.

Stragglers from the party that had landed trotted toward the shore behind Mithridates; a further number were still missing, from a quick estimate of those gathered on the boat or waiting to board her. Despite that, the *Florence*'s wheel was beginning to turn, and Baker was bellowing to the men to step aft and raise the bow.

A mob of shouting natives surged down the maze of streets. They weren't clearly hostile, but certainly they were as well-armed as they'd been when they greeted the strangers to begin with.

"Hold up!" Mithridates shouted, waving to call attention to the men yet to arrive.

"Push off, you in the water!" Baker shouted to the men still trying to board. "We'll have to leave—"

There was a squawk from the *Florence*'s deckhouse. The paddle wheel stopped rotating as it was taken out of gear. Kalhu held the throat of the black crewman at the controls.

"Go on, get aboard," Mithridates said to the woman. "They'll pass you forward; it isn't *that* great a panic."

Not like so many of the disasters that had struck armies of his, he thought as he turned coolly to survey the oncoming natives. Some of his own men were caught up in the crowd. There didn't seem to be any open hostility between the groups.

"I'll stay while you do," said AE.

"On deck!" Mithridates called over his shoulder. "Take a posture of defense, but don't start anything. And shut *off*— "

The steam whistle choked to a startled halt in the middle of a shriek.

"—that whistle!"

Kalhu smiled from the deckhouse.

Non-coms were lining the rails with armored Assyrians. Half a dozen riflemen scrambled to the roof of the deckhouse, where they had a line of fire above the helmets of their fellows.

"You're a fool!" Baker shouted. "These black beasts are cannibals! We have to stand off from the shore or we're lost!"

"I think we can board now," said AE calmly. "Unless you want to receive them from here."

"Thet's my cousin," said an American, leaning close to Baker. "Right thar, waving from the middle of them niggers. You planning to run off and leave him?"

He spoke in a tone of mild interrogation, but the muzzle of his rifle tapped the lobe of Baker's right ear.

"I don't see Munza in the first group," Mithridates said. "No, I think we'll board."

He turned and raised his hand toward the rail. Three bearded Assyrians grasped him simultaneously and jerked him aboard. AE, as tall as the king but lighter framed, flew onto the deck even more abruptly.

Stragglers started running when they saw the king board. The natives, more confused than their guests, ran easily alongside while shouting questions. Haste wasn't part of their chief's persona; Mithridates couldn't see Munza even from the higher vantage point of the deck.

"Hand them aboard," Mithridates ordered as a pair of worried-looking Assyrians slapped through the mud to the *Florence*.

"I stumbled into one of their foul kitchens," Baker said. "There were bones—freshly scraped skulls, there can't be any question of where they came from. I sounded the alarm immediately."

The American beside Baker reached down to help

his cousin, who'd lost his pants but still held his muzzle-loading rifle.

"Why is the noise?" cried a big Nyam-Nyam warrior. "Why is the *whee-whee*?" giving a good imitation of the steam whistle.

"They were greeting you as a fellow cannibal, you know, noble sir," said the Mandarin. He gave the king a look of amusement. With the troops formed shoulder-to-shoulder along both rails, there was comfortable room on the rest of the deck—behind the walls of mail shirts.

Mithridates glanced at him. "I do not eat human beings, Easterner," he said in a voice as full of metallic menace as a sword whispering out of its sheath.

"Where are you going, men with iron coats?" a woman demanded piercingly.

"Where are you going?" took up the crowd in thunderous unison.

"No, but you told the first village that you did," the Mandarin explained, without the mocking superiority of a moment before. "And they told the Nyam-Nyam—because the Nyam-Nyam would have been very angry at subject tribes who hid the coming of brothers like us, noble sir."

Of course. Drums. Couriers, even. The *Florence* chugged upstream more slowly than an experienced runner could run along the bank. . . .

An Assyrian who was trying to struggle through the packed natives found them resisting him. One of his fellows at the *Florence*'s rail nocked an arrow and began to put tension on his bow.

"Wah!" cried one of the warriors, lifting his spear

high so that the crowd itself didn't prevent him from thrusting.

"Good people!" Mithridates shouted. "Hosts and brothers! My god, who is the Fire, warns me that he will destroy all this place."

"Wah!" alternated with, "When!" The Assyrian slipped through without difficulty. His friend dropped his bow to lift the man aboard.

Two more stragglers, both Americans—their discipline wasn't nearly as good as that of the Assyrians, but neither man had lost his weapon—made their way to the boat as well, working their way around the edges of the crowd and wading in chest-deep water to board abaft the deckhouse.

There might be some men still missing, but Mithridates couldn't see any signs of them. He *could* see Munza, approaching in his former state with musicians—and with a bleak expression this time rather than a smile of greeting.

"Everyone shift to the stern," the king ordered over his shoulder. "Kalhu, back us away."

The deck trembled as the *Florence* wobbled on the mud beneath her keel. Shouting to the crowd in the voice he'd used to marshal his troops on the wind-swept plain of Cabira, Mithridates continued, "Flee before my god the Fire wastes you with this doomed place! Flee to your neighbors and beg their—"

The *Florence* broke the mud's grip with a slurping sound, bobbing into the stream on the wave her churning paddle wheel kicked up.

"Of course, we still don't have any supplies," Baker grumbled, as if he hadn't sounded the alarm himself.

"—forgiveness for your past cruelties! Flee before the Fire strikes!"

"Does he really expect a flame to sweep the village?" the Mandarin asked AE in amusement, loud enough for the king himself to hear.

"We can hope it does," AE said. She stared at the Chinaman with eyes as cold as her memory of the infant spraying blood. "We can certainly hope it does."

A herd of twenty or more impalas exploded from the water's edge where they had been drinking until the paddleboat startled them. The black-and-white flashes on their rumps floated in the air as momentary flags. Then the antelopes were gone into the high grass and acacias.

Mithridates released the tension on the bow he'd drawn just too late. Baker mumbled a curse. He lowered the gun from his shoulder, but his thumb hesitated before returning the hammers to half-cock—in case one of the impalas would bound back into sight for a moment.

AE tightened her lips; but a moment later she said, mostly to herself, "We need provisions badly. I can see that. But . . ."

One of the Assyrians loosed an arrow from the *Florence*'s deck, aiming at the tip of a horn above the waving grass—or perhaps shooting in frustration at the lack of a target.

"There's plenty of game out there," Baker said judiciously. "It's the racket the boat makes that frightens the beasts away before we can get a shot."

The thought made him start to cock his gun, but

he paused and eased the hammer back to the middle notch when intellect reasserted itself.

"We could beat," Mithridates said. "Certainly we've got enough men for that." His fingers began to play with the nocks of his arrows; he felt saliva form in his dry mouth.

"A bit wet, don't you think?" Baker said, his eyes narrowing as he peered at the land past which they chugged. The gold and green of new grass poking up through dead growth was blotched at frequent intervals by the sullen hue of reeds thrusting fingers of swamp deep into the low-lying plain. "Still, it's not as though the beaters have to move quickly. . . ."

A trio of zebras stepped out of the grass. Because both the leaders were eyeing the crew speculatively, they noticed the beasts only when a rifleman lifted his gun. The echoing *bang*! and the plume of white smoke hung in the air, but the zebras had disappeared even before the shot was fired.

Baker grimaced to stifle another curse. "Put in to shore!" Mithridates called to the black at the helm.

"And shut the engines down," Baker added. "We'll drive them straight to us!"

He tugged his beard as he looked back to the expectant faces of Mithridates' soldiers. "Well, *they'll* drive them straight to us," Baker amended.

AE looked from one man to the other. "We need *food*," she said angrily. "Not another—"

She broke off when she realized that nobody was listening to her except the Mandarin—and his face wore a cynical smile.

* * *

AE was frowning thoughtfully as she rejoined Mithridates, Baker, and the three blacks equipped to reload their master's guns when the drive began.

"The trail keeps going quite a long way," she said, gesturing inland, back the way she'd come. "The ground's fairly firm, at least for the half mile I followed it."

She paused before adding, "I found human footprints as well as hoofmarks."

"You shouldn't have gone so far," the king said angrily.

"You can wait for your slaughter if you must," AE retorted. "I'd rather take the chance of a lion or something than just sit here!"

"You could have disturbed the arrangements, spooked the game!" said Baker. "It takes time to set up a beat, and you walking through the middle of it may have ruined it all!"

"I didn't see—" AE began.

"I wonder," said Mithridates, "if there *will* be lions?"

"There might," said Baker, fingering the silver-inlaid locks of the gun he carried. "Yes, you'd think there would, wouldn't you?"

A musket boomed from deep in the swamp. Both leaders straightened and the blacks, waiting on their haunches, jumped to their feet.

"Can you see the flags?" the king murmured. The first man in each of the two lines of beaters carried a ten-foot pole with a scrap of cloth on it, to permit the leaders on the river bank to judge how near the lines were to linking up to start the drive.

"Not for half an hour," Baker replied. "We should have used longer poles."

"They couldn't *carry* longer poles through ground so soggy," AE interjected tartly.

"But they should have joined by now," Baker added in a hopeful voice. "They're signaling that they've started the drive."

Very faintly in the still air, Mithridates heard men begin to shout and the clashing of sticks.

Another musket boomed. This time he could see the puff of white smoke rise, more than a second before the sound of the shot.

Baker took off his hat and slapped it furiously against his left thigh. "They aren't supposed to be hunting!" he said. "They're supposed to be driving game to *us*!"

"Relax," the king said calmly, standing at leisure with an arrow nocked and pointed to the ground before him. When he raised the bow, the same motion would draw it to the full. "Shots work as well as shouting to drive the game. And there'll be plenty for everyone, I'm sure."

His fingers toyed with the bow, drawing it a few inches and relaxing, as though he were checking its tension.

"I wish that you'd limit—" AE began.

An impala cleared the edge of the high grass in a beautiful, arching leap that looked more like rubber bouncing than a living creature in motion. Before the antelope touched the ground, Mithridates placed an arrow above the right shoulder and out through the ribs on the other side of the slender body.

The impala changed direction as if it were a reflection of itself, bounding back toward the grass with fluid grace. AE cried out in surprise. The king's second arrow took the beast at kidney level near the spine as it was leaping away.

Baker fired.

"Bagged him!" the Briton cried as the impala seemed to collapse in on itself. It had been a female, but the next that arched out of the screen was a lyre-horned male whose buff-and-white chest splashed red as it caught the load of shot in Baker's right barrel.

The impalas had come straight toward them, almost down the path AE had followed a moment before, but the spotted cat was a hundred yards away when it stepped onto the strip of mud and grass stunted by flooding. It was looking back, toward the noise of the beaters.

"Don't!" Mithridates cried as Baker raised the loaded gun the black had just handed him, but Baker was closer to the cat than the king who had to jump forward to—

"You'll spoil the pelt!"

—aim, and the musket already slammed its load of buck-and-ball into the leopard's deep chest, overprinting a bloody rosette upon the spotted coat.

It didn't matter, because the cat's mate was only a half step behind and Mithridates' arrow took her through the eye, a lucky shot but a skillful one as well. She dropped like a statue while the male thrashed and bit his side, kicking up the bloody ground—

"You can't *eat* a leopard!" AE screamed.

—until Baker gave him the other barrel and knocked him into trembling quiescence.

The beaters were slogging closer, firing as they came. Mithridates could hear the snap of bowstrings as well as the thump of distance-muffled musketry. A Minie ball burred angrily overhead, skewed and deformed by a heavy bone or a horn-boss.

"Bloody fools!" Baker grumbled. "They'll *kill* one of us if they keep shooting—"

But the last of his words were drowned out by the blast of his shots and the screams of the zebras, one hit squarely and two peppered.

The sky was as yellow as aged urine. All the sounds moved slowly, as though they were traveling through baffles that ground off their edges.

AE looked back toward the *Florence*, moored two hundred yards downstream so that she wouldn't startle game when it burst from the grass. The Mandarin had been alone aboard the vessel—he'd refused to join the beaters, and there was no reason for him to stay with Baker and the king if he didn't want to do so.

But now the Mandarin was trotting toward them. Only the rags of his normal complacence remained: his hands were thrust into the opposite sleeves of his robe, and his pace was not quite a jog—but he looked over his shoulder at the paddleboat and toward the grass as though he expected something terrible to lunge from it and swallow him.

"Please," AE cried, touching both leaders on the arm. "*Please* stop this before . . ."

"A gun, damn you!" Baker bellowed to the black

who was fumbling to cap the second barrel of the weapon he'd just reloaded. "A *gun*!"

Mithridates hit the leader of the herd of topi, but the dark, hump-backed antelope were large animals. This one already carried three arrows in his withers; the splotch high on his chest was probably from a musket ball.

The shaft of the king's arrow shattered when the point hit bone. The herd changed direction, spurting back toward the beaters. Two more arrows and Baker's lead raked them from behind.

The air was bitter with powder-smoke and blood.

There were more shots and shouts from men hidden in the grass. They were quite close by now. Mithridates panted in the sullen air, massaging his string-scraped fingers against the silk of his trousers as he waited for another target to appear.

"Noble sirs, something is wrong!" the Mandarin cried.

Baker said, "Don't stand where you block my shot, you blackguard, or I'll—"

"Your *men*," the Mandarin continued with breathless insistence. "From the deckhouse I saw. Something's—"

An Assyrian fifty yards out into the grass flew high enough in the air that Mithridates could see his legs, muddy to the knees, as well as the bloody, fist-sized tear in the man's mail-coat.

"Back to the boat," the king ordered in a calm voice while his wide, empty eyes scanned the waving grass.

AE had been looking toward the *Florence*. "Mithri—" she said.

"Now, damn you!" he screamed.

The grass trembled. Bow up, arrow drawn to the head; Baker's eyes open and aiming past the brass bead between the muzzles of his gun.

Phelps, mud to the waist, stumbled into view, flailing a path through the grass with his repeating rifle. "Sir!" he shouted. "Sir!"

"Get ahold of yourself, man!" snapped Baker. "What's going— "

The grass parted again for the huge horned skeleton of an anchiceratops, stalking forward on feet that splayed to spread its weight over ground too marshy for a man to run without sinking. It bore a stubby spike over its nose and a pair of brow horns as long as a man's arm—the right one bloody, and blood also splashed over the sharp-edged frill that swept back from the great skull.

If the bones carried flesh, the beast would have weighed a ton, and the soft ground splashed beneath its charge as though that weight were still real.

Two of Baker's loaders threw down their guns and fled. The third stood as if frozen, the ramrod poised above the powder he'd just poured into the muzzle.

Phelps turned and fired without raising the rifle to his shoulder. Lead chipped a strut of the anchiceratops' bony frill, leaving a gray smear. Phelps worked the lever and shot again as Baker fired past his shoulder and Mithridates put a vain arrow into one of the empty eye-sockets an instant before the beast's nose horn hooked Phelps in the groin and flung him screaming ten feet in the air.

Phelps spun over the anchiceratops' back in a crumpled arc. He hit the mud where the grass was ankle high and already trampled by the beast's rush. His rifle was still in his hand, its brass frame winking in the harsh light.

Phelps didn't move after he hit.

Men from the downstream side of the beaters were rushing aboard the *Florence*, rocking her on her cradle of mud. The skeletal creature into which Mithridates continued to slap arrows must not have been the only monster loose beneath this yellow sky, though the king couldn't see what was driving those men.

The anchiceratops spun on its left hind leg, twisting its skeletal frame with the grace of an elephant turning and at least as quick. Mithridates' arrows penetrated a shoulder blade; sailed through the hollow chest cavity without ticking a rib at either side; and shattered at the base of the creature's spine.

Baker fired the gun he'd snatched from the remaining loader and capped himself. The muzzle lifted with the unexpectedly great recoil. The iron ramrod spiked the anchiceratops' frill.

AE darted past the creature to reach Phelps' body.

"No!" Mithridates said, his fingers reaching for another arrow and not finding one.

The anchiceratops reared as Baker's cap cracked on the left barrel that the black hadn't even started to reload. The skeletal dinosaur brought its hoofless forelegs down together on the Henry rifle, smashing the stock and bending the barrel and receiver into a U as it crushed them down into the muck.

Its huge head swept toward AE, bending over the body of Phelps, who'd been eviscerated when the horn threw him.

The woman's eyes met the empty sockets. The skeleton very deliberately rotated its blood-spattered, six-foot-long skull and lunged forward to spike Phelps with a brow horn. The body twitched like a sack of rice being pickaxed. AE screamed; the anchiceratops turned toward the leaders and lifted its head as if snuffling the air.

The creature trotted off down the river bank toward the *Florence*. Each of its skeletal footsteps shook muddy ripples from the ground.

"What?" muttered Baker. "W-what?"

Mithridates had started toward AE before the monster spun away from them, though he couldn't have imagined what he intended to accomplish with his bare hands. He'd even flung down his bow, useless as it'd proven even before he emptied his quiver.

"Get up, woman," he ordered harshly. "We have to . . ."

His voice trailed off while he tried to find a suitable conclusion for the sentence.

Kalhu staggered from the grass. He'd lost his spear. His eyes were blank with the exhaustion of having dragged his armored body through bogs, knowing the thing hunting him and his troops was able to surge after them faster than a man could run on dry ground.

"Here, reload this!" Baker ordered, thrusting his gun toward the black beside him.

The anchiceratops charged the *Florence* at a full gallop. Men on the boat's deck screamed. A puff of white smoke signaled a shot. The muzzle blast was answered by the howl of a Minie ball ricocheting from bone.

Baker's servant let the gun drop, then flung his bandolier of powder and shot into the river. He bolted into the grass and out of sight.

Baker swore and grabbed for the weapon, though its right barrel was bulged from firing the ramrod and it was only an awkward club without loading materials. Kalhu caught the Briton's wrist.

"Let—" Baker started, but even his flaming temper recognized the madness in the eyes of the Assyrian.

"No," said Kalhu. "It don't hurt us unarmed, you see? It don't hurt us." His voice was as soft as clouds streaming past a mountain top.

There was another shot from the *Florence* and at least a dozen wobbling arrows fired by those who hadn't lost their bows. The great skeleton paused as the men on deck ducked or tried to crawl into the deckhouse already packed with their fellows.

Another creature strode out of the grass near the boat, walking on two legs and holding the limp remains of a man in its skeletal jaws.

The anchiceratops leaped. The crash and screams were simultaneous. Yard-long splinters of decking lifted, followed by a fountain of brown water as the creature crashed through the hull as well.

The carnivore's skeleton turned as if eyeing Mithridates and his fellows.

"We've got to go!" the Mandarin cried, looking up at the yellow sky as if he hoped for succor from that precinct.

"Yes, all right," Mithridates said. "We'll go—"

The *Florence*'s boilers blew, flinging bits of those aboard her in all directions.

"No!" cried Baker. He snatched up his gun in his left hand and, holding it overhead by the balance, jumped into the stream.

The creatures they'd shot moments before were transforming. Their flesh melted, but the bones remained articulated. Mithridates thought he saw the claws of the leopard just upstream of them twitch as if retracting into pads that had disappeared.

"—inland along the path," the king continued as though those were the words he'd always intended. "We'll probably meet some other stragglers. In any case, that's our only—"

"Come," said Kalhu, dragging the slighter Mithridates toward the path with as little ceremony as he would have shown a balky dog. The anchiceratops had vanished when the boiler exploded, but the bipedal carnivore was stepping in their direction with the care of a robin who thinks he hears a worm.

"I found it!" Baker cried. His hair and beard dripped river water. The bandolier was gripped in his right hand.

Baker sloshed toward the bank. "I'll dry it and—"

Those on shore caught the rush of motion behind Baker, but even they didn't realize what was happening until the huge jaws closed over the Briton like a vault door, stifling his screams the moment they began.

Baker was a big man, but only his head and limbs stuck out beyond the interlocking teeth of the skeletal crocodile. The creature's skull was almost as long as that of the horned dinosaur; its tail lashed the river fifty feet from its snout.

It backed deeper into the stream to finish its victim.

The grinning curve of the crocodile's mouth was all the more hideous by contrast with Baker's expression. His eyes were still open when the river closed over him and the thing he had drawn to kill him, but his explorations would soon be over.

Until Satan reassigned him from the Undertaker's slab.

Even Kalhu had paused when the third skeleton surfaced to take its victim. He was staring, his eyes and mouth open, as bubbles rose through opaque water colored by reflection of the yellow sky.

The bipedal carnivore continued to mince in their direction.

"Let's go," Mithridates said in a hoarse whisper.

They were surely lost if the carnivore rushed them, but he didn't think it would. Both cat skeletons were writhing now, and the bones of the male impalas were rubbing their horns on the ground as if in preparation to use them.

"*We're* still alive," Mithridates added as he led the two other men and AE up the trail with no idea of what lay beyond.

It wasn't true that they were alive; but it made him feel better to pretend otherwise at times like these.

A wedge of the horizon glowed like molten sulphur, but apart from that, Mithridates was encircled with hellish darkness.

"Sir?" a voice called desperately from the night. "Sir? Is that you? *Somebody*?" Brush crackled toward them.

"Who goes there?" Kalhu bellowed as though he

had a line of archers ready to loose on an unsatisfactory reply. The Mandarin, who had been just in front of Mithridates and AE, suddenly drifted off to the side.

"Section Leader Kalhu? Oh, Nergal has blessed me!" blurted the voice. The speaker, another Assyrian straggler, stumbled onto the trail. "I'm Trooper Hashemer."

"Seven of us, now," Mithridates murmured; but what his mind reviewed was the number of his losses, almost the whole of his tiny army.

He should've been used to that, now. It had happened to every army he'd fielded in life. So near, but . . .

"Do you have your weapons, boy?" Kalhu demanded, gripping the straggler's shoulders to keep the man from embracing him.

Hashemer was the third of the beaters Mithridates' party had met as they followed the trail inland. All of them, veterans though they were, had been terrified by the sudden disaster in the marshes and the way Paradise had set like a guillotine to pack their lonely fears in shadows.

"N-no, Section Leader," Hashemer admitted.

"He wouldn't *be* here if he'd kept his weapons," AE said. "Certainly *you* know that, Kalhu."

"Yeah, guess I did," the section leader admitted.

His bulky form relaxed in silhouette against the sticky light on the horizon. "Just habit. Glad to have you with us, Hashemer." He patted the junior man on the back.

They started forward again, picking their way

through the thorns that edged inward from both sides of the trail.

"Ah, Section Leader?" Hashemer asked. He'd fallen in directly behind Kalhu. The other two Assyrian troopers were at the back of the short column, keeping so close to Mithridates and AE that they frequently blundered into the leaders. "Ah, where are we going?"

"Mind your own—" Kalhu began instinctively.

"We're heading toward the light, Trooper Hashemer," AE said. Her clear voice carried through the section leader's and silenced it. "The source of the light, that is."

"And just what might *that* be, lady?" Kalhu asked, in the thin tone of a disciplined man irritated that the rules had been changed on him. Good soldiers didn't ask questions. Good officers didn't *volunteer* information to nosy soldiers who'd just been told to belt up by their non-coms. But if questions were the order of the day . . .

"The Mandarin says it may be Babylon," Mithridates answered carefully.

"I said," the Mandarin protested, "the sky above—I never said Babylon, I said 'Zahhaq's palace'. . . . I said only that the sky above Zahhaq's palace burned like that at night because . . ."

The rest of the group waited a moment for their guide to finish the thought on which his voice had trailed off. He said nothing further.

"All right, why is the palace lighted?" Mithridates said, more tired than piqued.

"It isn't the palace itself," the Mandarin admitted.

"It's the river and moat surrounding the city. They, ah, burn."

Kalhu turned and stopped, blocking the Mandarin. Mithridates grabbed the Easterner and spun him around, though with the guide's back to the sullen light, his expression was no more than a pool of shadow.

"The city is aflame?" Mithridates asked, drawing the sibilants into a sound like stropping knifeblades. "Where are you taking us, Easterner?"

"Not the city," the Mandarin said quietly, earnestly. There was no escape except through convincing the deadly men surrounding him. "There is a moat of fire around the city, that is all. Protection for Zahhaq. Protection for those whom he takes beneath his mantle."

"There's no better place to head, you know?" AE said to the king gently. "We weren't going to stay in the swamp after what had happened."

Mithridates slowly lowered his hand from the Mandarin's shoulder.

"Wait a minute," Kalhu insisted. "If we left the river back there"—his gesture was merely a shrug of shadows in the darkness—"then how come it's this way too?"

"Anyway, that wasn't burning," Hashemer put in.

"Noble sir," the Mandarin said, bowing to the king before he turned. "Noble sirs, I do not say the river is the same as the river around Zahhaq's palace. I do not say that *is* Zahhaq's palace before us. But it *may* be, and if the power of Zahhaq is with us, it will be."

He bowed again.

No one moved or spoke for a moment that stretched on achingly.

"All right," Mithridates said at last. "We've been climbing since we left the river. When we reach the top of the ridge, we'll have a better view of where we're going."

"It'll be dawn, like enough," grumbled one of the soldiers in the rear. "We going to march all night?"

"We're going to march," AE said calmly while the king fought to control his white fury at being second-guessed by an underling. "Because if we don't, we have to spend the night here, with whatever else is here. Do you want that, soldier?"

"Nergal and Inanna bless," Hashemer muttered. "Not that. Nothing could be worse than that."

Mithridates smiled. "All right, let's go on, Section Leader," he said.

But the unspoken thought which had drawn his mouth into a sardonic rictus was, *Nothing could be worse? How amazingly naive.*

They came out of the hills through a notch and halted, staring in wonder at the plain beneath and the walled city that rose from it.

"It's huge," Mithridates said. "Mandarin, how many people live here?"

"I really can't estimate, noble sir," the Mandarin replied distantly. "I have never resided here, you understand. And quite honestly, I've never seen the city from beyond the walls. I've arrived through the tunnels, in the past."

"But we *are* here?" the king demanded sharply. "This *is* the right place?"

"Oh, yes," the Mandarin agreed. He seemed somewhat dazed by the circumstances, by the precise workings of what could only be called the Fate that brought them to this place after all the missteps. "The palace . . . and there beyond it, the ziggurat. . . ."

"Oh, yeah, that's Babylon," said Kalhu. "I been there. Except for the fire."

"Inanna bless us," Hashemer muttered. "*Look* at that fire."

The river of flame, which split the great walled rectangle into halves of roughly a square mile apiece, was a licking, sucking yellow. Its light was so intense that the structures nearest the fire were hard to see, like objects on the surviving portion of sun-struck photographic film.

"What's that on the pyramid?" AE asked. "It can't be birds at this distance, but I thought I saw—"

"The ziggurat," the Mandarin corrected smugly, his arms crossed before him again and his hands hidden in the flowing sleeves.

"—wings."

The seven survivors of the trek could see one another clearly in the glare of the river that issued from the rocks below them and far to their right. Eddies in the turgid flame showed that the stream was moving, though very slowly. Canals drew straight, glowing lines through the city, and the outer face of the city walls reflected the glare of its surrounding moat.

"The wings, Mandarin," AE repeated, turning her head to stare at their guide. "What were the wings I saw?"

The Mandarin looked at her. For a moment, it

seemed that he might refuse to answer; but he thought better of the idea and said, "Zahhaq stables winged lions on top of the ziggurat, noble lady. It is said that he has a car drawn by them, but I wouldn't know about that. About anything regarding the conduct of my lord Zahhaq."

He paused and cleared his throat. "Shall we descend?" he offered. He bared a hand to gesture at the paved road leading toward the walls from the barren gap in the rocks on which they stood.

"All right," Mithridates said, wondering how many times he had agreed with their guide's program for want of a better idea.

The roadway was forty feet wide—and pointless, purposeless in its magnificence. There should have been nothing more than a track—at most. The footprint AE thought she'd seen on her initial exploration was the only sign of human passage since they left the village of the Nyam-Nyam.

"Why isn't it dawn?" Hashemer asked.

They'd spread into a line abreast on the road, though Mithridates noticed that the soldiers on either end of the "formation" were keeping well away from the edges. The flames toward which they marched threw their shadows back, hideously distorted.

The Mandarin walked between Mithridates and Kalhu. "It's very hard to judge time here," he said in an emotionless, pedantic tone.

Kalhu turned and grabbed the Mandarin by either the throat or the front of his robe. He jerked upward so that the toes of the Easterner's sandals flicked like terrified sparrows above the pavement.

"What?" AE said, leaning forward to see past the king as everyone halted.

""Why isn't it dawn, you little bastard?" the section leader shouted in the Mandarin's face. "D'ye think I can't hear you lying, is that it? Why isn't it bloody dawn?"

"Let me down, please, noble sir," the Mandarin said, wheezing but able to speak—so Kalhu's fingers couldn't be buried in his throat. "I'm not lying. Let me down, noble sir, and I'll explain."

The section leader hesitated a moment, then dropped him.

The Mandarin staggered with surprise and relief but managed to keep his feet. His long fingers reached up to straighten his robe—but Kalhu reached for him again, and the Easterner blurted, "I must admit that I've never seen Paradise shine during the time—brief times—I've spent in my lord Zahhaq's palace. I—"

He looked at the surrounding faces. "There's no difficulty seeing with the, with the light from the canals. It never occurred to me that it was unusual because of the short duration of my visits."

"You're lying," Mithridates said simply. "You're not the sort who wouldn't notice."

"I'll take care of him, sir," Kalhu promised.

Mithridates caught the section leader's hand. "Don't," he said. "It doesn't matter."

"I wasn't certain, noble sirs," the Mandarin pleaded into his folded hands. "And I don't know what it means. When we came by tunnel each time before, I thought we were—very low, do you understand? Deep beneath the Hell that others knew. But if we aren't . . . I don't know."

Kalhu turned and tried to spit. His mouth was too dry. They were all dry, and the sickly yellow light was drinking what moisture the long march had left in their systems.

"We'll go on," the king said, stepping out crisply.

He was more pleased than not to learn their guide was at a loss as well. He'd had a feeling all along that the Mandarin was leading them into a trap; but if the fellow was *this* nervous and unsure, perhaps that, instead of treachery, was what Mithridates had been picking up.

"Does Zahhaq have that much power?" AE asked, her head close to the king's and her words meant for him alone. "To blank out Paradise above his kingdom?"

"My lord Zahhaq has the power to protect those who dedicate themselves to him," said the Mandarin before Mithridates could—or could decide what to—answer. "He has complete power over his kingdom. He can protect you from the anger even of Satan."

"Who *gives* him the power, then?" AE asked.

But the Mandarin didn't answer; and none of them thought their guide had an answer to give.

The walls were thirty feet high. The gatehouse piercing them was double that, looming like the jaws of a beast as the humans approached the city.

Light from the moat rippled across the glazed-brick facings, giving the fortifications the look of a living thing shifting in its sleep, or in ambush. Gilded figures were set against the background of dirty blue, but their shapes were doubtful in the trembling illumination.

They could see there was a bridge over the moat, but puffs of yellow vapor licked its edges occasionally.

Hashemer yelped and jumped sideways, staring at the pavement.

The lowering presence of the gate had absorbed the party's attention so completely that only now did Mithridates and the others look down. The road was bordered with slabs of red breccia, but the main paved expanse was of square limestone slabs, each of them a yard or more to a side. The rock was thick with ammonites, thunderstones, the twisted hornlike shells which remained of the armored squids of past ages after the soft parts had rotted away.

Except that here and there, a tentacle waved in a desperate attempt to snatch the ankles of the pedestrians.

None of them moved for a moment. Then Kalhu swore softly and stamped down on the pavement. His hobnails sparked. Dust rose, settled.

A tentacle twitched out of the dust and tugged vainly at the toe of Kalhu's boot.

"Let's go," Mithridates said, putting an arm around the section leader's shoulders. They walked on, the others following.

All of them kept their eyes fixed on the open gateway. That way they didn't have to look down.

The glazed facade reflected both the light and the dry, enveloping heat of the moat beneath the walls. The gilded figures *were* moving. Here and there, a lion grappled with a dragon, or a bull gored a spearman whose body dripped golden blood as it lifted slowly through the background of blue brick.

"I don't remember no gate like this," Hashemer

volunteered. "Even without the, the . . . you know." He lifted his bearded chin to indicate the writhing decorations.

"If this were Babylon," the Mandarin said, "the building would be after your time." He walked at a measured pace, and his voice stayed calm; but Mithridates noticed the Mandarin was as careful as the rest of them not to look at what was happening beneath his slippers.

"Why do you keep denying that it's Babylon?" AE asked unexpectedly. "The men who've been there say it is. You know it is, from the way you talk around it. Why?"

They'd reached the bridge over the moat. The curling flames drove the party closer together in the center of the roadway, but the fire's beckoning clutch didn't—couldn't—significantly increase the discomfort the humans already felt.

"Because it *isn't* Babylon!" the Mandarin insisted in sudden animation. "Because Babylon is in the upper world, not here. Because Babylon is dead and in ruins!"

Kalhu looked at their guide. "I'm dead," he said without emotion. "I remember the arrow going in." His finger massaged the base of his neck beneath his beard. "Fucking Kassite archer, it was. Just like ice. I reached up and my hand was all red with blood."

The flames chuckled. Kalhu cleared his throat, aware of the embarrassment he'd caused by discussing the one thing everyone in Hell had in common.

"Death and Eternity," Mithridates whispered. He could understand why their guide denied the city's reality, now. If Babylon was real, so was the Mandarin's own situation. . . .

"What I want to know," the section leader resumed loudly, "is where the guards are? The gates're spread like a whore's legs on payday and not a soul in sight."

"My lord Zahhaq," the Mandarin said, smirkingly pedantic again, "welcomes all travelers and refugees. He has no use for gates and guards."

The gatehouse was constructed with three chambers that visitors—or attackers—had to enter in turn. Spiked portcullises and iron-bound gate-leaves poised to close the arches separating the chambers, and the domed ceilings were slitted so that arrows and blazing oil could be poured down from the guardroom above.

The portcullises were raised. The gates were held open by iron hooks as massive as the defensive furniture. Through the last arch, the party could see a broad street raised like a causeway as it passed the two-story residences of mud brick on the left and the great stone front of the palace on their right.

The only sound they could hear was the mocking susurrus of the flames.

"I understand about the guards," AE said, articulating the thought that had occurred to Mithridates as well. "But where are the *people*, Mandarin?"

The king thought he saw the tip of the Chinaman's tongue touch his lips before he spoke. "The city is difficult of access, as you know," the Mandarin said. "There is ample room for the populace which subsists on my lord Zahhaq's bounty."

"There's *nobody*," AE pressed.

They'd walked to the inner face of the gatehouse, where they had a clear view into the city's interior. Nothing moved except the creeping light of the flames in the canals, silhouetting silent houses and public buildings.

"I have brought a few hundred persons to share my lord Zahhaq's protection," the Mandarin said. He would not meet his companions' eyes. "Stragglers like yourselves, refugees. I know nothing of my lord's other subjects."

He straightened. "I am my lord's servant, no more," he added firmly. "I will take you to him, where you can ask your questions if you choose."

He stepped out of the gatehouse, taking long, slow strides as if he were leading a procession down the boulevard's silent majesty. The remainder of the party looked at one another—

And followed.

The suction of the flames was a pillow to smother the little noises that would otherwise have formed the background as the party walked on. Vendors' cries, traffic sounds; raucous signals from the military barracks and the screaming arguments that explode between neighbors and housemates—

Or at least the echoes of the party's own footgear. The other sounds required there be a population to make them.

"Hey, I saw somebody!" said one of the Assyrian soldiers. "Up on a roof, looking at us!"

"You sure?" Kalhu asked enthusiastically. "Where?"

They scanned the residential buildings to their left. The boulevard on which they stood was above second-story height; AE lifted herself on tiptoes to peer over the low parapets where nothing seemed to move.

"Ah . . . ," said the soldier. "Ah. I guess I saw a reflection, you know. A shadow on one of them domes."

The Mandarin moved on without comment.

"This place doesn't look like a palace," AE said, eyeing the facade along which they walked. "It's a prison, isn't it?"

Mithridates stared sharply at the building: blank walls that looked high above even the raised boulevard, their straight line broken with shallow pilasters; stepped crenelations along the roof, fitfully illuminated by the moat and canals; ahead of them, the shadow of a single doorway guarded by huge, stone monsters. . . .

Of course it was a palace. If it had been a fortress, there would've been arrow slits at the upper levels. And what possible use would there be for a *prison* this big, when there were always quarries and chopping blocks for a ruler's enemies?

"The architect, noble lady," the Mandarin said without looking at AE, "did not feel a need to proclaim the throne's magnificence to the rabble *outside* the palace. I assure you, my lord Zahhaq does not dwell in a prison."

"You're properly formal about 'your lord' as we get closer," Mithridates noted ironically. "You weren't always so careful when you spoke."

The Mandarin shivered but kept his eyes straight ahead of him. His hands pressed together. "Then I misspoke," he said simply. "When I am distant from my lord's glory, then I sometimes speak with the pride of being the servant and tool of my lord in the greater universe."

"We're all in prison," AE said.

"These doors is open too," Kalhu muttered. "*Damn* but I wish there was guards. . . ."

Statues of wild bulls—aurochs with forward-pointing horns—flanked the palace entrance. They were twenty feet high at the withers, and they thrust their proud heads higher yet, out beyond the palace facade.

There were no doors or even door-posts to close the entranceway. Beyond was a courtyard and another opening, this one resting on the shoulders of scale-covered dragons.

The Mandarin continued on, the others following a half-stride behind. In the passage between the great bulls, they could at last hear their steps echo.

The courtyard was covered with glazed tile of dazzling splendor even in the uncertain light.

"As you see, noble lady," the Mandarin said, "the beauty of the palace is turned inward, for its occupants."

"What occupants?" Kalhu grunted.

"What beauty?" said AE.

The walls were sea-green, with geometric borders picked out in red and gold. Between the borders, oared vessels foundered in storms as their crews were devoured by serpents of golden fire. If you looked carefully, the figures seemed to move.

Mithridates wasn't conscious of lengthening his stride, but as the party crossed the courtyard, the Mandarin was lagging behind instead of leading as before.

The dragon statues flanking the second archway

had snake heads and snake scales, but they balanced their sinuous bodies on pairs of clawed legs like those of great birds of prey. Mithridates thought of the skeletal carnivore that had minced toward him as they fled after the loss of the *Florence*, but these were whole. And stone.

And much bigger than the skeleton would have been when fleshed out.

There was a second courtyard beyond the passage. On the other side of it was an archway guarded by stone lions.

The ground color of the walls here was brown. Between the gilt zig-zags and god's-eyes of the borders, a city of domes and parapets collapsed in an earthquake. Serpents of golden fire nosed through the rubble, swallowing those of the inhabitants with enough life in them to thrash their limbs.

Mithridates set his face. He touched Kalhu and AE—like him, on the verge of running.

"Slow it down, damn you," Kalhu snarled to the other Assyrians. "This ain't no race."

They crossed the courtyard at a moderate pace. The Mandarin said nothing, but his composure was as forced as that of any of the others.

The lion statues, both of thick-maned males, had a haughty magnificence that Mithridates never remembered seeing in the real beasts. Either the living cats sprawled with their bellies protruding, whether or not they had gorged recently—or they were engines of snarling fury, clawing forward as his arrows hit and hit and hit again, until he spurred his horse away and had to circle back to finish the job.

For a moment, hunting memories brightened the

king's expression . . . but like the other statues, these were twenty feet tall at the shoulder. An enraged lion of that size could demolish a city.

The third courtyard was as empty as the first two. Its walls were tiled in black. Light flickered against the surface without clinging, leaving only its absence and absolute nullity. There was no doorway facing the third entrance.

"This way," said the Mandarin, nodding to the left and leading the way.

"Oh . . . ," murmured AE as she followed.

That whisper of sound made Mithridates feel better. He'd momentarily imagined that they were lost in shadowed oblivion—that a gate would crash closed behind them and the ultimate black of the walls would drink them, drink him, the way it absorbed all light

Only a fool could think that. Only a fool could miss the archway in the wall to their left—three times the height of the other courtyard entrances, though without the embellishment of guardian statues.

But AE had missed the passage also, and from the way the Assyrian soldiers stepped forward at a near run, they too were glad to have a destination beyond the black walls.

"Please," the Mandarin said in horror as the soldiers clumped past him. "Please don't offend my lord Zahhaq by—"

He didn't know how to complete the sentence, but the Assyrians slowed with shamefaced looks at Mithridates. They knew better than to get spooked just because the walls looked funny. They'd seen worse things than *that*.

In line abreast, Mithridates and his party entered the throne room of Zahhaq's palace. Its splendor was as great a shock as the black sky above black walls had been in the entrance court.

The archway opened the hall in the center of one of the long sides. The ceiling was carried on a trio of great vaults with no intervening pillars.

Everything was covered with gold, not gilding but the raw, lustrous metal. Cressets flared at mid-height of all the walls to light the huge room like the heart of the sun.

"Oh . . . ," someone murmured—and it might have been all of them, including the Mandarin who knelt in obeisance.

The throne was lost at first impression in its enormous surroundings, though it was raised fifteen feet on a stepped dais and encrusted with precious stones on a background of ivory. A man with a handsome face and a full gray beard rested his forearms easily on the gleaming throne.

He was the first human Mithridates had seen, besides the members of his party, since they left the Nyam-Nyam village.

"Most noble lord Zahhaq," the Mandarin said, his face pressed against the floor—which was golden, just as the walls and ceiling.

"Rise, Mandarin," Zahhaq said in a kindly, cultured voice. "Bring in the rest of the suppliants."

The room's acoustics were unimaginably perfect. Though the throne was forty feet from the party at the entrance, Zahhaq's words were clearly audible without a noticeable echo.

"Most noble lord," the Mandarin whispered—but

Mithridates could hear him, and he was sure Zahhaq heard as well because the prince's expression remained one of kindly enquiry. "There are no others. There would have been *hundreds*, but they were lost because, because—"

He turned his face, doubled in the floor's reflection, to glare at Mithridates.

"Your gracious majesty," Mithridates said, taking two steps forward to focus all attention on himself. "I am Mithridates—late of Pontus, late of Hell's own administration. Now your suppliant, as you say, but a king in my own right."

The room's only architectural embellishment was an ornate latticework of gold on the wall behind the throne, covering the lower half of an arched opening like the cella in which the god's statue would be kept in a temple. The heads of two great golden serpents projected into the throne room from above the lattice.

"My welcome to you and all your party, noble prince," Zahhaq said with a gracious wave of his hand. Mithridates realized that though the ruler's face and limbs were perfect in all respects, Zahhaq was a hunchback. "My only regret is that I cannot offer my protection and hospitality to all those who started out with you. How were they lost?"

"Lord Zahhaq," said the Mandarin, "instead of paying the usual toll through the way station, he—urk!"

Mithridates glanced behind unintentionally because of the unexpected way the outburst had ended. The Mandarin's slippers dangled in the air while Kalhu held him by the throat.

"There's no need of that, Section Leader," Mithridates said calmly. "The Mandarin will permit two monarchs to continue their discussion without interrupting again, I'm sure."

He wondered if Zahhaq's power included the ability to fling thunderbolts. Because, though he looked like a man and sounded like an unusually kindly man, Zahhaq *glowed* with enormous, hellish power. . . .

"I refused to buy my way through your way station with the lives of my men, Prince Zahhaq," Mithridates said. Fear made his tone more forceful than he'd intended, but if Zahhaq wished to destroy him, there was enough excuse already. "My losses—our losses were heavy, but that was not through my choice."

"You are a good man, Prince Mithridates," Zahhaq said approvingly. "A man of principle. I look forward to making your closer acquaintance."

"I was a king . . . ," Mithridates said, his vision blurring with the strength of the emotion he felt. "May the holy Fire grant that I always act like a king, whatever my surroundings."

The flaming cressets burbled as with evil laughter from around him.

"Well, your journey can scarcely have been less than arduous," Zahhaq said, rising from his throne with a caution that belied the ease with which he seemed to sit. "All journeys here are arduous . . . but you have found safe haven, my brother. We'll dine and talk in the garden. The Mandarin will attend us, while Fremont arranges food and quarters for your entourage."

He glanced to his right, over the back of the throne glittering with faceted rubies, and called, "Fremont. Take care of my other guests as you would yourself."

As Zahhaq carefully descended the steps from his throne, a man appeared from a small door in the back corner, hidden by the room's immensity. He was in military uniform, blue frock-coat, and trousers. He carried a heavy saber in a brass-mounted sheath, and his high, gleamingly polished boots rang on the metal floor.

Fremont held himself stiffly erect, almost as if to emphasize his ruler's hunched back, but he had hunted, rat-like eyes.

Was he the *only* servant in this vast palace?

"Prince Zahhaq," Mithridates said, making an instantaneous decision and offering Zahhaq the support of his arm as he neared the floor. "My consort, the lady—"

"Amelia Earhart, your highness," AE said, stepping forward to the ruler's other side and extending her crooked arm as well: to be treated as a person, not as a woman or anyone's consort, not even a king's. . . . "But AE, if you will."

"Be pleased to join us, Lady AE," Zahhaq said. With his hands, he gently declined their offers of assistance. Except for his stooped posture, he would have been taller than either of them.

His eyes lingered on the woman's face, as though he were memorizing the pattern of pores and the way the cressets reddened the tight ringlets of her hair. "I'm sure you will add as much to my enjoyment as my brother Mithridates himself."

Zahhaq led them toward the door from which his servant Fremont had come. The ruler's face was composed, but the cressets continued to chuckle in amusement.

The roof garden's view out over the city was so striking that it was only after a moment of gasped wonder that Mithridates noticed the profusion of plants dangling and coiling around him from terraced beds. AE yelped as she brushed a Spanish bayonet.

"Yes, do be careful of those," Zahhaq murmured. "Be careful of all of them, I'm afraid, though many can do no harm to humans."

"I've never seen Venus' flytraps so big," AE said. "Those could hold a . . . hold a puppy."

"They seem to thrive here," Zahhaq agreed as he gestured his guests to two of the three couches arranged around a serving table, keeping the central one for himself. "I wish more pleasant vegetation did, but the underlying *nature* of the place is beyond anybody's changing.

"The nature of Jehennum," he added as he settled himself with the caution owed to infirmity. "The nature of Hell."

"Your city is huge," Mithridates said, easing himself onto his couch while his eyes continued to drink in the expanse lighted and delimited by the blazing canals. "How many subjects do you have?"

"Only a handful," Zahhaq said sadly. "There is plenty here for all who would come and escape Satan's tyranny; but the way is hard, and few succeed."

The Mandarin knelt with a tray and set crystal dishes of thin-sliced melon on the serving table before the diners. He showed no sign of irritation at being excluded from the meal. On the contrary, he performed his menial function with abject thankfulness.

"I wouldn't have thought that," Mithridates said, taking a slice of melon as soon as their host reached for one. "The things the Mandarin said on the way here, and the degree of organization at the way station . . . ?"

He let a raised eyebrow complete the question.

The tray clattered to the floor.

"Did he say that?" Zahhaq asked with an amused smile. "The Mandarin has been the most indefatigable of those I employ to publicize this refuge, but—"

"Lord, Lord," the Mandarin begged with his face pressed to the stone flags of the terrace. "You must believe me, I never—"

"—I'm afraid his success has not been as great as he may have implied," Zahhaq continued as if unaware that his servant was speaking. "As for the way station, it serves the purposes of many besides myself. And the purposes of Ahriman before all."

"Satan," AE translated.

"Ahriman," Mithridates agreed morosely.

They were high up above the houses and silent streets of the city. The individual dwellings tended to be one-and-a-half or two-and-a-half stories: the lower portion often with the additional headroom of a dome for dining during bad weather, while the roof of the higher part was flat and served the inhabitants as the palace's terraced roof gardens did their ruler.

Except that there were no signs at all of habitation. Just the houses, as void as bones in a desert.

The melon dissolved with a foul aftertaste in

Mithridates' mouth. It wasn't as cool as he'd hoped either. He took another slice anyway.

Zahhaq was right, of course. There was no denying the nature of Hell.

The Mandarin scurried off, carrying his tray. "The only service I require of those who place themselves under my protection," Zahhaq was saying, "is that they attend me in pairs for one night. After that, they're free to reside anywhere within the city—"

He smiled at AE, whose lips were pursing for a question. "Or to leave it, of course."

"Night?" Mithridates repeated.

"Oh, you mean that because Paradise doesn't cross our sky, there's no day or night here?" Zahhaq said. His tone suggested amusement, but his eyes were as bleak as the palace's final entrance court. "Our bodies have their sequences, my brother, whatever the skies above them are doing."

The Mandarin had returned, bringing platters of skewered lamb as well as cups and a ewer of yogurt. He picked up the dishes of melon. The fruit that remained uneaten was already slumping into putrescence.

"Bodies have their sequences," Zahhaq repeated softly. He shrugged as though he were trying to dispose his hump more comfortably. "And their demands . . ."

He put his slice of melon on the plate that the Mandarin was removing. Though Mithridates remembered Zahhaq raising it to his lips, his teeth didn't appear to have marked the dripping fruit.

"I'll tell Kalhu," Mithridates said. "He'll arrange it."

He tried a bite of the meat. It had the texture of braised lamb, but the flavor . . . A swig of yogurt modified the taste in his mouth without improving it.

AE swallowed with the resignation that came from experience of food in Hell. "The pyramid," she said, pointing with her skewer. "The ziggurat. I saw movement—a wing, I think?"

The men's eyes followed her gesture. The streets of the city were generally straight, but few of them met at right angles with one another. Across four or more irregular blocks of houses from the palace was a walled compound covering an area greater than that of the palace itself.

In the center of the enclosure was the seven-tiered ziggurat they'd seen as they crossed the hills that formed the boundary of Zahhaq's realm. A stepped ramp, built out from the front at a one-to-one slope, gave access to the small temple on top. It was a little higher than the palace garden, but Mithridates thought he too caught a shadow of movement over the parapet of the sixth tier.

"Yes," said Zahhaq. "My little pets, I suppose you could call them. Winged lions, quartered there because they love the heavens. It's selfish of me not to let them go, I suppose—let them find their own salvation in this underworld. But I give my subjects their privacy, and the dumb beasts are often my only companions." He smiled sadly.

The Mandarin was back with a bowl of rice gleaming with butter and sheep fat. Its odor preceded it. He set it down on the table.

"They're quite magnificent beasts," Zahhaq continued. "They have normal forelegs as well as splendid pinions—like the wings of very angels. Are you interested in natural philosophy, my brother, lady?"

AE shook her head. "I had other interests," Mithridates admitted with a shrug.

Zahhaq shrugged also. "It was a concern of mine throughout most of my life," he said diffidently. "It seems to me that the articulation of the skeletons must be quite wonderful. The way the disparate elements are linked beneath the flesh . . ."

He blinked as though he'd fallen into a reverie as his voice trailed off. "I'll show them to you," he said, molding a ball of rice with his right hand. Had he actually eaten any of the lamb? "In a day or two, I think."

Zahhaq smiled again.

The Mandarin turned away so quickly that one of the skewers he was removing fell off the tray. He bent to retrieve it, his back to the diners; but his fingers were so clumsy with nervousness that it took him three tries.

When Mithridates dined with his host the following "night," Zahhaq chose an ivory-inlaid room overlooking the palace's first entrance court. Despite his intentions, the king found himself watching the tiled horrors enacted on the walls below.

Their motion was, he realized, the only change in Zahhaq's city, save for the repetitious creep of the flames.

"Your men are satisfied with their accommodations?" Zahhaq asked as the Mandarin poured wine into Mithridates' cup.

"Scarcely an adequate word for their feelings,

Brother Zahhaq," Mithridates said, waiting for his host to be served before raising the goblet. It was of gold, and its bowl was built up from the coils of two ruby-eyed serpents that swallowed one another's tail.

"My section leader, Kalhu, calls me a genius and"—he flicked his hand in a gesture of deprecation —"a god for having led them here."

Mithridates looked at the Mandarin as he bent over Zahhaq's cup. His spouted jar was decorated with a scene of a woman being raped by a bull; perhaps intended to be Europa and Zeus, but executed with an unflinching appreciation of the differences in size—and what would result from them.

"Which of course," the king continued, "is quite undeserved. We owe it all to the Mandarin. I should be serving you both while he sits in my place."

The Mandarin splashed the serving table and floor with a stream of wine as purple as blood returning through the great veins of the chest.

"Leave it, Mandarin, leave it," Zahhaq said with gentle amusement as the Mandarin almost dropped the spouted jar in his haste to mop the mess with the hem of his robe. "You can clean up later."

Head bowed, scuttling rather than walking, the Easterner disappeared through the doorway. The doorposts had papyrus-frond capitals, reminding Mithridates uneasily of the route he'd taken to this refuge.

"My servants," Zahhaq said, "are happy with their lot. They tell me they take pleasure in ministering to my needs . . . which are negligible, even on occasions" —his cup lifted in a gesture as delicate as a crooked eyebrow—"such as this one, when we have guests in the palace."

"When will you dismiss the men who attended you yesterday?" Mithridates asked as he sipped his wine. It had a fruity taste as it first met his lips, but as it rolled back onto his palate the flavor began to change.

As he'd expected.

"Oh, I gave them leave to go when I arose this morning," Zahhaq said, "and I believe they left the palace. They'd asked Fremont to introduce them to some women."

Zahhaq smiled ruefully, then touched his cup to his lips. When he lowered it, he continued, "I don't know what luck they'll have; but as soon as they've paid me that one homage, all my subjects have absolute freedom."

Mithridates took a second mouthful of wine while he decided how to phrase his surprise. He hoped that if he swallowed quickly, the initial fruitiness would wash down the flavor of horse urine. He was unsuccessful in the attempt.

"Including you and your consort, of course," Zahhaq continued. "The lady AE is well, I trust?"

"She chose to dine alone," Mithridates said. "There hasn't been much opportunity for any of us to be alone since . . ." He shrugged. "Since we were thrown together. Since my coup failed."

Mithridates wasn't *sure* why AE had refused to eat with Zahhaq again; she hadn't said, even in private. He had no doubt that it was because of the prince's deformity, though. Whenever AE's eyes strayed near

Zahhaq during the previous meal, she'd stared at his hump.

A natural attitude; but not one Mithridates cared to offer to his host as a reason.

"If you're concerned to speak with your men," Zahhaq offered, "Fremont will no doubt be able to find them for you in a day or two. Of course"—he lifted his cup again—"by that time you'll have attended me at night also, and you'll be free to leave the palace."

"You expect *me*—" Mithridates said; and broke off, spluttering, because he'd inhaled some of the wine in his surprise and that was an even worse idea than drinking the noisome fluid. . . .

"I expect all my subjects to render me minimal homage," said Zahhaq, with only the least emphasis on "all" to indicate that he understood Mithridates' shock—and was unmoved by it. "That is a condition of my—independence here, one might say."

Mithridates stood up. "Very well, my lord," he said. "I've abased myself before lesser rulers in the past. My son-in-law, the king of Armenia, for example." He bowed. "What would you first have me do, my lord?"

"Please," Zahhaq said, "please, brother. I have no wish to cause you discomfort. Your only duties will be to stand before my throne for a night—and tomorrow, please; your section leader has already arranged for himself and the other common trooper to take care of the business tonight."

Mithridates bowed again. "Very well," he said stiffly. "In that case, I'll take my leave of you until then—your highness."

He strode toward the doorway. The Mandarin hovered just beyond the doorposts, his expression unreadable. He leaped back as Mithridates approached.

"Brother?" Zahhaq called.

Mithridates took a further step—then stopped and turned.

He was furious at himself for the vehemence of his reaction. He *was* a suppliant. Why should it bother him to be reminded of the fact?

Zahhaq had started to rise from his couch, looking frail and even more deformed than usual. "Brother," he said quietly, "I have taken pleasure in your company. I hope you believe that."

Mithridates swept out of the room without replying.

The corridor was lighted by narrow windows placed high in one wall. Either it was brighter than when Mithridates had walked along it at Zahhaq's slow pace, or he was paying more attention now to the decoration—

"There you are!" said AE, coming around a corner so quickly that her boots skidded on the tile. She braced herself on a dark green wall molded into broad corrugations—like a papyrus thicket. "I was . . ."

She stepped closer to the king and continued, "I was afraid it'd take longer to find you. I saw—"

She looked around.

"Where?" Mithridates demanded, staring up and down the corridor himself.

What he'd thought was movement within the wall was only a decoration catching the light. An inlay of raw yellow bone had been set at the base of a corrugation, as though something dead were striding through the papyrus stalks. . . .

"Where's Zahhaq?" she asked. "And that Chink?" As she spoke, she was drawing Mithridates with her back around the corner. A circular staircase led down from an alcove.

Mithridates shrugged. "Back there," he said without bothering to point. "They'll be on their way to the throne room, I suppose."

He was following AE's tug down the straight, dark stairway for want of a reason to refuse. It should lead directly to the first courtyard, so there was no likelihood they'd meet Zahhaq again.

"*We'll* be dancing attendance on our 'brother' tomorrow, you'll be pleased to know," he added bitterly. "Though I don't suppose we have a right to complain. Doesn't the saying go, beggars can't—"

"I saw Fremont," AE interrupted. "I think it was him. I was in the garden, looking at the city like yesterday. Climbing the pyramid with something heavy."

"With *what* heavy thing?"

"It's a long way to see in that light," AE said evasively. "I just think we ought to find out what he's doing."

The stairs circled tightly down a shaft cut in the palace's thick wall, lightless and dizzying. Vertigo might explain the breathiness in the woman's voice.

"Perhaps we should wait—" Mithridates suggested.

Beads rattled. There was light—more light, at any rate. A curtain of green glass closed the bottom of the stairwell, merging as well with the mural of sea and storm that Mithridates hadn't noticed in the alcove when they crossed the courtyard the first time.

Of course, he'd had other things on his mind.

"—until Fremont returns. Surely we won't be able to find him out in all the city?"

He glanced up at the balustraded loggia on which he'd dined with Zahhaq. It was as silent as the sky of eternal night above.

"It'll take him a long time to climb those steps," AE said. She strode across the courtyard with her hand in the crook of the king's elbow—not quite pulling him, but willing to if he resisted. "We'll hurry."

"All right," Mithridates said aloud.

What was Zahhaq going to do if they left his palace without permission? Damn them to Hell?

The boulevard seemed bright after the gloomy corridor between the stone bulls' flanks. The breath of the flaming canals was louder outside the palace, and the air even more suffocatingly dry.

"This way," said AE, speaking in order to be speaking. They were already headed down the boulevard in the only possible direction, moving at something between a walk and a jog. They were keyed up. Mithridates couldn't be sure whether he felt as he had the afternoon at Cabira that he led the charge that shattered the Roman line—

Or the morning at Pantacapeum, while he raised the poison to his lips as the mutineers approached.

He glanced over his shoulder. The street was empty, the buildings as they had been. "I thought," he said carefully, "that I saw the bulls' eyes move when we passed them. I suppose it was a trick of the light."

"I saw Zahhaq's back move," AE said grimly.

Mithridates blinked. "I don't understand," he admitted.

The ziggurat itself was visible only in snatches among the roofs of deserted houses. The wall enclosing the temple and its grounds lay a block ahead, across one of the canals.

"I mean I saw his back move," AE repeated. "At dinner, under his robe. And his arms weren't moving at all, just his back."

Even in their present haste and nervousness, the canal which the road crossed on a single arch made AE and Mithridates pause for a heartbeat before starting over. The breathy whisper of air throughout the city was here a snarl like that of a leopard baring its fangs.

"I see the entrance," Mithridates said, feeling the relief that came with stepping onto the solid ground beyond the bridge. He turned at the splash.

Fire vomited over the parapet behind them. A serpent the thickness of Mithridates' chest writhed at the center of the spout of flame.

The saffron blaze dribbled back through the bridge railings, but the golden wedge of the serpent's head turned toward the humans. Its tongue sampled the air from between lips closed in a permanent smile.

"We could run," Mithridates whispered from the side of his mouth; but neither he nor AE thought they could outrun a snake that size if it came after them. There must be a hundred feet of it still hidden. . . .

The creature slipped back into the roiling canal. Flame gouted, then closed as if the serpent had never existed. The fire hadn't affected the bridge, but where the golden belly-plates had slid over the parapet, the brickwork was cracked and discolored by heat.

"It doesn't matter," AE muttered as they entered the temple compound through plain brick gateposts. She spoke loudly enough for her companion to hear her; but he was fairly certain she'd been speaking to herself.

The river blazed as a flaming curtain behind the ziggurat, throwing into relief the angles of the seven tiers. The stairs rose with the structure's whole mass between them and the river. . . . Light off the canals and scattered from buildings illuminated the treads—

And at the top, the figure of a man entering the temple that formed the topmost level; foreshortened by the angle, but bent as well beneath the weight of the heavy burden across his shoulders.

"I think you're right," Mithridates said in a distant, emotionless voice. The steps were about eight feet broad, comfortably wide for them both together to take two at a time. "I'm afraid you're right."

Their boots clacked on the treads. The bricks were fired but not glazed or otherwise decorated. AE reached out for Mithridates' hand. The contact helped both of them balance as they continued upward in calf-straining jumps.

"About it being Fremont, you mean?" she said.

"That too." Mithridates had his mouth fully open, not gasping but breathing as deeply as he could even before he needed the excess. "The mountings of his scabbard caught the light."

"I'd forgotten that sword," said the woman.

"I hadn't," Mithridates said with grim assurance.

They both knew they should keep their heads raised so that they would see if Fremont—or whoever might be with him—looked out of the temple. That was impossible. The climb was agonizing, and under that strain, neither of them could look at anything higher than the step on which they'd next put a foot—unless they stumbled.

Which the king did twice, and his companion three times; each caught by the other, braced and pausing for a moment while their lungs burned and fire pulsed in their calves and thighs.

Then on, for to hesitate longer would be to let muscles knot into shapes that only hours of massaging could undo.

From the base of the sixth tier, they had an even better view of the city than from the palace's roof garden; and they could hear the roaring from the temple still above them.

Mithridates risked a glance toward the palace, wondering if eyes were watching them the way AE had watched Fremont climb earlier. Viewed from this eminence, the third courtyard was a faint rectangle as the throne room's cressets spilled light through the archway.

Mithridates and AE paused just below the final tier. A man shouted wordless anger from the temple. AE held up three fingers to her companion. Lowered one; lowered a second; lowered the third as they staggered together through the door.

The winged lions bellowed, but they were already thundering through the open roof as if to wake the blank heavens. Fremont's back was to the doorway.

He laughed and tossed one of the chained beasts its food, a lower quarter of a human being.

The upper section remained, head and shoulders crudely separated from the rest of the body by the bloody saber in Fremont's right hand. The victim was Hashemer. His face was blank, unnaturally relaxed.

The lions roared and slammed their black pinions. Their chain harnesses clashed, and the bronze tongue to which the harness was attached rang against the body of the chariot.

AE had paused in horror, but Mithridates stepped forward. The moment was clear; every action was planned a fraction of a second ahead, a lifetime ahead.

Fremont was bending for the last section of meat. He saw the motion out of the corner of his eye; but before Fremont started to turn, the king gripped his right forearm and his hand on the saber hilt.

A scrap of shinbone protruded from an Assyrian boot in a corner of the square enclosure, flung there by one of the lions earlier. It didn't belong to Hashemer.

"Get away from me, you—" Fremont screamed, terror distorting his face. Blood from his butchery speckled his face and goatee.

Motion—the trip-hammer swipe of a lion's fore-paw. As Fremont turned, he stepped too close to the beasts he'd been feeding. Four black claws as sharp as meat-hooks sank into his collarbone and the base of his neck.

Fremont's scream became wordless. Mithridates couldn't have prevented the man from being dragged back into the jaws of the lions if he'd wanted to.

But the bloody saber came away in the king's hand.

AE knelt beside the fragment of Hashemer. She tugged Mithridates' sleeve for attention, though by shouting they could make themselves understood above the throaty growls of the feeding lions.

Hashemer's face looked relaxed because the back of his scalp—and the back of his skull—had been eaten away.

Mithridates said, "All right. We'll go back to the palace. We'll find our remaining—"

"I'll stay here," AE said, still-faced, as she rose to bring her lips closer to her companion's ear.

"Yes, of course," agreed the king, wondering why he felt surprised. She was a woman, after all, scarcely to be expected to undergo willingly the risks of—

"Mithridates," she continued, forming the words with the organized calm of a heavy machinegun walloping through its belt of ammunition, "this cart is meant to fly. That's the only way it could get in or out of this"—she gestured at the open ceiling—"room, the door's too small. I'm going to learn how to do it while you bring Kalhu."

Mithridates looked at the pawing, snarling lions. They were splendid beasts, as Zahhaq had said. Bigger than the lions he'd hunted in life, and truly gigantic to watch when they fluffed their mighty sable wings. Learn to rule *them*?

Not, he would have thought, within the capacity of any human; but woman's work if a woman did it.

Mithridates nodded and sprang through the doorway, extending his left arm wide to balance the weight of the curved sword in his right. He was feeling loose—giddy, even, from the hormones with which his body had charged itself in the past moments.

Another lion snagged its claws into Fremont's thigh as the beast which made the kill devoured it. They tugged and snarled at the ends of their harnesses until the corpse separated, even more crudely than Fremont had butchered out previous victims.

The stone bulls guarding the gateway were haughty and still as Mithridates entered; their eyes and spear-sharp horns faced forward. Even the scene of storm and shipwreck on the tiled walls moved with glacial torpidity if it moved at all.

The eyes of the gilt serpents winked when Mithridates' shadow brushed them. His fingers flexed on the saber hilt as he passed them and strode through the dragon entrance of the second courtyard.

The earthquake-toppling city on the walls within was as motionless as if it were no more than a tile mural and the serpents in its streets were only painted gold. All that Mithridates had seen there before was a snowflake memory, belied by the flat surfaces he walked past now.

The stone lions were as big as the king remembered, but they didn't have the power to impress him so soon after seeing their winged fellows on the ziggurat. Even the black tile walls of the third courtyard were lost in the red fury growing in Mithridate's mind as he entered the throne room.

The cressets had slumped to a dimly glowing line high on the walls; the throne was empty.

"Kalhu!" Mithridates shouted. His legs were spread, his saber across his chest at high port.

The cressets flared.

Kalhu and another Assyrian—the only other, now—sat against the base of the throne with their legs sprawled before them. Their faces were blank; rhytons of gold and cloisonne had spilled the remainder of their drugged wine when they slipped from the soldiers' nerveless fingers.

Zahhaq knelt between the men, on the lowest of the steps mounting to the throne. His head was bowed, and from his shoulders—

"Kalhu!" Mithridates screamed as he ran toward the motionless tableau with his saber rising.

Zahhaq lifted his sad, handsome face and said, "I am Kalhu, brother. I am all those who enter the kingdom Ahriman granted me here—for the same price he made me king in the upper world."

Kalhu's body slumped over on its face. The snake which grew from Zahhaq's right shoulder blade withdrew its head from the section leader's skull. It hissed at Mithridates. The scaly lips dripped blood and brains.

The saber whistled in the air, but that sound was lost in the shriek from Mithridates' throat as he swung the weapon. He caught Zahhaq's neck with the belly of the blade, a chunk-*zing*! as Mithridates followed through, sawing on the draw-stroke the bone that hadn't parted on impact. He knew curved blades. He'd been raised to be king of a nation of horse-warriors. . . .

Zahhaq's head fell to the golden floor, blood soaking the gray beard and spouting from the neck stump as the torso rose slowly to a standing position.

The snake growing from Zahhaq's left shoulder

lifted from the other Assyrian's half-eaten skull and said, "Everything here is changeless, brother Mithridates. Have you killed Fremont? Take his place. Live forever—"

Mithridates' back-stroke lopped the snake apart at an angle. The head and six inches of the neck/body spun to the floor while the remainder writhed against the robe from which it had emerged to feed. Flecks of severed scales quivered in the air.

"—as I do," concluded the remaining snake.

"Never!" Mithridates cried as he slashed down.

"Never!" as he lifted the blade again, sure of nothing except that he would keep hacking at the body until something changed—

But it did change when the second snake fell in pieces. Zahhaq's corpse fell forward, rigid as men sometimes are when their spines are severed. The blood from the stump was a pulseless trickle, and the severed snakes were as limp as yarn toys.

Mithridates leaned back, using his sword for support by gouging its point into the floor. His breath wheezed through his nose and open mouth. He was the only living being in a golden charnel house.

The screen covering in the rear wall collapsed sidewards as the serpents thrusting through it moved. They grew from the shoulders of a golden statue of Zahhaq, kneeling in the alcove behind the throne.

"Join me and live forever," croaked the statue in a voice like distant thunder. It began to stand up, very slowly. It would touch the sixty-foot ceiling of the room when it was fully erect.

Mithridates turned and ran. The Mandarin stood

in the throne-room entrance, his eyes as wide and round as the circle of his lips.

Mithridates raised his saber, instinct rather than anger: a need to escape, and someone in the way.

"No!" the Mandarin cried as he turned and gestured. "I'll lead you out! You'll need me to escape! But we have to run!"

Because flight rather than slaughter ruled Mithridates' reflexes, his arm stayed its motion as soon as the Mandarin shifted out of his way; and then there was time to appreciate that what the Easterner said could be true.

Mithridates didn't respond at once; but he let the Mandarin run alongside him, across the courtyard whose walls were a void, instead of disemboweling him with casual expertise.

One of the lions growled as they ran through the passageway. The statues' lower legs still seemed to be stone, but their chests heaved and the air was rank with the odor of carnivores.

"Quickly," the Mandarin pleaded. "Quickly."

The dragons were moving. Scraps of stone fell into the passageway, pattering on the heads of the men.

Mithridates' arms pumped, emphasizing the saber's unbalanced weight. He should throw it away. It was as useless now as a crown would be . . . but the burden was comforting, despite the stitch it pulled in his side.

The final archway out of the palace darkened. The bulls were turning their heads to view the humans running toward them.

The Mandarin hopped a step and paused. Mithridates thought the Easterner would stop rather than chance the passage; but when Mithridates sprinted between the beasts with his head lowered, he saw the Mandarin just behind him.

The bulls' breath smelled as if the animals had been eating old bones.

As they plunged out of the palace, Mithridates glanced toward the city gate by reflex.

The Mandarin seized his arm and pointed the other way. "Not there," he cried. "We have to climb the—"

A portcullis slammed across one of the triple gateways; the other two followed so closely that their ringing echoes merged for the moment before the sets of gate-leaves closed and barred themselves of their own accord.

"—ziggurat," the Mandarin completed.

Mithridates had neither the breath nor the inclination to say that had been his destination in any event. He'd lost all his power, all his followers. . . .

He would not lose her as well.

Stone crashed within the palace. A cloud of dust and rubble spouted as if a bomb had gone off in the building's heart. Out of the dust climbed a lion big enough to carry an obelisk in its jaws. It saw the men running down the boulevard and coughed twice, shatteringly, as it gathered its haunches beneath it to spring.

Two dragons rose with thunderclaps of shearing stone. One fastened its beak onto the lion's throat while the other's raptorial claws gouged the cat's withers. The lion roared in pain while the dragon on its back raised its beak to heaven and hissed past its forked tongue.

The front of the palace collapsed as the bulls walked out from under it, stepping together as though they were yokemates. They paused as brick and stone cascaded into the street around them. One looked toward the city gate.

The other's eyes followed the running men for a moment. It began to pace after them with slow ten-foot strides. Behind the bull, another lion raised a paw for purchase on the highest remaining portion of the palace, the room of the throne room.

"Quickly," repeated the Mandarin as a prayer; but he knew, they both knew, that the walking bull would catch them before they reached the ziggurat, no matter what they did.

They began to run anyway.

The bridge was before them, quivering in the heat of the canal. Mithridates was sure he could smell the bull's stinking breath, but he didn't dare look back. Would the horns toss him, or would a cleft hoof slice down and spread him across the pavement?

Flame slapped the bridge parapet ahead of them. A ruby-eyed serpent writhed from the center of it. Its head was oval, like a cobra's, and it flowed across the pavement as if metal were pouring from a casting kettle.

"Don't—" Mithridates said with his hand frozen in mid-motion as he reached for the Mandarin's shoulder "—move."

Fear or simultaneous realization already held the Mandarin rigid; as motionless as the statues in the gateways had been when first Mithridates led his troop into the palace.

The bull snorted explosively. The serpent, motionless

for an instant while gummy flame leaked through the bridge railing, slid forward like a dance of golden lightning. Its torso radiated heat that was shocking even on the edge of the blazing canal.

"Now!" cried Mithridates as he broke into a run and the two giants crashed together behind the men. The serpent clamped its jaws on the bull's shoulder and tried to throw a coil around its opponent's great chest. Yards of the serpent's body were still steaming out of the flames, but the bull's hooves left broad gouges on the golden scales.

Mithridates threw his bloody saber into the canal. He could no longer even pretend that he might have a use for it here.

The ziggurat's steps had been torture to climb the first time. Pain had become a meaningless concept, but Mithridates' exhaustion threw him sprawling on the third step . . . and the tenth . . . and so up the steep stairway, none of it mattering so long as he was higher each time he fell.

The Mandarin, though less strained by the events of the night thus far, lagged a body's length behind the king. But he came on, wheezing and using his hands like forepaws; Mithridates could see that every time he fell and he looked back of necessity.

The bull and the serpent still battled, the strains so nearly matched that the beasts moved in slow motion. The bull had hooked one of its horns into the serpent's side, but the gleaming coils hid almost all of the bull's body. Its knees were buckling, and it could not raise its head to complete the horn-stroke.

A lion was prowling the roofs of residences across

the boulevard. Occasionally a beam gave under the cat's weight, puffing plaster and brick-dust.

"Quickly . . . ," the Mandarin gasped through lips made white by dust and tension.

The roof of the throne room lifted with the cataclysmic effortlessness of a volcano blowing a plug of ancient lava. Something huge and golden winked in the midst of the destruction.

Mithridates stumbled through the door of the temple. His eyes were fixed before him; he was almost too exhausted to catch himself before he pitched into the bellowing maw of the nearest lion.

A pole with some sort of framework on the end had been pivoted up from the center of the chariot. When Mithridates had been in the temple before, that pole had lain along the tongue to which the lions were harnessed. He'd thought it was just part of that apparatus, normal to any vehicle drawn by beasts.

So AE had been working with the vehicle as she'd said she would. And now she must be—

Mithridates turned. He hadn't heard the shouts over the roaring. The Mandarin stood behind him with a raised dagger. Its blade was eight inches long, and its point could split a beam of light.

AE had been bending over beside the doorway when Mithridates lurched through. She'd dropped a coil of rope in time to grab the knife the Mandarin was slipping from his sleeve as he followed.

AE held the knife wrist-high and crooked her other arm around the Easterner's throat from behind. The lions subsided into rasping growls as they crouched at the limits of their harness, waiting for the moment that would bring them more food. They had eaten tonight, but men were small prey for creatures as huge and ravenous as these. . . .

The Mandarin shrieked wordlessly. AE did not speak at all, concentrating on the wrist that she drew back steadily despite the desperate drumming of the Mandarin's heels on her shins.

Mithridates gauged the distance, then kicked the Mandarin in the groin. The Easterner tried to hunch over, but AE held him too firmly.

Mithridates kicked him again. The dagger dropped; when the king's hand swept the weapon up, AE released the slumping Mandarin as well.

Mithridates gripped the Mandarin's pigtail and drew the head into position. For a moment, the king gasped to get control of his muscles. Then he reached down with the dagger, and—

AE caught his wrist. "Please," she said. "Please don't."

He straightened, letting the Mandarin fall. "Are you mad?" he shouted. "Shall I spare this filth who led us here? Who betrayed me yet again when I spared him before?"

"Please," she said, her eyes as determined as they had been while she wrestled the Mandarin's arm back. "There's been enough killing. Killing and anger."

"I wouldn't have hurt you," the Mandarin whispered. He'd fallen on his face, and his lips were puffed and bloody. "Only there has to be meat to guide the lions, to get them to draw the chariot . . . and I have to leave quickly."

"He's right," said AE. "I'm going to tie myself onto the, the pole. You'll guide it—"

"No you won't," said the king.

He slid the dagger under his sash, then pulled the Mandarin to his feet. "Mandarin, do you want to live?"

The Mandarin looked at Mithridates, then at the chariot. He balled his hands at his sides and began to weep. Mithridates muscled him roughly toward the back of the vehicle, out of the lions' reach, and said, "How do we get the basket down?"

"It cranks," AE answered distantly. "But I'll—"

"*No, you won't!*" the king shouted. "He will! Now, get *back* here and help me, woman."

She smiled, though there was more irony than humor in the expression. "Yes," she said as she slipped into the car ahead of Mithridates and their sobbing prisoner. "Of course you're right."

She began to turn one of the two bronze cranks set at right angles to one another at the base of the pole. The handles were chased with delicate silver figures, a pair of wild dogs tearing out a fawn's lungs.

As she cranked, the pole telescoped and the lions resumed bellowing and ramping upward against their chains. The chariot rocked but did not lift from the enclosure as the king had half expected.

"Brother Mithridates!" boomed the voice of an earthquake.

"There's rope!" AE cried.

"No time," said the king.

And there wasn't. The basket at the end of the pole was meant for dead meat, not living; but the spring-loaded hooks closed over the Mandarin's chest and held him when Mithridates slammed his prisoner into their grip.

The Mandarin's screams couldn't have risen louder

than they were already . . . and anyway, almost nothing could be heard over the roars of the lions.

Zahhaq's "Join me and live forever!" shook the ziggurat itself. Nearer now, very near.

"I'll turn!" Mithridates cried as AE, tight-lipped, began to hoist the basket.

"No!" she screamed back over the beasts and the sounds of a city being demolished. "That pin—"

Her foot gestured. A wrist-thick eye-bolt rose through a slit in the floor of the cart. The eye was closed with an even sturdier cross-bolt which rang but did not bend as the lions tried to drag the vehicle skyward.

"*Not yet*!" AE continued, putting her shoulders into the crank. Then, "When I say—"

The ziggurat trembled; its bricks were crumbling under more weight than they could bear. Golden light gleamed above the lip of the enclosure.

Mithridates kicked the pin away.

The chariot lurched, lifted ten inches. The loops of harness chain gathered by the eye-bolt fell loose with a jangle like that of a statue struck by lightning.

The Mandarin shrieked as the lions, trained and waiting, lunged upward together. Their wings hammered the narrow walls of the enclosure for the instant before they rose above the stone—

Their claws were shredding the Mandarin's ankles as the woman cranked fiercely to lift the bait out of the beasts' range and the chariot wheels bounced on the lip of the enclosure.

The roofless temple collapsed behind them, gripped by Zahhaq's golden hands.

"Brother Mithridates!" shouted three mouths in

unison, the sad-faced human giant and the golden snakes growing from his shoulder blades.

Zahhaq's hand opened and reached for the chariot. AE gripped the other crank and spun it, angling the pole to the right. The lions, their sable pinions slamming, banked to follow the screaming Mandarin. The chariot, dancing through the air, curved around the giant's grasp.

They were gaining height slowly, but they were clear of Zahhaq. Mithridates clung to the chariot's side and looked down at the city.

Where the palace had been was a mass of blazing rubble. In the heart of it, the lion battled the pair of dragons; dying together, but concerned with nothing except their last opportunity to kill. The bridge near the ziggurat had collapsed; there was no sign of the serpent or its prey, but the flames boiled fiercely between the abutments.

The remaining lion was locked in a death struggle with a bull; when they rolled, buildings powdered beneath them.

AE put a hand on Mithridates' shoulder. Her eyes sparkled. "Where?" she asked over the wind-rush. "Do you want me to turn and fly us back the way we came?"

When her mouth formed, "fly us," her face became transfigured.

"Brother Mithridates," called the three-tongued giant. "Stay with me. . . ." The words were too distant to be deafening.

The chariot lurched as one of the lions fouled another. AE fought the reins, bringing the beasts back into smooth control.

"No," the king said. "Go on as we're headed. Before long we should return to the light."

"Do you know what lies this way?" AE asked.

"Not yet," said Mithridates. "But we will. Soon we will."

The chariot bucked again, flinging Mithridates forward. He opened his mouth, but his forehead banged the metal frame before he could cry out.

For a moment there was light inside his skull, blazing like the memory of pain. Then his consciousness spiraled down through a blackness deeper than the nights of Hell; and at every twist, the souls of Mithridates' tens of thousands of victims plucked at him and gibbered.

It was still dark, but he was awake again in a greater Hell than that of his own unconscious mind.

"Didn't you think it was strange what Zahhaq said—that he was selfish not to let the winged lions go, so that they could find their own salvation in this underworld?" AE was yelling over the wind that whipped back from the lions' wings as they flew.

"Strange, AE?" Mithridates called back, across the chariot's width to a woman he could no longer see in the dark. "As compared to what? The destruction of Babylon? Zahhaq and his snakes? What?"

AE didn't answer. Or her words were lost to the wind boxing his ears. In the blackness that had engulfed them, only the wing-beaten regularity of the gusts and the occasional shudder of the airborne chariot were proof that they still flew high above the fundament. But Mithridates' body didn't need visual proof. Every fiber of his being knew it rode through the air in the chariot of his vanquished enemy, drawn by sable-winged lions. And his body didn't like it one bit.

He'd vomited twice over the side. Each time the chariot had swayed terrifyingly, and AE had remonstrated that he must keep still or the cart could lose its balance, lions or no lions, and turn over in the air, pitching them groundward.

After that, he'd vomited miserably upon his own feet, showering them with hot water and lumps that must be pure bile, since his stomach had long since given up all it had.

AE called this "air sickness" and promised it would end. It had—when they'd flown into a black cloud . . . or into a part of Hell as black as night.

Now that he couldn't see the ground below or the lions' haunches straining before, or the Mandarin in the basket that dangled just out of the lions' reach, his stomach had settled. Oh, yes.

It sat in his body, empty and sore. But it ached. And the muscles of his trunk ached. And his windpipe ached. His throat felt as if it had been scalded by the acid water he'd vomited. It was hard to talk, let alone yell, over the roaring wind.

For a man who'd poisoned so many, this bodily plight brought back too many ugly memories. He closed his eyes as if there were daylight to shut out, concentrating on the slap of the icy wind and banishing memories from his time among the living. Why were those memories so much more poignant than those he'd accrued in Hell? Was it because everyone in Hell deserved no better than to be here, living a shadow life?

Or was it so because the things he'd done in life

had gotten him here, where rulers of long-dead cities had snakes living in their bodies, growing out of their flesh, and those snakes had wills of their own? In life, what he'd done had been, he'd thought, not any worse than others had done to him. He'd fled from his mother's clutches, from all her evil, from a will she'd forged that said his father had left the empire to her and his hateful brothers—and his sister.

He'd become a fugitive. He'd schemed and planned. He'd put brave words in his mouth and cultivated the youngest warriors, the most gullible men in the hinterlands, who could be roused to his cause with talk of holy war and the smell of blood.

With these forces, he fell upon his mother's capital of Sinope. There he imprisoned her, killed his brothers, then married his sister, Laodice. His sister was only the start of his mighty harem, which he undertook to build with her "understanding." But there had been no understanding in her heart, once he'd begun shaming her. Nor in his.

Poison was his great fear, his great tool. He did as his father would have—expanded the empire. And as he did, he found men who were knowledgeable in poisons, and undertook to make himself immune to their effect before he died of one.

He acquired many countries, many soldiers. He took the Euxine's shore, then Lesser Armenia, eastern Pontus, Colchis.

That put him eye to eye with Rome and butt to butt with Nicomedes of Bithynia.

There followed the First Mithridatic War, wherein dissident Romans made him at home in Asia Minor and all over the Aegean isles but on Rhodes. Even into Greece had he ventured.

Then Sulla came and drove him back, and this his heart could not endure. His reprisals were legend, thereafter, and from that moment, if not from the moment he destroyed his mother and married his sister in order to betray her with myriad women, his way to Hell was cast in bronze.

He'd styled himself Mithridates the Great in Alexandrian fashion, as if words could make it so. He'd been wrong, of course. Words could not make it so. He was small of heart and small of mind. It took more than a lucky birth and a yawning inferiority complex, more than disinheritance by the father and treachery from the mother, to make a man great.

Not even becoming fearful did the trick. He could not become all powerful. Therefore he collected enemies smarter than he, who bided their time and worse. Those men he obsessed about, those enemies he chose, had better things to do than think only of him. Thus they grew beyond his power, and when he would attack them, they met his blows, but that was all.

They did not think only of revenge. They were not blinded to the truth. They knew how many men were in their armies, and in his, and never misrecalled the odds, because more than passion drove them.

Not Mithridates. He was a man obsessed with revenge, with power, with control. After Sulla drove him out of Greece, and the revolt against him in Asia which he put down with horrors only a Persian could stomach, he had to make peace—on Sulla's terms—and give up all the territory he'd won.

He'd been a monarch whose fears that other monarchs were as unforgiving as he had caused him to perpetrate horrors at home and abroad. He'd been so frightened of how others saw him, so fearful of being unmasked as an incompetent, a pretender, a stupid little man doing evil out of fear of evil, that he'd become a buyer of hearts, a terrorizer of souls.

Men served him out of greed or out of fear, and all of them professed friendship, but none were his friends. When Sulla's lieutenant raided against him, he repelled the treacherous fool. Once he'd won the Second Mithridatic War against the lying Romans, he made an alliance with men more his sort, he thought: with pirate leaders, from whom he tithed great stores of treasure for his coming old age.

No better men than pirates, by then, would treat with him. When Rome set out to annex Bithynia, he went to war a third time.

The Third Mithridatic War saw him the occupier of Bithynia, but cost him his army: the Roman enemy cut off his supply train and destroyed his young and war-hungry pirate boys and warrior-shepherds.

When he subsequently was expelled from Pontus, he knew in his heart that he hadn't the strength of arms to stand against the Romans when they came again.

Which they did. His depredations in former times had assured that they would. He'd bought his own fate, poisoning this advisor and that retainer, and ordering the execution of the other supporter upon the way.

His final defeat had come at Nicopolis, and from there he fled to Colchis, home of witches and wily warrior-women. And to make it clear to the gods and the people of Colchis that he knew about the evils of women, he ordered the massacre of his entire harem then, as an object lesson.

What he learned from that was that he couldn't sleep a wink in Colchis, where the Medean witch cult looked at him with baleful eyes. He fled to the Crimea, where his back felt the unyielding wall of Fate's cold touch.

There he couldn't manage even to die with grace: all the poison he'd eaten over the years had made him immune to assassination by that means, though many tried. He was sick all the time from their attempts. Finally, it was a guard who slew him with a sword that ended his life when he was sixty-nine.

But the end of life didn't mean the end of suffering. He'd been a poor strategist, a man who could not keep the loyalty of his subordinates: this he'd expected. Since his father had passed over him, and his mother had falsified his father's will, he'd known that there was no one he could trust where power was concerned.

Toward the end of his life he'd known he had no friends. And he'd known why: he did not deserve them. His first wife he'd long ago driven to tears and death, and all other wives and concubines and lesser whores of his administration served him only for what they could get or in fear of what they might lose—until he killed them.

But he couldn't kill all who looked at him and through his mask and deep into his heart, where nothing lay but fear. Fear of discovery: that he wasn't so smart or so brave as he pretended; that he was struggling just to survive, weak and riddled with illness brought on his body by the illness of his soul; that his passions were only reactions to his fears.

No one had been left who cared one bit for Mithridates when he died—not even his son, the inheritor of a life's work and a kingship that had made him less than a man.

Alone as he'd always feared he'd be, after destroying so many who'd seen through him, a well-worn blade destroyed him. Because he couldn't destroy them all, not all his enemies, no matter how many men he ordered tortured and murdered—because he'd failed to make enough friends along the way. No matter how many careers he ruined and vendettas he mounted against his rivals, nothing eased the wounds to his pride and to the hurt and vicious child beneath.

No one had loved him in life. Those who served him were the venal and the slow-witted—whoever he could buy or trick, and whomever he could ensare sufficiently that they dared not leave his service. Those who'd said yes to him in life, no matter how foolish his plans or his pontifications, spat on his corpse when he died. In the end, he had lost everything: all human virtue had been dissolved by a lifetime of animal gratification and animal fear.

No one had loved him, in the end, because he'd driven from himself everyone capable of love, keeping only those who could be bought or trapped or enflamed with the Iranian idea of superiority by blood. And those all despised him, finally, even his own armies.

No one dared, in life, tell him to his face that he was wrong or he was frightened, or that he was mad with his lust for a power no man could accrue—or even that loyalty was a different thing than slavish obedience secured from dogs and footsoldiers in the field.

At last, when death closed his eyes, he was alone with his misery. His sister, his first wife, was long gone, the whores who came after were cold in the ground with his despite upon their graves, or long gone with whatever they could steal. His advisors were the least qualified of men, for all the wise and honorable ones he'd chased from his country or outright murdered when they defied him by trying to inject some reason into his senseless rages or his endless self-aggrandizing speeches.

So when he'd come to Hell, he'd thought it was his life that had poisoned him with its emptiness. It was his life that killed him, with its foul misery spread far and wide; it was his life that choked the life from him. Dying on his retainer's sword, he'd realized that every evil he'd done was now a weight bearing him down to Hell.

Every sin of his, no matter how subtle or unsuccessful, balled up in his throat and the mass of them was so great he could not breathe . . . and darkness descended upon the lonely soul of Mithridates . . .

So he came to Hell, gasping for breath, full of fear, a puffed-up, pompous toad who went straight to work, tunneling into Administration where he could gain power enough to pay back the Roman enemy for all that Rome had done to him.

Now, in the dark, where the wind wailed and the cart below him shivered and threatened to dump him into the black and Hell-spawned sky, he regretted having spent so much of his afterlife plotting to destroy the Roman West. Rome was smarter. It had always been.

Rome was at the root of his peril, even now. He could feel the cold sweat break out on his brow and dry in the gale. He could hear the creak of the lions' harness as they bore him onward through the blackness. And he could hear the thud of his own heart, whispering that as Zahhaq had been destroyed in treacherous Babylon, so would he be destroyed.

And destroyed and destroyed, neverendingly. All that had happened to him so far was proof of that. And where was he? He had escaped the serpents and the fires, only to be aloft at the mercy of a woman—a woman who had come to him he knew not how.

Rome was smarter. The woman, AE, was smarter. The woman who had seemed to be his friend was . . . what? No woman would help him, not after what he'd done to women in life. She was using him for her own purposes—or, worse, for Rome's.

He kept seeing the sad face of the afflicted giant, Zahhaq, and in it he saw his own misery, his own fate, his own foolishness.

When the three-tongued giant that had been Zahhaq had called to him to stay in Babylon, he'd refused. And he'd said to AE, the driver of his winged chariot, "Go on as we're headed. Before long we should return to the light."

And AE had asked, oh so innocently, "Do you know what lies this way?"

To this he had responded as a king: "Not yet. But we will. Soon we will."

And now, his head throbbing with the blow it had

taken, he looked askance at his female charioteer, racing his cart through the black clouds of night, and he wondered how he ever could have said those things.

There was no light, not here. He never should have told her what he wanted. Nothing had gone right since they had met. If she was a Roman agent, so be it. He could deal with that. But what if she were more?

What if she were worse? She was a female, an indictment in itself. What had come over him to trust such a one? When no one in Hell was ever who they seemed. *AE* was *EA* spelled backwards, he suddenly realized with a start. Was she Ea, primordial god of wisdom, cunning, spells, and water, come to exact payment from him where he languished?

Ea could be a woman if he chose. Or was she the Iranian god/goddess Zurvan, the hermaphrodite deity who existed prior to Heaven, earth, Hell, and everything else? Or was she merely AE, a modern woman from a time beyond his, who loved only the sky god and was an innocent in Hell?

And if she was an innocent in Hell, how had such an error come to be? Or were all women subhuman creatures like his mother and his filthy sister, scheming tools of the gods who never had souls but souls borrowed from Hell in the first place?

All manner of fears assailed him in that dark which whipped at him with windy palms, slapping his face this way, then slapping it that way. He was not the cleverest of men, and this was what had made him fearful. He looked into every heart and saw never what was there, and thus what that man might do, but only what he, Mithridates, would do were he in the other's place. And this made him a blind hippo charging through a temple.

But though he was blind, he wasn't deaf. He might be dumb, but in Hell he had resolved to even his score not only with Rome, but with all of Heaven.

He told himself that AE was not Ea, was not Zurvan, was not any trickster god or goddess whatsoever, but only a woman wearing pantaloons and boots.

This calmed him, but what she'd done yet remained: he was totally in her power, flying through air as dark as his sister's grave.

And she had not responded to his question, in all this long time of introspection. He wanted to reach over and grab her by her shoulder, shake it, demand to know why she thought it was strange that Zahhaq had made such a comment about the lions.

But to do that, he would have had to uncurl one aching fist from the rim of the chariot's cart. This would have been difficult, but not as difficult as continuing to be flown through a dark and featureless void by someone he could not see, or touch, or hear, driving winged lions who chased a basket of meat in the person of the Mandarin.

Or was he anywhere, with anyone, at all?

This fear, a sudden and complete terror of nothingness, overcame him and his knees began to quake. Was AE still there, to his right? Was he alone in a chariot pulled by winged lions gone wild? He could feel the rim of the cart, the polished wood, so that was truly there. Which meant he had a body also, for his fists to ache and his knees to quake.

But no more could he determine, unless he tried.

He yelled as loudly as he cloud: "AE! Let us land upon solid ground."

There was no answer.

He called again, "AE, do you hear me?" The wind ate his words.

He steeled himself, remembering that he must not overbalance the flying cart. Slowly and with infinite pain he uncurled his fingers from the chariot's rim. Each was stiff and unwieldy; each burned like fire as he straightened it after so much sustained clenching.

When his hand was free, he felt with it for AE's shoulder. And felt nothing. And felt around. And felt again. And then heard in his ears an awful sobbing.

This sobbing, as he patted the empty air he couldn't see, grew louder.

He realized then that it was his own, an awful soughing cry: half wheeze, half funereal moan. He clamped his jaws shut, and the terrible sound ceased.

Then again he felt the air, and finally gave up. His hand dropped down, as if to slap his side, and struck something.

Something hard, it was, with a softness on its surface. He snatched his hand away, even as he heard a muffled, "Damn, Mithridates, you scared me."

Suddenly the chariot rocked beneath his feet and he clutched its rim again.

As she rose from the shelter of the cart's curving wall, AE yelled, "Sorry, I fell asleep. What's up?"

"Up?" he yelled back, fury lending him strength, and relief upstepping his rage. "*Up?*" He snarled again. "*We're* up, you foolish twat—up in the middle of the air! And you go to sleep? Put us on solid ground! On land, I say!"

She yelled back something he didn't catch.

He demanded: "What? What did you say?"

Her skull slammed into his nose and the chariot rocked leftward, almost pitching him over the side.

AE shouted in his face, "I said, 'What land?' Do you want to try just anywhere?"

"Try!" he bellowed. "I command it!"

She moved away from him abruptly, and the chariot rocked again so that the lions growled. Or something growled.

"Hold on," AE warned, and all things slanted downward.

The chariot's floor angled beneath his feet. His belly hit the cart's rim. He nearly pitched overboard, doubled on the curve.

He thought he heard, from beyond the lions' heads, a faint "Aiiyeee!" as if the Mandarin had screamed in anguish or in terror.

But he didn't care about the Mandarin in the basket—if he were still alive. He cared only about Mithridates, whether he, the Great King, the lord of many lands, would still be "alive" in the way that he had accustomed himself to thinking of afterlife.

His body was his temple, here—all he could command, all he could survey. He didn't want to lose it. He didn't want to awake, broken and helpless, upon the Undertaker's table, back in New Hell where the Romans held sway.

Nothing, he told himself, not even falling forever in blackness, or crashing onto rocks of misery, could be worse than being reborn in New Hell, where the Julian Romans would have him at their mercy.

The thought sustained him on that stomach-wrenching descent through darkness.

How deep was Hell? Where did it end? Did it end? Were the deeper hells as different from the higher as Babylon, the way station, was from New Hell?

Did it matter?

He was telling himself that if he could merely feel solid ground beneath his feet, he would never ask more from his hereditary gods, when the chariot hit something. For a moment, he was sure it would come apart, a deathwagon of shattering spokes and splintered floorboards that would impale him. The axle screamed. Wheels jolted. Lions roared like thunder.

Then he knew that he had heard all those things, that the wind no longer boxed his ears.

And that he heard AE cursing like a soldier as she struggled, bounced against him, tripped, and sprawled on the chariot's floor.

He was tangled in something, he realized. Then he sorted out AE's yelling and the roaring of the beasts and the jolting of the car and recognized that he was sitting on the crank that held the basket before the lions, and that his limbs were tangled in the chariot's reins.

He rolled off them as AE pummeled him and pushed at him, demanding that he "Move! Move, Shit-for-brains! Move!"

He moved, and then he moved again, pulling himself up; on his knees, on his feet.

Without warning, the chariot lurched forward. Overbalanced, he careened backward. One step. Two. Then his heel caught on empty air and he fell back, arms pinwheeling.

For an instant, he was suspended in the air, screaming. Then his body hit the ground with an appreciable *thud* that knocked the wind from his lungs.

The pain was overwhelming. It seemed as if a giant were squeezing his chest. If he could get air into his lungs, he would live. If he could not, he would die. The desire to take one breath overcame every other thought, every other impulse. He struggled, mouth open, lying on his back, tearing at his chest, as if his clothes were keeping him from breathing.

The breath he finally forced down into his lungs was a breath of knives, so painful was it as his lungs filled. He heard the woman calling his name, but he was unconcerned, presently.

He needed that breath. He wasn't going to waste it on an answer.

But he heard the words she was calling, and understood what she meant at last: "Mithridates? Where are you? I can't find you in the dark if you don't answer! The lions will find salvation, if left to it. I want to fly them, Mithridates—it's the only hope. Please, if you're there, yell. Otherwise . . ."

He understood now, oh yes. Zahhaq had said that he should have let the winged lions go to find their own salvation in the underworld. AE was a flyer. AE was letting the lions fly wherever they chose—had been, until he demanded to land.

And she would again. She was going to leave him here, while she flew off to salvation.

He wanted to call out now. He truly did. But the lions were growling and someone was screaming, "No, don't let them eat any more of me! Don't let them reach me! I beg you, no!"

It was the Mandarin's voice, and beneath it was the sound of the chariot crank being winched.

She was going to leave him! AE was going to leave him and fly off into that black sky, in search of what salvation the winged lions could find.

He wanted to forbid her. He wanted to demand that she stay with him. He wanted to . . .

He tried to find the breath to yell out, to force his body to obey his mind. But his lungs were greedy and his body was unwilling to scramble to its feet the way he wished.

Had he broken something? His neck? His back? His heart?

He called out, as loudly as he could, "AE, do not leave me! Am I not Great King? Obey me!"

But the lions were roaring and the chariot wheels were rolling, making a racket over the rock-strewn ground on which he lay, prostrate, face to the unremitting black of the vault above.

Again he called out, "AE, you can't leave me! I'm your friend!" But he knew he wasn't. He wasn't anyone's friend. No one could sustain loyalty to him, any more than he could to another.

He remembered how AE had smiled at him with irony and no humor in her expression when he'd ordered her to get back into the chariot and help him, when he'd called her "woman" and she'd looked from him to the sobbing Mandarin and said, "Of course you're right."

AE loved only the sky, like the winged lions she drove. She would drive them up to salvation, up to Heaven, or die happy in the attempt. And she wouldn't lose her chance in order to save him, not after what she'd seen him do to the Mandarin. Why should she?

But she called back, "If you can hear me, Mithridates, go west. There's light there. I can see it." Her voice was fading as the lions' wings carried the chariot further and further into the heavens. "That's what you wanted, you said—to return to the light."

So then he realized that she hadn't even heard him call out to her. But it did not excuse the fact that she'd left him, showed disloyalty for which Hell would surely punish her.

But then, Hell punished everyone. Eternally. Lying on the rough and rock-strewn ground whose extent he could not see, in total darkness, aware of the cold and the mulchy smell and his own battered body's pain, Mithridates began to lament loudly, in the fashion of his kind, a fate worse, so he proclaimed, than he deserved.

When Mithridates awoke, there was light. The light came from the west, and it spoked through the clouds in rays that made him sit bolt upright, despite his battered body's pain.

Had his whole time in Hell been an awful nightmare, a reaction to some Bithynian poison, a drunken stupor, or a purge of guilt?

For one glorious moment he hoped so. He hoped

passionately. He hoped with every fiber of his being. He hoped as he had never hoped before.

The clouds above were massive thunderheads, a great mountain in the sky—the very abode of Zeus, he told himself. If that were so, the rays that spoked through those clouds like sunlight through giant chariot wheels were true light, Apollo's light, the sun chariot's own light.

If that were so, he was somewhere in his beloved kingdom, or in a territory of his, or left on some wheel-rutted battlefield by yet another cowardly driver. . . .

He must remember where he was. He must remember what driver, what chariot, what battle.

And then he did remember AE, and the winged chariot, and shook his head fiercely to shake that dream-memory away. He was in Colchis, surely. Or in Pontus, with luck. The jagged mountains he saw could be the mountains of Luristan, of northwest Iran . . . of Persia.

If only those rays would brighten from red to gold, from gold to white. If only the sky would lighten from ominous to sun-licked, from the dusty rose of dawn to the bright blue of heaven. . . . If only.

He got his legs under him, and it was a struggle he was proud to endure. He clenched his teeth and used his hands to help his legs move, grabbing each thigh, then each ankle in turn, until he was cross-legged, propped up by stiff arms.

Then he surveyed the ground about him for the tracks of chariot wheels, for the ruts of battle, for the divots of cavalry, for the humps of corpses, for the weapons of fallen fighters.

But all he saw on that dark and rugged plain was a single set of chariot tracks, directly ahead, that came from nowhere and went nowhere, as if a chariot had come down from Heaven, landed briefly, and departed.

He imagined he could see parallel score marks around the tracks, sets of lines, white marks in the rocks as if a lion had been sharpening his claws there.

And then he began to weep. He wept freely. He took his hands from the rocks and wrapped them about his belly and he rocked as he wept. Mithridates rocked back and forth, alone on the dark and stony plain, and howled to Heaven to have pity on him.

But Heaven did not, although Paradise rose while he wept, a bloodshot eye in the sky of Hell. Paradise peered down on him unblinkingly and she did not soften unto him.

The sky reddened but did not turn blue. The clouds above massed, and thunder rolled.

Thunder was the gods' displeasure, all men knew that. Mithridates would have gotten up and run for shelter—if he could run in his condition, and if there were shelter to be seen.

But as it was, he sat there cross-legged on the empty plain as the storm massed and lightning flashed and thunder rolled across the countryside, shaking loose rocks and quaking the very ground.

He had learned to count the time between the thunder and its lightning, in New Hell. He had learned that thunder and lightning were one thing, not two separate things. He raised his face to the vault as the red sky turned purple and a torrent began to plummet from the clouds.

Then it was that Mithridates called to the powers of Hell: "Take me, if you want me! All things belong to Zeus, even Hell! Zeus of the Lightning, of the Mount, of the Wrath, I am your lonely instrument! Take me! Let me bring repentance upon all those who have betrayed me! Make me thine instrument! Make the world quake before me!"

Lightning struck the ground less than a man's length from his right foot. He scrabbled backward, and his pain followed after him, dulled only slightly by his fear.

He gathered in his bruised and torn limbs and crouched there, sitting on his heels, his hands locked around his ankles, his head between his knees. The rain pelted him and froze him and numbed his hurt. It soaked his clothes and washed his scrapes and cuts. It cooled his bruises.

But it could do nothing for his soul. He was alone out here, amidst nothing, without even a sheltering overhang of rock. Lightning was forking to his left, forking to his right, stabbing the ground all around him.

He found his mouth open and a ululation coming out of it, as if he were a woman. His tongue spat out the particulated sound and it was lost in the rain, but it made him feel better. He howled at the heavens, and the sky spat back thunder.

He began to shiver and to shake where he sat. Water from the mountains was running down the hills, a distant roaring. Water was collecting on the plain in rivulets that met, and grew, branched, and grew again. The sound of rushing water was mixing with the sound of the torrent, like the downpour mixed with the runoff. Soon enough all sight and sound were one rush of wet and pervasive force.

The water was up to his hips when he realized he was no longer howling at the sky. It was up to his bellybutton when he noticed that the whole plain was bouncing and jouncing.

He wiped his drenched face and looked again, shielding his eyes with his hands. There was no plain to be seen, only water falling, water hitting water, rainwater bouncing as it struck the surface so that there was a miasma of spray that danced above the rock-punctuated water.

This was all he could see of land now, but for distant mountains: the occasional rock, sticking up. The mountains were lending their white stripes of running water, and the brown water of muddy run-off. The deluge had reached his waist.

When it got to his knees, even with his chin, he knew he must swim for it or die where he sat in sodden clothes that would weigh him down as the mud collected on them and gravel filled his pockets. . . .

Mithridates was not a man for a slow and reflective death. He raised one fist to the stormclouds and called again, "Zeus of the lightning bolt, I am yours. Do not waste me!"

Then he started taking off his clothes. This was harder than it seemed: his fingers were numb; his clothing was soaked; the currents in the swirling, muddy, debris-carrying waters were strong.

But eventually he was naked as a babe, divested of

all rainment, all artifice, and cursing as he tried to swim against the current.

He needed to reach the mountains. But they were far away and he was hurt. The water was cold, too, and numbing. He knew, after a while, that he would not make it. He turned on his back, and floated under the stormy sky. He would die with his eyes on the unattainable, like all men. He wanted to see Paradise, at least once more, if only to spit in its eye. He wanted to see Olympus, from where this torrent came, and tell Zeus what a waste his loss was, even to a god.

He wanted somebody, somewhere, to care about him, he thought at last, as he floated on his back with only his chin, his toes, and the tip of his penis breaking the water's surface. But there was no one whose name came to mind. There was no one he could think of who loved him. Not even AE, surely not the Mandarin; not Fremont; and most especially no one from his life on earth whose name he could speak, in the eyes of gods, and say that this one or that one would pray for him.

Nobody would. Some might be distressed, in New Hell, if he were to be reborn there, but that was nothing more than expediency: should he turn up, whatever goods of his that had been distributed would have to be given back. Whatever ursurpation of his power base that had taken place must be relinquished.

But he didn't want to go back to New Hell. Could a man ask for death in such circumstances and receive it? He forbore: Hell tended to give a man what that man wanted least, not most.

He floated on his back, without a thought to where

the currents might be taking him, and he wished evil upon everyone who'd had a hand in bringing him here. He wished evil upon AE, telling Zeus that, in view of Mithridates' sworn vassalage, the god should make sure that AE did not escape with the lions into salvation, let alone unto Heaven.

He prayed that the Mandarin would be eaten by the lions, and that the lions would then be eaten by Zeus' hungry horses, and that AE would be eaten last of all.

And he prayed that all his enemies would suffer more than he was suffering. He prayed for revenge. He prayed for destruction. He prayed for an end to all the powers of Hell that had conspired to put him here, a naked king stripped of everything that kingship implies and demands: honor, glory, adherents, advisors, wealth, constituency, land, valuables, gold, renown, power. Power. Power.

The power to destroy. The power to humble. The power to ordain and the power to cast down. The power to punish, oh yes. This was the power that Mithridates, thrown back on his personality's life-forged basic attributes, wanted most.

He'd always said, "Don't get mad, get even." He'd gotten even with everyone, for everything, throughout his life. This had destroyed him and brought him to Hell, but it was his way. He lived on vituperation; he was stirred to his greatest deeds by jealousy, by vengeance, by the urge to destroy.

He had humbled his mother, taken from her everything she valued. He had killed his brothers, who conspired with his mother to cheat him. He had married his sister and deflowered her, screaming, on their marriage bed. He had stripped her of all her pride and all her primacy, taking woman after woman into his harem, and letting her know she no longer pleased him by succumbing, in her presence, to wenches half her age.

He had seen suffering, in the years of his youth, and he had learned to strike out at the first sign of disloyalty. He could not bear to fail, so he thrust from him any and all people wise enough to see that he was not perfect, calling them incompetent, devaluing their work in his behalf, and taking to him any and all who would, for a time, follow him unquestioningly, no matter the foolhardiness of what he said or what he asked.

A man is the man his soul creates, and it is that man, no other, who comes to Hell. In Hell, Mithridates had struggled against the Roman West, and therefore against Satan himself. He had set himself up to support the Dissidents, burrowing into the very Pentagram itself to destroy whatever he could of the Romans' power.

The Dissidents wanted to supplant the sole rule of Satan with a kinder regime as they waited for final judgment. The Romans were aligned with Authority.

Fighting the Romans was fighting Lucifer Himself. Mithridates had been told, but refused to listen. And then, when the Romans captured him, he had shut down the questioning part of his mind, merely taking one step, then another; dealing with things as they came.

His head went under water. He let it sink. Perhaps he could die like this, in this sudden sea, and not be reborn in New Hell. If willpower were all it took, perhaps he could . . .

But he hadn't even enough willpower to drown himself. He came coughing and sputtering to the muddy surface, hands slapping the water like paddles.

His feet thrashed beneath him, trying to find purchase. How long had he been floating? The mountain walls seemed closer, now.

They were, he decided, closer now. They were so close that as his feet kicked, he scraped a rock protrusion with his big toe. He couldn't see the damage, but he knew from the feel his toe was bleeding.

Yet he was much heartened. He swam in that direction, thanking Zeus (his new and self-proclaimed patron god, god of the thunder and the lightning, even here). He thanked Zeus that he was still alive. He thanked the Lightning for the storm that had picked him up and carried him across the endless rocky plain that was probably Tartaros. He thanked Zeus for allowing him to reach into his soul and find a residue of hate from which to build a new fire under his arse.

He knew that Zeus was a jealous and a cruel god, a manipulative god, a primal god. Only the old Iranian gods had such attributes, and they had never spread far enough to have power here.

But Zeus had power over the Romans, who still believed in him. And Zeus had power over the heavens and the earth, or else the lightning would not have encircled him the way it did: never hurting him, only alerting him. Nor would the torrent have come down from the mountains and lifted him up and carried him to safety. Nor would the waters of the god have refused to drown him.

He told himself that Zeus and he were kindred souls, that he had no reason to repent his nature—that in Hell, where everything was evil by definition, a god of power had been drawn to his aid.

Therefore, he'd always been right. He need regret nothing that he had done—only the piteous nature of human beings, the flaws in other people that made it necessary for him to teach them the lessons that the gods had in mind.

You cannot separate a man from his gods, even in Hell. All the local rulers had learned that. Here the gods and the demons and the devils all roamed the land, and no one was safe from the monsters that belief brought into being.

Something grabbed him from beneath the surface. Its fingers were sharp like bones, unyielding like rigor mortis, cold like the grave. He kicked his way from its grip. A tree root, or a skeleton, or a demon from the deeps: what did it matter?

Mithridates was alive! Reborn! Reunited with his old self, the self that had made him a great king, and a great lover, and helped him live to a great old age! No more would be rue the "evils" that had brought him here.

A god had given him a sign, and not just any god—the great Father, Zeus!

He swam with new vigor. His elbow, then his knee, scraped sandy bottom. He cautiously felt the depth under him, and estimated that he could stand.

He waded shoreward. When the water was no deeper than his knees, he noticed that the torrent was abating. The sea behind him, as he turned to survey its expanse, was drying up.

Its choppy brown expanse was circling centerward, as if someone had pulled the plug in a bath. Mithridates watched for a time, fascinated, naked in water up to his calves.

Then he felt the tug of the water at his ankles, the suck of the current toward the center—and he ran up the shore.

He ran until he found a solid outcropping of rock. There he leaned, one hand on the rock, feet on solid ground, as the flood continued to abate before his eyes.

It was only when the sea of rain and mud was totally gone, and the sinkhole where it went no longer discernable in the middle of the plain, that Mithridates heard whispers, and then giggles, behind him.

The outcropping hid a cave. In the cave, he saw two pairs of eyes.

Slaves' eyes, he realized when he called them out and they didn't move, but scurried off into a darkness of tunnels. Slave children.

"Good," he told them. "Run from me. I am Mithridates the Great. You have reason to fear me. I am just become a son of Zeus!" He raised his fist then, filled with the glory of survival, and shouted Zeus' name so loudly and so proudly that it must, he thought, have been heard on distant Olympus and on Paradise itself.

The single word echoed over the great plain ringed with mountains, and came back to him: ZeusZeusZeuszeuseuseusus.

When the last echo faded, so did his newfound courage. Mithridates remembered that he was a naked, cold, mud-encrusted man standing on a treacherous slope, the sort of slope that a mudslide can create and destroy in an instant.

He began, then, as Paradise settled behind the mountains and darkness fell, climbing as best he could and as rapidly as he could, looking for a safe spot to curl up and spend the night.

When he reached the first ledge, it seemed too exposed to him, so he climbed to a second in the dusk. There was no telling how long it would take Paradise to set—if it did truly set here. The interval of dusk might last a long time, or even forever.

So he was considering climbing on when he finished exploring this second ledge, much wider than the first, if he found no dry cave or pine tree from which to make a bower.

As he was scrambling about so carefully, always making sure he had a good handhold, he chanced to look down the far side.

And he froze there, shocked and dumbstruck. The place he saw below him looked familiar: two outcroppings of rock, nearly meeting, a crack of light from the Hellish Phlegethon where she dived into subterranean realms, illuminating . . . a nightmare. He would not look.

He peeked. He closed his eyes tight. He would not look again.

Then he did. He fought the realization as long as he could, and then he crawled back out of sight, along the ledge, and there he huddled, shivering in the dusk.

Below was a work camp—perhaps the very work camp he'd escaped from. It looked like that one. It looked like the place where the Preacher had blazed on the rock. But it looked different, too.

He must not be caught, if it was the same camp. He must not lose the opportunity to secure help, food, clothing, and whatever power he could if it were not the same camp, but the camp of some other faction.

He couldn't tell whose camp it might be, not in the dusk, not while he was so tired, after so trying an adventure.

Bravery was never precipitate, he told himself, although the truth was that Mithridates hated going into any new situation—he hated crowds, he hated places where he was unknown and therefore not duly respected, he hated embarrassment of every sort.

There would certainly be embarrassment if he went scrambling down the cliffside, naked as a harem girl, and begged for some warm soup and a blanket.

As much as he wanted that soup and that blanket, he hid on the ledge for hours, trying to decide whether he should go down into the camp, or run as fast as he could away from here.

When Zeus intervened, or sent him a sign, then he would decide—if his stomach and his shivering flesh could hold out that long.

How long had it been, before that sign from Zeus appeared, plummeting out of the sky?

Mithridates was not certain. He wasn't certain of anything but the chill in his bones and the hunger gnawing his vitals. All he could say for sure was that the sky was yet an ill-tempered red when out of it came a screaming dot that grew.

The dot was screaming *Aiyeeee!* as it hurtled toward him, larger and larger still.

He blinked at it. He shaded his eyes with his hand to see it better. When that hardly helped, he made a circle of his thumb and forefinger, and looked through the tiny aperture ringed by his flesh.

All this time, the screaming and the dot were growing greater.

Soon he was certain it was no dot at all. It was longer than it was wide, and then it was wider than it was long: it was tumbling as it fell.

Fascinated, he squinted at it, black and growing larger, larger.

Soon he began to have a suspicion as to what the screaming oblong was: his sign from Zeus.

But by then he was becoming concerned: the thing was falling fast. It would hit hard, when it hit. He must not be under it when it crashed.

And it was heading straight toward him. Its size was indeterminate, for there was nothing against which to measure it but his intuition.

If the plummeting object was what he suspected it to be, Zeus had sent it to him as a sign, as a proof of favor—even if not as a literal answer to his prayer.

But no matter its nature or its provenance, if it fell upon him it would squish him like an ant under foot, and then there would be no more bargain with Father Zeus—no more anything but the Undertaker's table, if the jelly he'd by then have become could be reconstructed into anything even vaguely resembling a man. . . .

Mithridates got up hurriedly and backed toward the place where the ledge met the mountainside. He flattened himself against the mud and rock.

He was an archer of renown. His eye was legend. He kept that eye upon the object, tracking it as it fell, trying to estimate its trajectory.

But an estimate is only an estimate. He thought he was safe. He hoped he was safe. He prayed, for good measure, to Father Zeus that he be safe.

Meanwhile, his searching hands found a place in the mountainside where the face curved in. He hunkered down there, squeezing his body into a shallow place over which a lip of rock protruded.

And there he waited, to see how right he'd been.

What had first appeared as a dot was now a great boulder hurtling from the vault. It cast a malevolent shadow, even in the diffuse and sullen light. Wind whistled and crackled around it as it fell.

It would strike close to him, so close that it might as well be a missile sent from Paradise. He knew this as clearly as he knew how every abrasion on his battered body hurt. But there was nowhere to run: if he were not safely out of the impact area now, then he didn't know where else on this (suddenly) dangerously narrow ledge he would be safe.

He must stay where he was. He must trust his judgment. As an archer, he knew that the wind should be considered, and the arc, which he could not estimate, when adjudging point of impact.

He kept Father Zeus firmly in his mind. He kept his Luck firmly in his mind. He kept the curses he had uttered in his deepest misery firmly in his mind.

And he shook like a leaf in a gale, waiting for the missile to land.

It sounded like a New Hell engine, now, as it came close. It seemed, for a moment, not to be getting any closer, not to be falling or getting larger at all. And at this realization, he almost bolted.

If something seems not to be growing as it falls, then not to be falling as it approaches, it is headed straight for you. This he had learned from the LURPs in his service in New Hell, those who knew the magic of the Recoilless Projectile Guns, those masters of the New Dead's killing ways.

The thing was so close now that it cast a dizzying shadow. That shadow spun as it fell and for instants of its spin he was sure he could see the Mandarin's basket, or the lions' furled wings, still as stone, or the cart they drew.

But never in the entire and agonizingly fear-slowed time he watched the falling object did he catch sight of AE, only of the chariot's polished rim.

And then it was upon him—or almost upon him. The gust of its passing was horrifying, a token of its force.

Mithridates quailed before it, his arms going up of their own accord to shield his face, as if soft human flesh and human bone would be any protection from the splintering of the chariot when it would strike him or strike close on the pitifully narrow ledge he'd chosen for his martyrdom. . . .

But it did not strike him. It did not hit the ledge at all. As it roared past, he had a glimpse of basalt-black lions' wings, of massive haunches, and of the Mandarin's gray and contorted face, mouth open in a blood-curdling scream he couldn't hear over the rush of wind.

The chariot went by in a roar and then there was silence. There was no crash. There was no splintering of wood and blood or spattering of bone. There was only a resumption of the scream he'd heard, which changed pitch as it passed.

And continued falling.

He ran to the ledge's edge and peered over. How could he have misjudged its trajectory so, famed archer that he'd been?

The chariot was falling free, falling into the crack, into the crevice where two lips of rock nearly met but didn't, falling into the split from whence Phlegethon's light poured—falling toward the work camp far below.

Now he heard crashes: caroming thuds and horrible scraping sounds like fingers on a slate as parts of the chariot struck the closed-sided rock.

By then, though, he could no longer see it. It was out of sight beyond the rocky lips.

When it struck, he told himself, he would not hear it—not from so far above, not with the overhanging rock walls in between.

But Mithridates did not need to hear the fall. He had his sign from Zeus. Although he had asked that the Mandarin be eaten by the lions, and the lions eaten by Zeus' hungry horses, and AE eaten last of all, he assured himself that Zeus had not failed him, only sent him a sign he could not misconstrue.

If there was anything left of the chariot, of the Mandarin, of AE—anything left of them at all—then a long and horrible death was probably awaiting them in Phlegethon's blazing currents. Or someplace worse. He had cursed them, and his curse had been heard by Zeus, who struck them from the sky with a swat of his giant hand.

Who knew just what the god had in his mind?

Mithridates was careful not to be ungrateful. Whatever the fate of his enemies, it was at his behest that they had been cast down from salvation. This he knew like he knew the absolute pleasure of safety as his bowels relaxed. This he knew as he knew that he must now, in good faith, venture down into the camp.

Father Zeus had used the chariot that had fallen from the vault as an oracular sign, and the traitors who'd stolen it and left him to die as pointers.

He must only follow where the god's pointer led.

His Luck waited, far below. His new god awaited. And since Father Zeus had given him a sign that the power to punish his enemies was now in Mithridates' hands, he hastened down the ledge with only a little trepidation.

Even if this was the selfsame work camp where the Roman henchman had made of his life an ignominious torture, all that would now be changed. Father Zeus was making his power felt in Hell through his instrument, Mithridates the Great.

With a god on his side, how could he fail? All the years of his life, when he'd tried to style himself in Alexander's image, he'd never had the favor of Zeus, as Alexander had had.

Now he did. Everything would be different, from this moment on.

* * *

The camp was a shambles when he got there. In the middle of the trustees' tents was the chariot, although it was no longer that selfsame chariot, a conveyance of wood and iron and leather drawn by beasts of flesh and blood.

It was shattered. It was crumbled. It was in pieces and under every piece lay a guard or a lackey, but this was not the most startling thing Mithridates saw.

The most startling thing was that the chariot, and the lions who drew it with great black wings, and the Mandarin in his basket, and the car of polished wood—and even AE in her boots—were all turned to stone. All was broken statuary, chunks of black basalt.

Mithridates, in the confusion at the impact crater, in the tricky light of Phlegethon, slipped through the crowd and picked up the chunk that once had been AE's head. The look on that stone face was not one of fear, but of beatitude.

The head fell from his fingers, which were growing clumsy as they held the stone head of AE, as if his own fingers were turning to stone as well.

He massaged his hands, examining his nails, his knuckles, his palms for any sign of petrification while his pulse thudded in his ears.

His fingers were pale and cold, but human fingers yet. He flexed them with sudden affection and a possessive joy in their mobility.

Then he kicked the head at his feet and it rolled until it came to rest face up. AE's basalt eyes stared at him.

He wanted to kick the head again, kick it to shards, but there were others milling about, frightened guards, some as naked as he. And these trustees were talking loudly, swearing bold oaths through mouths dry with fear at what had come hurtling from Heaven to strike down some of their number with no warning.

He must not become an object of curiosity, naked as he was there. He must not become remarkable in the confusion because he displayed none. He'd strode boldly among them, as if he had some right to be here, staunch in his purpose.

Now . . . he was vulnerable, naked among his former captors. He should move away, now. He should slide through the squatting men and the kneeling men and the stalking men and the men stuffing their feet into boots and buttoning shirts and belting on weapons, past others who pulled at the mashed limbs of fallen comrades, or cradled crushed skulls in their arms.

But he did not. The stare of AE's basalt head transfixed him as if she were Medusa. What right did AE have to display such a look of peace and glorious triumph upon her shameful face?

He forced himself to look away, and spied what was left of the Mandarin, freed from his basket by the crash. What right did the Mandarin have, not to be eaten alive?

He shifted his eyes and his gaze fell upon the stone lions. What right did the great winged lions have, to fall to earth as temple statuary, as Babylonian fetishes, as mere works of art?

Mithridates staggered back from the wide-strewn pile of rubble, and bumped someone as he did.

The someone elbowed him back and muttered, "Watch where yer goin', fella."

Mithridates murmured an apology and stiffened

for the yell of recognition, the call to surrender, the hue and cry of guards come upon an escaped prisoner.

But nothing of the sort happened. Here he was, naked as a baby, amid so many milling guards, and no one seemed to give him a second glance.

Then he understood why, when he saw another guard, pulling on his breeches as he came: No one up here could be a slave; this was where only trustworthy minions and guards slept and ate and did what they willed with the unfortunate workers.

Mithridates continued to retreat, toward a tent chosen at random. As he did, he searched the faces of the frightened, worried men who craned their necks to squint up through the crack at the sky.

He recognized none of them. Yet he recognized the camp, he was nearly positive. This must be, he decided, because these were all different men. His escape must have caused a shakeup in personnel here.

Now he retreated with bolder steps. If these men were all new, perhaps he had a chance of blending in, of at least pilfering clothes, if not rank itself. . . .

This scenario pleased him. This plan, he wanted to believe, was workable. He was a king; not an omnipotent king or an omniscient king, but a king nonetheless. As a king must, Mithridates considered again the possibility of error.

This might yet be a different camp. Who knew how many similar camps existed in all of Hell? Not Mithridates. All he could say for certain was that he knew none of the guards by sight. Only the lay of the land seemed the same. Perhaps it was a different place after all. . . .

But then, from the yawning cavern where the work gangs languished, a demon swaggered up and out. Blue and ratty, with a dangling penis that shot sparks: this demon he well remembered.

He turned his face away and scuttled as boldly as he dared for an open tent flap, every muscle of his stiffened back twitching, anticipating the burning clasp of claws upon his shoulder.

But no claws impaled him. No demon breathed down his neck or even raised an alarm. He ducked beneath the tenting, through the flaps.

Inside was everything he needed. Well, not really, but enough from which to choose. He would make do. He thanked his adopted father, Zeus, and struggled into New Dead clothes: tight pants with a hair-eating zipper, a khaki shirt, a wide cartridge belt with a heavy pistol depending from it in a leather scabbard.

The man whose clothes these were had a wallet in his hip pocket, and orders open upon his campaign chest.

Mithridates looked nothing like the picture on the owner's photo-ID, not really. But he wouldn't be here long enough for that to matter. He pulled the picture from the wallet and stuffed the ID-card in a pot of tea that was brewing above the cookfire.

When he took it out, the picture well enough resembled him, as much as it resembled any man. The text, as he had hoped, was still readable.

If he needed to, he could impersonate this lieutenant of the guard. Until the man himself returned, of course.

He put socks on his feet and sighed, closing his

eyes at the sudden comfort. The lure of such luxury was almost overpowering. He wanted to sleep, to drink the tea brewing here, to eat the fine white bread. . . .

He forced himself to hurry. The shoes of Lieutenant Calley were too large, but not if he donned a second pair of socks.

When he was shod, he looked around further. In Hell, when you assumed a man's identity, did you also assume that man's fate?

It was a question that made someone of Mithridates' nature pause to reflect. His spine grew cold with an ominous and stiffening chill. He fought the paralyzing notion that he could inherit the fate of a man when he was totally ignorant of the man's fate. It was not like robbing a grave, since even were Calley dead under the basalt chariot, he would live again in New Hell, soon enough. Therefore, Calley either lurked beyond the tent flaps, chin-deep in his fate, or soon enough would resume afterlife if the basalt had bludgeoned it from him, resuming the enactment of his fate in Hell as well.

Ergo, I am safe, Mithridates told himself, shaking off the paralysis of fear with a physical shiver like a dog shedding water from his fur. Then he began robbing the grave goods of Calley, or the tent to which Calley might yet return to find a looter within.

He took a padded jacket with patches on its sleeves; he took a Skorpion in a sling and clips for it, and slung those over his shoulder. He took a black bandana and tied it around his head as many of the New Dead soldiers did.

Then he stepped boldly out of the tent, his finger

on the trigger of the Skorpion, to hunt for the real Calley.

He must find the man and kill Calley if he still lived, lest Mithridates' identity be discovered. He could force the soldier to Phlegethon, shoot him there. The flaming river would take the body as a sacrifice to Zeus, he would make sure of that.

And then he would learn what he could of this place, and why Zeus had brought him here.

For he *had* been brought by the Thrower of Lightning. Mithridates had not been Great King for nothing; any monarch of his day knew an omen when he stumbled over one. In all his years of kingship, no god of Persia had ever served him with so direct a warrant. Not in the whole of his youth, when he had worshiped all Alexander's gods in hope of currying equal favor, had Zeus so much as winked in his direction. Now there had come to him favor from Olympus.

In Hell, he had been blessed. From the abyss had come this bond with a god too great to be banished from even Hell's deepest recesses.

There was a spring in Mithridates' step as he ducked out of the tent and into the confusion.

Men were still pulling bodies from the wreckage—human bodies, struck down by the chariot as it fell, shattering into a rain of razor-sharp exploding missiles.

Mithridates walked among the guards, thumbs stuck in his belt, grunting monosyllables of profanity in English and in German and in Dutch. It was not hard to sound like one of the New Dead; it had never been hard to sound like a soldier; even easier to sound like a lackey, or a fool.

He even tried giving an order, then another. He was helping the cause, he told himself: clearing the wreckage could answer a pressing question of his own.

And then, two grunting privates of the guard pulled a chunk of basalt lion haunch off a pair of corpses, and there lay the real Calley, his limbs entwined with a slave boy over whom he'd fallen.

Calley was as naked as Mithridates had been, and the position of the boy and the man made clear what had been going on when the missile from Heaven interrupted.

Some things in Hell were eternal. "Take the corpses to the river, out of the way. We don't need 'em decomposing here. Move your asses," Mithridates snarled in English, and stomped away to watch covertly while his will was done.

When the real Calley was put into the burning waters of Phlegethon with the others, a private came up to him, his brow furrowed.

The private said, "Lieutenant? Sir, we got a problem."

"This is something new?" Mithridates responded, aware that his dialect was not quite appropriate.

"Yeah, I hear ya, sir: nothin' works right, includin' simple math, I guess. But ya see, there's one more body than we c'n account fer casualties. . . ."

"Somebody screwed up, Private? Bring him to me."

"Ah . . . shit, sir. We'll never figger out where the extra came from—somebody didn't count something, somewhere. . . ."

"Don't ask me to cover for you, Private. I don't know anything about—"

"Nothin', yeah, I know. Okay, sir, just so's you know it wasn't me, that I told ya . . . okay?"

"Okay." Mithridates was out of his stock English idioms now, and trying his best to bluff the matter through. Why wouldn't the private just go away and lie about the numbers?

The youngster scratched with a pencil behind one red ear and said, "Want I should make it come out right?"

"I don't want to . . . hear anything more about it. When you do your report, let there be nothing amiss."

"Nothing . . . amiss?" The private squinted at him. "Yessuh. I hear ya." The private slouched away, looking back over his shoulder twice at Mithridates.

He must do better, next time. He would do better. He had had many Americans under his command, at one time or another in Hell. He moved along the shore of Phlegethon, watching the bodies burn and sink.

A dozen had died in the crash of the basalt chariot, not counting the Mandarin and AE.

His mind threw up a vision of AE's black basalt face, and the look upon it. She had no right to have that look of beatitude upon her treacherous countenance. She had betrayed him. He found himself headed back toward the crash site.

What happened to someone in Hell who was turned to stone? How were such souls resurrected? Were they resurrected? Could it be that, if the head of AE and the body of AE were left apart, mere pieces of stone that had shattered, her person would languish in that form? Did one need at least most of a body to secure a resurrection? Or human flesh parts of a body, to start the process?

There was one way to find out: experimentation. On the way back to the crash site, Mithridates passed the cave mouth leading into the excavation. He could hear Liszt's organ playing. He could smell the charnel smoke. The smoke reminded him again of the eighty thousand Roman civilians he'd ordered slaughtered.

Life was shit, the New Dead said, and then in afterlife you couldn't. But you could burn, in earthly life and in the next. The corpses Mithridates/Calley had ordered carried to the river would burn only a little faster because they'd been dumped into Phlegethon. Perhaps they would suffer more in the river's flames than in the spontaneous combustion that cleared the corpses that otherwise would litter Hell so deep there'd be no standing on anything but bodies.

Perhaps not. But he wanted to find the head of AE. He needed to find the basalt head of AE. The smiling head, the beatific and beautiful black basalt head of AE, and see if it burned, or turned to wet and smoking jelly that sank into the ground. . . .

If it didn't, then he would be sure that the god Zeus had made him a gift of her traitorous soul, a gift more precious than life: the gift of death. If AE's head could be mounted on a block of marble, and put in Calley's tent, and if it would stay there . . .

Then AE would never return to afterlife. The head would be proof. His god would have given him a sign that none could misread. He, Mithridates, King of Kings, Great King, King of Pontus, of Persia itself, would be the single man in Hell qualified to dispense death forever.

Death of the sort he'd thought he was dealing, when he'd ordered those civilians massacred. Death of the sort he'd meted out in the jungle, burning those huts, the whole village of enemies—old enemies, young enemies, enemy women, and enemy babies who, if they'd been allowed to grow up, would have been another generation of enemies. . . .

He shook unfamiliar memories away. He blinked and staggered as he moved. He didn't remember huts like that, though of course there must have been some. He didn't remember flamethrowers like that, burning the jungle and the straw. . . .

But then, he'd been in Hell for thousands of years, and each resurrection brought with it wisps of error. Errors in memory, errors in forgetfulness. He'd been in jungles, he'd killed more civilians than anyone else in his outfit . . .

In his time, he corrected himself savagely. And what was this sudden differentiation? An enemy people was an enemy people—every person among them was at best a slave, a potential deportee, a hostage . . . or a corpse. Every peasant and farmer and witch and grandmother who succored and supported the enemy was an enemy. There were no noncombatants. The teeming population of Hell was testament to that.

And if his men had sacked and burned, then so what? God sacked and burned, didn't he, through men? All the gods, he amended. Before the Fire cult, which had been a way to unify the people, the Iranian gods had known what to do with fire. As did the gods of Hell, and Zurvan, the God of Gods, the primal lord who had created Heaven and Hell, and sustained them.

If the dead caught fire in Hell when they died, then death by fire was pleasing in the sight of Heaven. Therefore, death was pleasing in the sight of Heaven, which allowed Hell and sustained it—allowed death and made it man's destined end, his ticket to Hell or Heaven.

There was something wrong with this logic and Mithridates tripped over a human hand, just beginning to smoke, as he reached the pile of rubble, so abstracted was he in thought.

If death was god's gift to man, then why was he here because he'd delivered it? Why did the messenger suffer for bringing the message?

The hand in the rubble was continuing to smoke. He called out hoarsely, "Yo, get this dink outta here!" without knowing what he did. He had a deep and abiding horror of seeing human flesh burn.

And this was odd. He'd never felt that way before. All the dead burned in Hell, if they didn't melt or explode once afterlife had fled. . . .

Corporals and privates came dog-trotting to do his bidding. One said, "Easy, sir, okay? We just missed one, is all."

It was the same private he'd encountered at the riverbank. He said, "Get it away from me! Get it to the river. If it burns in Phlegethon, it ain't my fault. It's . . ."

"Okay, sir; okay." The private had on asbestos gloves; so did the corporal. They pulled black bandanas up over their noses as they bent to the steaming corpse.

He couldn't bring himself to step over the body. Nor was there a way around it, among the jagged chunks of rubble. He waited until they'd moved it, backing up as the two men hoisted the corpse between them.

The body was beginning to glow as it steamed; juice was seeping to its skin. The sweet smell caught in his throat and gagged him. He closed his eyes. He didn't want to see the skin blacken. He didn't want to see the eyes pop. He didn't want to see the lips draw back as they blistered, and charred, and curled. . . .

He kept seeing a blackened face with white eyeholes and heat-browned teeth, even with his own eyes closed.

When he opened them, he was shaking and sweating as if it were his flesh that was starting to burn from within.

But it wasn't. He must remember that. He didn't understand the strange fear of death that had come over him. Was he not Mithridates the Great, who had died in life and died in Hell and meted out death to the multitude of living and afterliving souls?

He gathered his courage and stepped boldly through the rubble where the corpse had been removed. He knew what he wanted. He must find it.

The head of AE was still smiling that horrid smile. The basalt of her face was black/gray, black/green, black/red . . . and beautiful.

He picked up the head and clasped it against his side, cradling it with his elbow. He was going to have her mounted. He was going to make sure that she stayed dead, if keeping her head apart from her shattered body would do the trick.

And she would thank him, no doubt. He grinned a grin he'd had on his face while surveying the carnage his Pontiac warriors had wrought long ago in life.

He was King of Kings. Whatever jungle huts he now recalled, whatever brown and primitive folk he'd roasted there . . . well, they just hadn't been consequential enough to recollect until the smell of Phlegethon's marshy banks receiving the dead had triggered a memory. He'd been many places in his afterlife and times.

And none were better than this place, now that he had assumed the identity of the trusted officer, Lieutenant Calley.

He made straight for his tent, where Calley's orders awaited him, laid out in simple English. In his Pentagram years, he'd become fluent in written English, even if his spoken idiom was weak.

He ducked into Calley's tent, unlaced the flaps and jerked them down, sighing as soon as he was safe from prying eyes.

Then he took the head of AE from under his arm and placed it on the campaign chest, taking up Calley's orders instead.

He sat by the cookfire, reading the orders and drinking Calley's Asian tea, until his eyes ached. Then he brewed more tea and read them again.

He rubbed his eyes, having read the document a second time. Then he began to chuckle. He got up. He stretched. He took time to shrug off the Skorpion, the clips, and to unbuckle the gunbelt from his waist.

He was sweating, but he ignored that: the tea was hot, the tent confines close; the air was muggy, and purple mud squished under his feet as he secured his weapons and unfolded his cot.

He lay on the cot, his orders folded on his chest, looking at AE's amazing face. He'd have the workers fashion a marble plinth for her; he'd mount her like a Phidian fragment. He'd drive a steel rod into her neck to keep her on her plinth.

He scratched his chest under the sheaf of orders, and dogtags jingled there. He didn't remember putting on Calley's dogtags, but he must have . . . and the olive t-shirt, too.

Everything was going better than even the King of Pontus had a right to expect. He should make a sacrifice. Maybe a dog, if he could find one. He licked his lips and then they twisted. A dog? Where had such a thought come from? An ox, perhaps . . . the fatted thigh of a great bullock, for Father Zeus, maybe; but . . . a dog?

Dog was unclean. Dog was not tasty. Dog was not something to salivate over. Dog was surely no sacrifice. But roast dog with rice and mung beans . . .

He crumpled the orders in his fist, and sat up abruptly. He ran one hand through his hair and that hair was spiky, shorter. His stomach lurched and he didn't know why. His vision was blurring. The combat boots on his feet had laces that were undulating like deadly vipers. . . .

"AE," he said in a hoarse and determined voice, struggling to see the basalt head through the fog over his vision. "AE, do you know what these orders say? They're secret, you know?" He grinned a wide, fierce and humorless grin that made his cheeks ache and split his sun-dried lips so that blood spurted from the cracks.

The basalt head under the mottled green tenting did not answer.

"Says here," he continued in a slurred English dialect he hadn't been able to summon at the crash site, "that Satan's got it in his mind to, like, raise Zeus—the old god from mythology, y'know. So that's the mission—that's what you and me and the Mandarin and Fremont an' the rest of the POWs is—was—here for: dig out this petrified god, like."

He paused, in case AE's severed head would comment. It didn't. His dogtags jingled as he leaned forward to confide the rest of his secret orders in a low tone. Elbows on his knees, paper shivering between in his hands, he licked the blood from his lips and looked up at her black/green/red/glorious head and said, "Y'know, you'd a burned in Hell, so's to speak—over and over. Y'oughta thank me."

The head of AE didn't.

"Look," he said, licking his lips again because the splits hurt, trying not to hear the desperation in his tone. "You really got no call to be mad at me, AE. Look at you—peaceful like, safe from everything. Beyond the pain. Like it should be, right? There's no way outta here—dead or alive: that's what they say. But I got you out. You don't have to suffer no more. You can sleep. We used to think that the dinks got a ticket out o' them damn rice paddies, too. Friend o' mine used to love to shoot the little brown things when they jumped into the paddies . . . from his

Huey, that's all they was. Extended twice, till we . . ."

Mithridates clamped his mouth shut. He stared at the crumpled orders in his shaking hands.

He smoothed them, stroking the paper flat meticulously. Then he read aloud: " '. . . dig the entire basalt colossus from the pit without error. Scratch nothing. Crack nothing. Raise the basalt Zeus onto his feet. Then send word to Satan's office that this has been done. And make no comment or disparagement, no curse or derisive remark, in the process. This statue of Zeus shall live again, by order of His Satanic Majesty.' "

The words he read wriggled before his eyes. He looked again at AE. Her expression had not changed. Why did he expect it would? She wasn't alive. She was a head of rock. . . . Wasn't she?

But the implication of Calley's orders was that the statue of Zeus in the pit was more than just a statue. He'd worked in that pit; he'd seen the giant curve of a thigh, hewn as no human could manage, the articulation of muscle there so vast and mighty.

He resumed reading aloud: "When you have raised the statue, say unto it, 'In the name of Lucifer, Lord of Hell, we His damned minions welcome you, Thunderer, to the eternal afterlife. Bide here until Satan Himself arrives to welcome you as His Ally against the fools in Heaven.' Can you dig it, AE?"

He scratched his lice-infested brush cut. AE's head still had an expression on it more suited to a church than a bivouac. He tugged on his dogtags, an unconscious habit. He folded the orders he held and leaned farther forward, to where the cookfire burned low, his dented pot steaming over it.

He touched the secret orders to the coals, and the edges of the paper began to blacken. Then they turned red and yellow; they caught, flamed, and he pushed the sheaf into the fire, under the pot, and sat back to watch it burn.

The hungry flame licked high as it ate the paper; the firelight reflected off AE's black face as if her eyes glowed.

"Shit," he said, and jammed his hands into his back pockets as he got up to leave. From the tent's doorway he added, "Don't figure, huh, AE? Satan makin' an ally out of Zeus—you oughta know what Zeus is about. He ain't playin' the Devil's game, not for nothin'."

He let the tent flap fall when AE didn't answer.

He wanted to go down into the pit and see how the exhumation of a god was progressing. The exhumation of *his* god, he reminded himself as his steps began to drag when he got close to the excavation's mouth.

To get down there, he'd have to pass Liszt's disgusting organ; he'd have to pass the burning martyrs, and the rest.

Stupid martyrs. What difference did it make when you burned? What was the point of burning alive on purpose, when you burned in the end anyway?

He knew all about burning alive. . . .

Or did he?

Mithridates didn't realize that he was slumped against the cave-like entrance to the excavation until someone said, "Are you unwell, Lieutenant?"

"Naw . . . I—" Within Mithridates, a struggle for control of more than simply language was taking place. His mind sorted memories of horses screaming in battle and napalm delivery systems screaming under smoke-filled skies. He was Mithridates, King of Kings. He was not a New Dead lieutenant who'd killed a mere handful in some mismanaged border war fought in mud. . . .

For an instant, he couldn't see the cavern, or any part of Hell. All he could see was mud: yellow mud, red mud, purple mud. And mud running with blood.

He shook his head again. He could not let his mind play such tricks. He was not Calley. He was Mithridates, Great King, King of Kings, King of . . .

"Sir? *Sir!*"

Yet Calley's knowledge was invaluable, perhaps crucial to his survival here and now. As he very slowly and very determinedly opened his tight-shut eyes, he was saying, "Hold your water, soldier. Just a little too much wacky weed, is all."

But it was not a soldier he confronted when he could see who spoke to him. It was a demon, shouldering aside a private with a worried look on his face.

The demon had breath that smelled like the underside of a water buffalo's tail. He was blue and mangy and one of his eyes was dripping fluid. He kept wiping it and lashing his tail, which threw sparks. He said, "Lieutenant, you're late for your shift!" *Slap!* went the demon's tail. *Slap! Slap!* "What have you got to say for yourself?"

"We had a little disturbance, or maybe you didn't notice down there. What, this project's on schedule or somethin, that you're bitchin' at me? What's your name—I can't never tell you guys apart!"

"Zuzit, I am," said the demon on a noxious breath. His tail was lashing harder now, making it seem that fireflies hovered around his haunches. "How dare you speak so to me, you human refuse? When you address a demon lord, you do so humbly!"

Smack! The demon's clawed forepaw backhanded Mithridates across the jaw. He staggered, grabbed the wall for support.

"Listen, you rat-furred piece of shit," Mithridates heard himself saying as his body stepped forward, hands reaching for weapons he'd left in his tent and clenching on empty air. "You touch me again, and you'll have to send all the way back to New Hell for a copy of the secret orders I just burned and somebody qualified to do what they said. Them orders was from Satan's own fuckin' office, and there ain't a demon can execute 'em. You need ol' Calley fer that!"

And he was right, Mithridates realized. Calley, or someone like Calley, would be needed to supplicate Zeus, who was a god of man, not of demons; who must be groveled before and sacrificed to, all in advance of any meeting with Satan, who was neither a groveler nor a sacrificer.

Yet Mithridates tensed himself for the inevitable result of speaking thus to a demon overseer of the pits.

He winced as the demon opened wide its jaws, seeing the sudden end of everything he'd planned.

But the demon only growled at him, "Then hurry,

semen-bag. If you have a task to perform, come and do it. The thing in the rock needs attention."

And the part of him that had access to Calley's twisted wisdom said with sullen pleasure, "When I'm damned good and ready, muff-face."

The demon's tail lashed more furiously, back and forth in the cave-like entrance. Chunks of rock began to crumble where the spiked tail struck, then to fall.

"Now, doomed soul!" Behind the demon, Mithridates could see pale human faces: the private he recognized, others with the black bandanas of the trusted.

"Keep your hide on, I'm comin'. There's nothing down there can't wait." The demon was from MACV, you bet. Slimy shit from Saigon, with his head-wedged orders. Orders never made sense worth a damn; cut by guys who never got enough mud on to know what was shakin'; guys who never heard the quiet that came when the rain fell.

So quiet, in the rain, even the bugs shut up. You could hear the rice grow. You could hear your hair fall out. You could hear the dinks breathing. . . .

Mithridates/Calley saw the scared eyes of the private behind the blue dink and the other prisoners—behind the private with those too-scared eyes that kept him awake nights. You had to kill the damned enemy; takin' prisoners was cruel and unusual punishment on both sides.

He jumped for the blue dink's throat, bare hands out, and slammed upward with his skull and the entire force of his leap, catching the jaw with the top of his head and ramming it up and back as his hands closed around its neck. He heard the neck snap even as he and the snaggle-toothed dink went down in a heap.

He scrambled off it, as soon as he could. He could feel the lice jumping ship, from the dink onto him. He hated the lice worst of all. . . .

The private and two grunts behind him were all huddled up, whispering.

"It's cool," he said. He already had one mother of a headache that went all the way down into his neck, into his shoulders, right down his spine to his butt.

"It's okay," he said again, realizing he was straddling the demon and stepping over the blue corpse, already starting to smoke. "You didn't see nothin', right? Right? *All right?* That's a fucking order, dickheads!"

And he strode past them, into the tunnel, and off toward the excavation, alone with his headache and his memories.

He heard the boys scrambling in his wake. They'd be all right. They'd get over it. They were as guilty as he was. DX-ing the demon was just the thing to do right then, that was all. You had to do something about all this suffering. You couldn't let your people take all these hits and do nothin'.

You had to do some damned thing.

The screaming of the souls stretched on Liszt's organ was fading in the distance, a barely noticed curiosity back up the incline, when Mithridates regained control.

Calley's feet—his feet, the feet of Mithridates, Great King—were slipping and sliding down the final ramp, which was steeper now than when he'd dug here.

The soldiers following him were still whispering together. You couldn't trust whisperers, the king knew that. How had he allowed himself to jeopardize everything he'd struggled for by losing his temper?

Had he truly killed a demon, barehanded? Or was it a nightmare, a slur of Calley's thoughts in his brain? For the first time, Mithridates admitted to himself that those thoughts were not his own; that those memories were not his own.

He reached up and felt his spiky brush cut. He scratched the lice that infested him. Then he stopped. His boots were too tight. He sat down there, on the edge of the excavation's deepest pit, amid numb and miserable workers who came and went with their baskets, up the ladders.

There he stripped off his boots and then the second pair of socks he'd put on when those boots were too large.

Now they fit him. His hands, as he relaced the boots with casual familiarity, were too scarred, too square in the fingers, too broad and too strong.

He was a king, not a peltast or an infantryman. He had no right to have such hands. But have them he did, and they played with the dogtags around his neck as he sat, staring down into the pit, swinging his dangling legs, and humming to himself.

The thing in the bottom of the pit was ten times the size of a man, and nearly out of the rock. The workers were on their knees, chipping at the body of the god with hand tools, brushes, and picks, scraping around its giant arse. Ladders went everywhere, up and down and across the excavation.

There were three blue-furred demons in the pit, and one of them pointed at him and called "Hi! Calley!"

He waved casually. Let them dig his god from the rubble of time. He was ready. He knew what to do. And Calley was empowered to do it. Say the words, make the sacrifices, raise the physical person of Zeus in Hell.

How could he refuse?

He had been brought here and transmuted in every way necessary to perform the sacrifice. He had asked, begged on the flooding plain of Tartaros, for the honor. And Father Zeus had heard him. His tutelary god was lying in a body of stone in the deepest depths of Hell.

Mithridates knew that the affairs of gods were impenetrable to the minds of men. He also knew that someone had made a grievous error, if that someone, somewhere high in Authority, thought that Zeus himself, Father Zeus of the Lightning, would serve any other power, even Lucifer himself.

Was Satan so distressed by the damned that he needed an ally? This couldn't be. Nothing so modest as Mithridates' coup could have precipitated this endeavor.

He nodded to himself, and waved again as the demon who'd noticed him started for one of the ladders to the pit's rim.

Behind him, he could hear the private and his friends, whispering, whispering. Was that private his aide? Did he rank one?

He waited for Calley's memories to answer his question, but they remained silent. It didn't matter. Nothing mattered but freeing his god, who languished in the pit. Bringing Zeus to life in Hell, under Satan's orders . . .

Would the Fallen Angel have demanded such a thing if Satan understood even so much of the nature of Zeus as did Mithridates?

Zeus was no man's ally against any threat. To request such support, Satan must be hard-pressed. What enemy could Satan be facing?

Mithridates stared down silently into the pit, and from the pit, it seemed, came a silent scream that was his answer: *Against God! Against the selfish god of modern man, who wants all power to himself! Against the One God, who has starved all the other gods of all the other heavens for so very long!*

The sounds in his head hadn't gotten there through his ears; they'd come from the thing in the pit. They'd come from the great form of stone there, whose noble head was bearded, whose magnificent beard and hair curled around a massive neck, whose mouth was as willful as creation and whose eyes were as sensual as copulation, staring at him out of that hole.

It was as if the god had answered, Mithridates thought. The god who had a face like Elvis with a beard and a hippie haircut on the body of a wrestler. . . .

Mithridates stopped swinging his legs and got up from the pit's edge. He didn't know who Elvis was, but he knew it was foolhardy to sit over a two-hundred-meter drop with guys behind you, even if those guys were supposed to be on your side.

Nobody was on his side; nobody'd ever been. His boys needed him, but that was only for now. He could hear the whispers. They were going to tell on him. . . . Like they didn't have anything to do with what happened, with the massacre . . .

Mithridates, who'd massacred hundreds of thousands, who'd ridden and driven in his chariot through worse than Calley had ever imagined, turned on the men behind him and ordered: "You! You! Both of you, let's go. Down there. You first."

He needed sacrifices, human sacrifices. He spied one more soldier, hanging back, who'd seen the affair with the demon at the cave's mouth.

"You! Soldier," he called. "Get me a bullock, or an ox, or a cow or a water buffalo, or the closest thing you can find. Bring it down, alive. I don't care how much butt you have to kick, or whether you have to make a sling to winch it down, but I want an animal in good health down there. And three jugs of oil. And a half a cord of firewood—good, dry wood; cypress, preferably."

If they were going to make a sacrifice, he and Calley in this single body they shared, the least they could do was perform it correctly.

And the least that the Calley memories could do was wait until they were needed, until he called upon them. He was Mithridates, Great King. He outranked the lieutenant whose flesh had become his flesh.

He didn't understand how the transmutation had occurred, or what it meant. Men did not understand the workings of Hell. It was becoming increasingly clear to Mithridates that even Authority itself was riddled with error.

Satan was out of his Infernal mind, thinking he could make an ally of Father Zeus and survive as Sole Ruler. But that wasn't Mithridates' business. His job was to do as he'd promised and perform the sacrifice, bring his god to full power here.

With Satan's blessing. With written orders to that effect. What happened then was not Mithridates' problem. Satan had done Mithridates no favors, over the years. Neither had his Roman bureaucracy.

No man loved Hell less than Mithridates, yet on that downward climb, behind his soldiers of the moment, he was invaded with qualms.

He told himself at first that these were crazy Calley's paranoid memories, twisted into new shapes by what was happening before both their eyes. But he didn't believe it. Zeus was not a god for Hell. Zeus would remake the heavens of old with such power, reestablish Olympus in its place. And destroy Hell in the process.

Zeus hated evil other than his own; he'd had rivals in the Underworld. Part of Hell contained that Underworld. To destroy Poseidon, to destroy Hephaestus, to destroy all the aspects of Hades, Zeus would stop at nothing once the power to manifest here was truly his.

Was afterlife worth saving? Was Satan capable of even understanding his peril, should Mithridates try to communicate his doubts? Would it be so bad to put an end to misery that seemed, to all the suffering souls here, endless?

And what would happen to Mithridates, if he went back on his word, if he failed the power that had saved him—had heard his prayers? Zeus had done great things for Alexander of Macedon.

Now Zeus was giving Mithridates the chance to become the destroyer of Hell.

Somewhere in the back of his mind, Calley's memories whispered that you couldn't trust authority, that the blame for everything was going to fall on the man who acted, that there was no way out but what seemed right at the time, that you saved your own skin, and did the best you could for your buddies, and didn't ever listen to those rear-echelon ratfuckers because they didn't have any idea what the hell was going on, let alone what to do about it.

If Zeus were freed from that rock, and the soldiers in front of him offered as sacrifices to the god, then everything in Hell would change, that was sure.

The question was, would it change for the worse or for the better? Not just for Hell as an institution, but for Mithridates himself?

And Calley's reasoning was that any change was better than continuing the way things were.

But then, Calley didn't have a discrete body any longer; he was only a ghost in the back of Mithridates' skull who was trying to take over the mind of a king the way he'd transmuted the body of the king.

As he descended into the pit, Mithridates reached up and jerked the dogtags from his neck, breaking the chain, then letting tags and chain fall to the dusty rock floor, still far below.

When he was almost down there, where the colossus lay, a blinding light flashed before his eyes and a clash like thunder boxed his ears.

He staggered, on the stone steps hewn into the

rock on this side of the excavation. His palms covered his ears. But the lightning came again and the thunder rang loudly in his head.

And the thunder said, *Bring me AE for my pleasure!*

The soldiers in front were asking if he was all right. They hadn't heard anything; they hadn't seen anything. He didn't have to ask: He could see the concern in their faces: They were worried that Calley was losing his grip.

Well, Calley wasn't. Mithridates might be. He didn't want to give up the head of AE, for now he understood why she'd been turned to basalt and not been allowed to die.

Zeus was a rapist of legend. He was ten times the size of a man. Even a basalt AE shouldn't have to suffer so.

Then Mithridates laughed out loud at his own cowardice, and quieted the men who looked at him askance.

"Go on, get down there. Y'all worry about yer own selves. Let the brass worry about the brass."

They went before him, shoulders slumped, trudging down the rock-hewn staircase as if down a jungle path.

AE wasn't a noncombatant. The Calley in him had a silly notion that white women were somehow to be protected. AE had left Mithridates to die alone, to suffer alone on Tartaros while she flew the winged lions to Heaven.

If Zeus wanted to rape a stone woman as part of his rebirth ritual, who was Mithridates to argue?

Still, he was uneasy, trudging down into the pit where the stone colossus lay.

* * *

When Mithridates stood by the gargantuan head of Zeus, the Calley in him fell silent. Perhaps it was awed by the power lying in the bowels of Hell. Perhaps the American soul was frightened. Or perhaps it had something to do with ripping off the dogtags. Howsoever, Mithridates felt more himself.

He said under his breath, "Thank you, Father Zeus, for banishing the spirit that possessed me," hoping words would make it so, never thinking what it would mean if Calley totally vanished from him—from his person, from his aspect, from his face, hands and feet, taking familiarity and vocabulary with him when he went.

Mithridates wanted to stand tall before his god. He needed to negotiate his bargain carefully, if bargain there was still to make. How deeply was he committed by the words he'd howled in Tartaros?

How deeply, by his actions since?

He looked around covertly. The demons were busy with the work gangs, down by the colossus's groin. The guard he'd sent for the bullock had disappeared. The private and his companion were standing to one side like bodyguards. And they were still whispering.

This made his flesh crawl as he knelt down beside the ear of Zeus to make himself known to his god.

"Father Zeus," he said with his lips next to that great ear, "hear my plea once again. I will say the words and raise you from this place and your ignominy, but you must give me a sign that this is what you wish, that you are pleased with your servant, Mithridates. I must know that our bargain will be kept, that power to destroy my enemies will be mine, and that I myself will live to—"

In his head, a paean of sound exploded: *Mortal king and murderer of masses, do you doubt me? Is not the power to punish your enemies almost within your grasp? All Hell will crumble, and every soul you hate will vanish with this travesty called Hell! There will be no underworld, no overlords within it, no suffering damned! Only my glory will persist! Now, go you to your tent and bring me the head of AE, that I may reconstruct a woman for my pleasure . . . like Ganymede, like Europa, like the rest . . . a female to seal the bargain, to write humanity's fate in blood.*

He wanted to say that AE was stone, not flesh and blood, but Mithridates' mouth would not move and his mind was full of what he'd learned.

He had his orders. Or Calley did. Without Calley so intimately inside him, he couldn't quite remember how those orders went.

But he remembered what Zeus had said, and it made his knees like jelly. If the power to destroy Mithridates' enemies equaled the end of Hell, then where would Mithridates find himself a place to stand when all the dying was done?

He knew what he was; he'd faced his sins in the flood of Tartaros. Whatever Heaven might contain, there was not a soul as wasted as his within its borders. And whatever Olympus might be like, no human murderers lived as lords there.

The unmoving chest of Zeus was wider than Mithridates was long. It seemed to swell as he watched, as if the god took a breath. And in his head he heard

Zeus say, *Do not disappoint me, mortal. I have made immortals of lesser men than you—the blood-soaked heroes of the Iliad, like Achilles, have I raised up. Do thy part, and rewards will come to thee. Do not quail before Me, your freely chosen God.*

Mithridates bowed his head, his mind carefully focused on Calley, and backed away from the god's ear, scrabbling like a slave upon his knees.

When he rose up, he dusted himself off and bawled, "Find my dogtags, Private! They're down here somewhere—they must have fallen from my neck."

Then he stomped toward the rock-hewn steps as if he knew what he was doing, rather than the opposite. Up them he climbed, a frightened king with a carefully quieted mind, waiting for Calley's madness to come upon him once again, praying for the invasion of that modern mind to manifest and protect his thoughts from the cunning all-knowingness of Father Zeus.

Mithridates knew damned well that he didn't want to share Achilles' fate: Achilles, or the greater part of Achilles, was among the devil's finest servants here in Hell. His Zeus-given immortality hadn't saved the greater part of him from one whit of the fate he'd earned.

Zeus was still attached to the bedrock of Hell. If he had been free, perhaps he could have made good his promises to Achilles, largely unkept from ancient times. Perhaps Zeus could, once the sacrifice was done, make good his promise to Mithridates.

But should he do so, all of Hell would be destroyed. And worse: Satan would be disappointed. Satan wanted an ally against God Himself. Mithridates wanted only power over his enemies.

Zeus wanted autocracy over everything that was, is, or could have been—and would destroy with all his primordial hatred everything and every soul that ever had displeased him.

The grudges of Olympus: how wide were they, how old, how far back and forward in the continuum that man inhabits could they reach?

If Zeus was capable of fooling Satan, what chance did Mithridates have of getting what he'd asked for from the Greek Overmind, rather than what he did well and truly deserve?

Mithridates had never been the smartest man, but he had always told himself he'd never become too complete a fool. Unlike those of greater wit, he feared foolishness too much. Next to Satan, he was a humble being. Next to those cocks on Authority's walk who'd concocted this plan to challenge Heaven itself, he was a veritable genius.

But he was a genius in a trap, and he needed help to find some way out.

"Private," he bawled again, from halfway up the staircase, "I'm going back to my tent, to review my orders and bring something I forgot. When you find my tags, bring them there."

The private waved. "Yo, sir. You bet."

"You," he called to the other soldier there. "Stay here. Await your compatriot, who'll bring the bull and oil and the wood. The two of you construct two pyres, one on the right of Zeus' head, one on his left. But do not light them. Wait for my return."

Mithridates *knew* those words weren't chosen carefully enough, that Calley never would have spoken so to his troops.

So did the two in the pit. They shaded their eyes and squinted up at him. But neither said a word about it, and Mithridates hurried on.

He didn't know that one of the pit-boss demons had followed until he heard the scrape of claws on the stone stairs, as he reached the top.

There he turned to face the demon, who wanted to know, "Are these what you're looking for, Man?"

The dogtags dangled from the clawed hand. He reached for them.

The blue demon pulled its paw back, just out of reach, and swung the tags on their broken chain before his eyes. "These give you power? They are important to you? Maybe me keep them; maybe they important to me, give me power."

The demon's forked cyan tongue darted out from between warty lips; the forks caught the tags between them and licked them so that they jingled. It cocked its head, watching blatantly for his reaction, and as it tongued the tags toward its maw it made a noise that sounded very much like a muffled "Yum, yum, yum."

"Look . . . you can't eat those if you . . . wish me to be at my best," Mithridates said quickly, hating the desperation in his voice and the difficulty of finding words characteristic of a New Dead trustee. *Where* was Calley's presence when Mithridates needed it? "Demon, sir: we're on the same side, isn't this so? I'm the only one here who knows the ritual to breathe life into that." He indicated the colossus below.

Retracting its tongue, the demon said, "Maybe don't want this done." Then it cocked its head again to regard him with a burning, baleful eye. "Something wrong, yes? With you? With it?" It ran the chain of the tags through its claws and the sound made Mithridates' teeth water.

"Calley," the demon read. "Calley, something not right." He swung the tags on their chain before Mithridates' eyes.

Mithridates snatched for them. His fist closed around them. He jerked them from the demon's grasp.

The demon hissed at him, spraying him with spittle. "Some demon broken, above. Some human pay, you bet." It drew back its lips in something resembling a smile.

"If Father Zeus is broken by ineptitude, Satan will make all demons pay," Mithridates said as he tied a knot in the chain of Calley's dogtags and slipped them over his head.

Then he turned, every back muscle twitching, and strode away from the demon, toward the upper levels of the excavation and Calley's tent, where the head of AE waited.

"Calley?" Mithridates said aloud. In his skull was only quiet.

Silently, he repeated the name of the entity who had previously invaded his person. It didn't answer. But then, it never had. He could only hope that the dogtags would bring back the magic—the disguise that Calley's spirit-presence gave him.

He watched his hands and feet, hoping his boots would start to fit again and his hands would grow strong again. Before he confronted another demon, he wanted to have the right persona to display and the right words on his tongue.

It was Calley, after all, who'd killed the blue demon, not Mithridates. The least the ghost could do was come back and see the matter through.

On the trustee level, under the overhanging rock where it began to widen into the canyon marking the way back to New Hell, a firing squad had formed by the time Mithridates climbed out of the excavation.

The climb had taken longer than he expected because Calley was once more within him. Of this Mithridates hadn't been certain until he passed by Liszt's organ, and from a side tunnel there a whore had propositioned him.

As a prisoner, Mithridates had never noticed the guards' whores in their barred caves, like animals in a zoo. This one was rubbing herself against the bars and thrusting outstretched arms toward him.

He'd felt a rustling in his pants and quickened his steps, closing his ears to the woman's supplications, which were barely discernable over the souls playing "The Mephisto Waltz" for the umpteenth time.

But so piteous was the woman's begging and so young and firm her breasts and thighs against the bars, so white her skin, that he stopped, transfixed.

"What do you want, woman?" he said and *Whoosh*, in rushed the knowledge of Calley and the cynicism of Calley and the strangely confuted mind of Calley, so that he laughed uproariously at his own joke.

The woman was begging him to "Put a coin in the slot, Officer. A coin in the slot!" Her eyes were ringed with deep black circles; her swollen mouth was like a red slash.

Calley was still chuckling through Mithridates' lips, and across Mithridates' mind flashed images of long-haired, dark-skinned B-girls dancing in giant birdcages.

"Or somethin' in the slot, hey?" Mithridates heard himself say, as his fingers went to his hip pocket. Calley knew that such women were as desperate as they seemed. Each coin in the pay-slot on the cave's rightmost bar upstepped a lust and a love that could only be excited, never satiated, by the money or the man paying it.

Other women, down the line, now stretched their arms through the bars toward him. Calley started to walk on, along the barred wall, coins ready for the next girl's pay-slot, and the next.

Mithridates was a king who'd never had a woman who wanted him in all his years. The white skin of the first young courtesan attracted him like no other: down the length of barred caves, the arms outstretched to him were black or brown or red or yellow; many were old arms, loose-skinned arms, arms ending in long, clawed nails.

He already had his belt loosened and his zipper down when Calley balked: "I don't screw no white women; won't screw none o' ya: can't tell what I'd catch. It's all the same to you, right? It's the spare change that gets you hot and keeps you hot. . . ."

Mithridates was a king who knew better than the mad mind sharing his skull. He forced Calley's objections away, stepped up to the bars of the first cage where the white woman was pressed against them, and moved between her ready, glistening thighs.

But try as he might, push as he did against the woman lifting herself to him between the bars, he could do nothing to satisfy her. She moaned and swooned; her fingers twisted around her bars; she thrust her breasts toward him, pushing them between the spaces in the iron. Her eyes rolled; her lips slobbered; her legs shook.

And she whispered in a throaty voice, "Another coin, Officer! Put another coin in my slot! Quick. Quick!"

By now, he wanted to finish what was no longer an easy stop for pleasure. But he could not.

Nor could he, he found when he tried, back away. He was caught inside her. She was clamped upon him so that even his sudden terror of spending the rest of eternity thus could not shrink him to slide out of her.

It was Calley who grunted, "Side-slit bitch, here's your coin," and with one hand pulling her buttocks toward him, thrust a piaster in her slot.

With an explosive sigh, she slumped down. Released, he stumbled backward, all his lust spraying uselessly upon the cage bars.

Calley said, "Some things never change. Just looked white, is all," as he stuffed himself in his pants and strode away, leaving the B-girl licking her bars and calling "Joe, Joe!"

Hell was Hell for everyone; there were no victims, only perpetrators: women who'd feigned lust and love for wealth and advantage, or refused their bodies to men until their will was done, or B-girls of every nationality who'd used their favors to demoralize, entrap, and weaken the enemy, all found in Hell that they lived out their earthly lies.

Calley, in his seeming madness, had been the wise

one: "Ain't no white women in Hell, fool," he muttered as if to himself. Mithridates didn't understand the soldier's concern for the effect of the paid woman upon his health.

There was no poison that Mithridates had not immunized himself against, save the poison of the soul. And that poison ran through Calley's mind like fire, raising a fever in the brain: it was not the color of the whore's skin that determined "whiteness" in Calley's eyes, but matters of linguistics and birthright, of culture and acculturation, of an image of Woman, constructed out of training and psychological warfare that could never be matched in flesh, on earth, or in Hell.

Thus, for Calley, there were no white women in Hell, and he was destitute: at the bottom of all his striving was an image that had powered acts unspeakable to his soul and excused them in his mind: the women of his land, the children of that place, the place itself that must not be dishonored.

On the rest of that climb to the uppermost level, it was Mithridates who laughed silently, if sadly. He who was once a king knew better than any how empty were the values for which Calley had given even his soul: viewed from the throne of kingship, men such as Calley were pawns, fools, dogs trained to guard the magazines, eunuchs trained to guard the harem.

All the Calleys of all the ages had served only the power and the avarice of the man smart enough or lucky enough to manage to equate himself, in his soldiers' eyes, with those soldiers' nationality.

"Become a cause," Mithridates' father had once

said to him: "Become a king and you become a nation; once a nation, men will lay down their lives for you, for you are their Luck, incarnate. Riches and luxury and pure power will be yours, if only you can transmute yourself into a symbol of all that men hold dear, and they will forfeit it all gladly to preserve you, for you are their image, their immortality, the hopes of their children and their grandchildren."

Mithridates' father had been no fool. That was why he left his kingdom to a woman. The penis that Mithridates shared with Calley was aching and sore; the scrotum beneath felt enflamed.

But Mithridates worried over none of that: he had so seldom reached orgasm in Hell that Calley's feelings and the peril to the sexual organ they shared were minor considerations.

He was a king and he had performed like a king. And he had seen Zeus in himself as he did; and himself in the whore between the bars, and in the wisdom of his father.

Should he give over all his allegiance to any other, even Father Zeus, then he deserved what then befell him. He had known better, once. He had nearly become Sole Ruler of the Underworld, himself. He had mounted a coup against Satan that had failed only by the hair's breadth. . . .

As everything in Hell must fail. Even Satan, he supposed as he flinched at the shots echoing from the curving stone walls of the canyon, and Calley's instincts threw their shared flesh to the ground.

He struggled to his feet, trying not to worry about the firing squad, now breaking up, or what its actions might portend.

The men in it were straggling his way. His tent, and AE, lay in the direction from which the men were coming. To get there, he must risk confronting some of them.

And he didn't want to confirm the suspicion he had of what the firing squad was doing. But in Hell you faced your worst fears daily. Like the already dripping organ in his pants, every lust had its price, every pleasure was but a lure into error and into pain.

Three of the soldiers crossed his path as he headed for his tent. One wore a cheetah helmet and carried a Garand in one long black hand. His other hand was to his lips; he sucked his thumb and then looked at it, critically, his eyes watering.

The Nubian's thumbnail was as black as the skin around it, and bleeding.

Beside him was a Roman soldier and a shorter, red-haired and freckled non-com in jeans and an IRA t-shirt who was saying, ". . . asshole, Dudu, or you'd learn that M-1 thumb isn't just a joke. How many times have you done that to yourself? You're going to lose your whole hand from gangrene. . . . Calley, Mary be praised, is that you, m'boy? We've been searching high and low—"

"Low is where, Mick. What's shakin'? I been down in the pit, puttin' a little somethin' together for the brass."

"Those 'secret' orders? Well, nothing secret about that." The Irishman jerked his curly head toward the firing squad's victims, smoking heaps at the canyon's mouth. "Somebody killed Zuzil—that brass-balled demon wasn't anybody's friend, but it seems some damned soldier did it."

"Seems? Soldier? Those are dead guys, out there—what do you mean, 'seemed?' "

"Well, nobody confessed, so we picked six at random. . . ." The Irishman looked down. "War's hell, y'know?" He said it very softly and then he looked up. "I think we got one of your grunts in the sweep, sorry about that. Some corporal said he was after a 'bullock' for yourself's pleasure."

"Great. Thanks a shitload, Mick." Calley's stomach turned. You didn't just shoot anybody, simply because you couldn't find the guilty party or make somebody likely confess. Not if you were Calley's kind, you didn't. It should have been his body, the one he and Mithridates shared, out there. . . .

The Nubian sucking his thumb took it out of his mouth once more and said, "Noble lieutenant, are you ill?"

"Gimme that Garand, soldier, and I'll show you how to keep your thumb out of harm's way."

Mithridates was overwhelmed by Calley's emotions, swept away by them, unable to stop what was about to happen or to retake control.

Calley threw the M-1 up against his cheek and sidled around, cocking it as if in a demonstration, so that the Nubian could look over his shoulder. When the barrel was pointing at Mick's heart, he squeezed the trigger, firing a live round through the red-haired non-com's chest.

At point-blank range, the body jumped backward, its chest disappearing in a wash of red, hands and arms and legs splaying out.

The Irishman landed on his butt like a sack of flour. He was still alive. He touched the hole in his chest and looked from the blood on his hand to Calley, surprise on his face. He might have been forming the word "Why?" when he fell over onto his back.

His legs were still kicking when Calley thrust the M-1's length against the Nubian's chest and said: "That's two lessons: Number One's how to avoid M-1 thumb; Number Two's don't take command decisions just because nobody better's on hand. We don't kill just anybody, not my goddamn unit, not for body count, not to satisfy Satan himself. Got that, Bubba?"

He stalked away, leaving the Nubian and the other non-com, who hadn't said a word the entire time, staring after him.

When he looked back, they were still watching. He called over his shoulder: "You'all shot my gofer. I still need that bullock. And a cord of cypress and two barrels of oil—down in the pit. Now, 'cause yesterday's gone. You, Roman! Move your ass and get that stuff down there. I don't want to see you anywhere but there, next time I see you."

The Nubian's Roman companion put one hand on his right hip, where his short-sword was slung, as if he were going to shout a response. Then he didn't. He just took off his transverse-crested helmet and wiped his forehead with his wrist before he clapped the Nubian on the back, stepped over the shot Irishman, and trudged away.

Once it seemed that his orders were going to be obeyed, there was no reason to stand there, in the middle of open ground, watching a body detail come to deal with the corpses that the firing squad had made.

Those men had died because of Calley's actions. Mithridates knew that afterlife was a cycle, that it should not matter, but the body he shared with the American was trembling as he forced it to walk unconcernedly toward the tent he sought.

AE's head was safe, that was a reason to praise his Luck, if not Zeus himself.

But Mithridates didn't feel like praising anyone. His stomach was upset; his loins were aching; his back twitched with fear that soldiers would come rushing in, saying they'd made a mistake and there was a second firing squad waiting just for him.

Calley hadn't thought twice about the consequences of killing Zuzit, the blue-furred demon. What was going to happen when the damned thing was resurrected? It knew who killed it. It'd probably be shipped right back here to finger him, as Calley would have said.

What would he say then? That he was Mithridates, of course. He fingered the dogtags that brought two men of two ages together in one body barely capable of containing two such disparate personalities.

His fingers closed around the tags as if to discard them a second time. Here he could bury them in the campaign chest, in case later Mithridates needed to become Calley. . . .

He should do that. Calley surely couldn't be reborn without his soul, and the wearing of the tags kept that soul tethered to a fleshly hotel in which it never belonged.

He was about to jerk the chain from his neck a second time when the head of AE caught his eye.

It wasn't smiling. It had lost its beatific aspect. It stared at him from stony eyes with a severe and worried look upon its countenance.

That couldn't be. He misremembered it. He got up, the forgotten dogtags jingling against his t-shirt.

"AE?" he said.

The head of AE regarded him from atop the campaign chest in silence.

He reached down to take it. Take it and return to the pit. That was what he'd come here for. But his hands wouldn't close over it.

His stomach felt as if it were rolling downhill. His knees trembled as if he were slogging through ice cold, muddy water.

He knelt down there. "This ain't right," he told the head of AE. "Something here ain't right."

She didn't answer Calley, and Mithridates forced the shared hands of flesh to close around the head. He staggered to his feet, the head under his arm. Calley didn't understand. Calley was looking for a white woman to protect, as if there was any soul in Hell worth protecting.

The head of AE was black as night, black as the vault over the pit, black as Satan's heart. He stared down at it, cradled in his crooked arm.

And as he did, he remembered the whores in their cages near Liszt's organ. Why wouldn't one of them suit Zeus' needs well enough?

But men did not disobey the strict demands of ritual, if they wished to serve a god.

He wanted all that he'd ever wanted, still, did

Mithridates. He wanted to humble his enemies, destroy those who'd offended him as Calley had destroyed the Irishman—without thought beyond the moment.

And yet, everything in afterlife had repercussions. If not for Calley's murder of the demon Zuzit, the firing squad would not have been formed, to find itself in need of targets. . . .

Men forgot how much evil was their doing, and not the gods'. Zuzit would return, if Luck went against Mithridates, and recognize the body in which two souls were sandwiched. So Calley, at this juncture, had to go.

Before worse came of his uncontrolled emotions. Before the weaknesses of latter-day man crept into Mithridates and ate away at the bedrock of the king in him.

Calley was full of remorse, full of repentance, full of confusion and regrets. His past overwhelmed them both, as real or more real than the afterliving present.

The wisdom Mithridates was gaining from the ghost of a twentieth-century man was not enough to justify the risk. He took the tags from his neck, this time determined not to be swayed, or frightened into hiding behind Calley, or lured by circumstance into inheriting Calley's fate.

He was about to toss them into the campaign chest when the head of AE said "No!"

He nearly dropped the head under his arm.

He sank down on top of the chest and put it on his knees.

Looking hard at the basalt head that had no

body and could not be any more than stone, he said, "What did you say?" very slowly and very carefully.

The mouth of the head of AE opened. He could feel the neck of AE, on his knees, shift as stone musculature came into play.

"No," said the head of AE again.

"No what?" he said to the statue. "No, don't leave the dogtags of Calley to Calley's fate? Or no, don't give you to the god, who wants to make of you his queen?"

The head didn't speak again. This was a relief. He chided himself that he'd thought it had ever spoken.

How could the head of AE be speaking? It was impossible. It was his imagination. Worse, it was some trick. It was some trick of Calley's to avoid whatever his fate had in store. Mithridates dropped the dogtags between his booted feet as if they were white-hot.

He got up quickly, stuffing the head under his arm, clasping it against his side, and strode from the tent.

He was in too desperate a situation to take any more chances. He would give AE to the god, and all the power of Hell would be his.

It was what he had wanted for so long. In a way, it was what he had always wanted. No one would snicker at him behind his back, because he was shorter than some, or less kingly than others, because he was a mongrel, because his father had thought him unworthy, because his mother had ridden him like a mule, because he could not inspire trust or loyalty beyond what fear could engender. . . .

Not in any but the poorest of men and the most

frightened of men and the meanest of men and the greediest of men had he ever managed to trust. So why now should he trust a stone head? So whyever should he have trusted a crazed and damned soul who had never left an earthly jungle?

What had he been thinking of, trusting anyone to help him?

He stalked blindly across the trustees' camp, AE's head clamped under his arm, and into the cave that led down into the excavation.

When the deeper dark of unbroken rock overhead enveloped him, a muffled voice said, "How can you trust a trickster, the god of another race? Don't give me to Zeus, Mithridates."

He ignored it, even though he could feel the head move under his arm.

"How can you give me to Zeus, when you will destroy all the afterlife thereby?" said the head of AE.

Without breaking stride, he turned the head so that its mouth was against his arm.

"How could you have left me on the plain of Tartaros to die, while you flew the winged lions to salvation, AE?" he said, his voice full of resentment and trembling with the desire to inflict pain greater than the pain she'd inflicted on him.

"Don't give me to Zeus, Mithridates. After all I did to help, how can you treat me this way?"

"Treat you?" he said. They were coming to the caged whores and he had to speak loudly if he wanted the head of AE to hear him. He shouted above the prostitutes and above the wafting strains of shrieking organ music. "What do you mean, treat you? You haven't even a body. You're just a fragment, a piece of stone, a thing of no consequence. Don't I deserve what I will from you, who deserted me? Who disobeyed me? Who was disloyal? You are nothing to me, AE, nor were you ever."

His boot heels stomped loudly on the rock as he passed the white-skinned woman's cage. "Joe," she sighed. "Joe, my Joe, you've come back to me. Put money in my slot, best Joe. Put coins in my slot. . . ."

He stopped there and dropped his pants, setting AE's head where, if she could see, she must watch. This would teach her what a woman was, what a woman was for, what great affection had been between them. . . .

Without crazy Calley in his mind, it was an easy and a quick matter to reach through the bars, take two handfuls of the white woman's buttocks, and pull her into position.

This time, he put only one coin in the slot and another where he put his organ. He didn't wait for her to sigh and rub against him, he didn't wait for her thighs to glisten.

His fingers dug in her haunches and he slammed her onto him, against the bars.

He'd never had a quicker success, not in Hell or in Pontus. He thrust the white-skinned whore back from him and left her crying out for more of him.

As he leaned down to jerk his pants up and scoop AE back under his arm, he noticed the green dribble on his thigh. This he ignored.

The look on AE's stone face was worth whatever later discomfort he'd endure. He could see he had hurt her. Her stone forehead was furrowed.

"And there's more to come, AE. Your turn, you see. I don't want you, you must understand. You're of no particular importance to me. After all, you don't even have a body. When you did, it was never offered to me freely. You just teased me with your pretense of honor, of loyalty, of bravery. You're of no importance except as a sacrifice to a god who happens to like his women made of stone."

Was there a tear glistening on AE's stone face? Or was it a dribble of green that had fallen there, a meandering wetness that only looked like a tear because of the black/green color of her cheeks.

He wanted it to be a tear. He wanted her to know that she was of no importance to him. He wanted her to know that even sacrificing her to the god wasn't important to him—only to Zeus.

And without Calley inside him, he was managing. Mithridates didn't have to worry about the disposition of every soul in Hell. If he'd succeeded in his coup and replaced Satan, then he would have made it his business. But now, his business was the business of getting Mithridates out of this work camp and back into power.

And time was getting short. If the demon that Calley had killed didn't return to find him, then someone else would spot him, eventually, without the shade of Calley masking his identity.

He had no choice, in his terms. He kept telling himself that, all the way down to the excavation's floor where the colossus languished.

He had no choice. It wasn't that he was taking pleasure in destroying AE. It certainly wasn't that. He'd never hurt himself just to hurt another worse.

But he couldn't forgive the unforgivable. AE had left him to languish in Hell. She'd made a fool of him. He'd admired her, coveted her, done all he could for her. . . .

Now he would do what he must for Mithridates, King of Kings, with no regard, one way or the other, to the fate of the severed basalt head of a statue which once had been a woman whom he'd overestimated.

It was as simple as that.

When he reached the pit's floor, the demon bosses were hunkered down over their lunchboxes, and three of his men were positioning the wood and the oil jars as he'd ordered.

The bullock wasn't in the pit yet, though.

He ordered the private and his companions to "Take your rest," knowing the wording wasn't quite right, but telling himself that they were getting used to his new speech patterns.

Once the sacrifices were made, the power to punish Mithridates' enemies would be his. What did it matter to him if that equaled the destruction of Hell? He'd destroyed as many kingdoms of his enemies in life as he'd been able. This was no different.

Zeus would make a place for him on Olympus. He looked into the beautiful, gigantic face of the god and he was certain of it.

Or so he told himself as, once the private and the others had retreated, he leaned down by Zeus' head and said, "I have her. I have brought AE as you requested."

The god didn't acknowledge him, or give any further instructions. What should he do now? He put the head of AE on the chest of Zeus, facing the god's head, and sat back on his haunches.

Then the god said in his mind, *Free my flesh. Free my great self. And face her the other way. Put her upon my loins and get thee back from me.*

Mithridates hardened his heart to the horror beginning to rise in him. He was a man who had a core of superstitious awe. He wasn't sure he wanted to see what might happen next. He wasn't sure, now, so close to the mighty lord of Olympus, if even his need to punish AE was sufficient reason to risk all of the afterlife.

But then, men risked their afterlives in earthly battle, for earthly honor and earthly immortality. He ought to know: he'd wagered that there was no afterlife, or that his kingship could secure him a safe place in one, and he'd lost.

As he reached out to do the god's bidding, the head of AE suddenly said, "Mithridates, how can you do this? How small a man must you be?" And now she had eye-whites, not simply black orbs in a black face.

She had eye-sockets with moving eyes in them. His hands froze before they could lift her head from the chest of Zeus.

Was this a living being, after all? This AE, who had betrayed him. And if so, what difference did that make? He wanted to say, "You must understand how badly mankind has treated me—its women most of all. You must understand, I am a king. I cannot be trifled with."

He wanted to say, "Humble yourself before me,

AE. Abase yourself, and we will make things as they were before."

But he couldn't. How could he? He was Mithridates, King of Kings, and she was . . . not even a woman, merely a basalt head with liquid, human eyes.

"Mithridates!" the head of AE called again, its features contorted with fear—and with desperation. "Don't do this. Don't leave me defenseless, with this . . . thing."

"Why shouldn't I, after Tartaros?" He stood up to prove that he would leave her, defenseless, helpless, exactly as she'd left him—and that she'd suffer worse than he ever had.

"Why shouldn't you?" the head of AE wanted to know. "Because I helped you so. Because I took such risks for you—the escape, and after: I lent you my strength, my wisdom. You profited. Whatever you think I did to you, I did nothing out of malice! Please!"

"Beg, go ahead," he said, taking a step backward and another. "You mean nothing to me. You did nothing for me. I did everything for you, and you thanked me with betrayal. This is your fate, you earned it."

"How can you let your hatred and vengeance blind you?" said the head of AE on the chest of Zeus. It jittered there as its mouth moved. It rocked. It teetered.

If it fell and broke, would Zeus still be able to bring AE to life in the way the god wanted?

For that was what was happening: her mouth was

turning red and feminine; her basalt skin was lightening, becoming human.

He didn't need the god's urging in his ears to reach out and grab the head where it rocked, to replace it where the god had suggested, at the meeting place of those mighty thighs.

As he put AE's head down there, she bit him.

"Ow!" he yelped, and dropped her head in surprise. It rolled nose down into the crack and he stepped back again. Two steps. Three.

There he paused and surveyed his work. A miasma was issuing from the god's navel. In it, he thought he saw shapes moving, things forming. He blinked. He was not certain now what he saw.

But the miasma was crawling toward AE's head and her muffled cries were reaching his ears. He couldn't stand the mewling of women.

He turned away.

And then he saw that the bullock he'd demanded was being winched down into the pit on a sling.

The big-eared private and his companions were standing under it with ropes, guiding its descent. And the centurion who'd brought it was trotting down the hewn steps at pitside, waving to the lunching pit demons as he came.

Mithridates looked back once more at the cloud over AE's head and Zeus' loins, and strode over to his men to help.

The bullock's head was hanging; its feet dangled: it was obviously drugged. As they winched it down and its feet touched the ground, it bellowed mournfully and looked straight at Mithridates.

The eyes of beast and man met, and in the eyes of

the bullock Mithridates saw himself. Not simply his reflection, but his fate.

The bullock's member hung below his knees; in his drugged state, he couldn't control it. He knew with animal certainty that his future was in the hands of the two-legged gods called men, and he knew he couldn't trust them.

But neither could he fight them. The bullock's eyes were wide, white-walled, glazed with fear and frustration. He was beaten, doped beyond real resistance, unable to do more than bellow as horror approached that he did not understand, horror decreed by man for the benefit of man—a horror of which the bullock was about to become an unwilling, uncomprehending part.

It was too close a parallel, looking into the eyes of the sacrificial animal that Zeus had demanded, then past the bullock at the dumb private and his two companions, all of whom Mithridates meant to sacrifice along with the bullock, to the hungry stone deity, Zeus.

He closed his eyes and walked unseeingly away. What was this sudden quailing? Had he lost his mind? His strength? His courage at this crucial moment? What was it to him if the ghost-blood of three doomed souls was needed to wash life into the stone carcass of a god? What was it to him if the bullock had left behind cows in his pasture? What was it to him, who had slaughtered so many—his entire harem among the total?

No flesh would be wasted here: the pit slaves could eat of the bullock; the pit-boss demons would eat the carcasses of the men, if they didn't burn first.

And all would be reborn, Mithridates was almost certain. . . .

Reborn to more torment, to myriad afterlives and other deaths, if Hell survived.

If Hell survived . . .

He turned his back on the men steadying the wobbly bullock with their own shoulders, leaning against the beast, one to hold its head up, one to keep its forequarters tracking, one to keep its hind legs from folding under it.

The centurion was talking to the pit bosses.

Mithridates hated Romans the most, but this Roman had done him a service. Unlike AE, the Roman had performed a function as ordered.

Yet he could not look at the Roman. It had been a Roman who murdered him, a Roman, he told himself. Or one of his own, you never could be certain. A guard, like all these guards. He clenched his fists over the yawning pit of his own memories.

He must not become like Calley, who didn't know life from afterlife, who was lost in might-have-beens and the sins of his journeying.

He was Mithridates, Great King. He must act like a king. No king would be afraid to look upon his god. No king would be afraid to look upon the designated sacrifices to that god, to walk among his dead, whom he commanded in the field. Or to walk upon that field, with those he'd ordered to their deaths when next dawn broke.

These were the burdens of consciousness, of command, of kingship.

He strode back toward Zeus rather than look behind him.

The cloud over the god's loins had something moving in it: something white and the length of a person. This something resembled a person, all of a person: it had legs and arms and it was flailing those legs and arms wildly, helplessly.

It was crying, too. Mithridates closed his ears to the sobs of suffering coming from the loins of Zeus. He slitted his eyes against the horrid sight masked by a curtain of mist.

He yelled to the men, "Pour the oil on the wood."

And with those words, he committed himself to performing the sacrifice, as he watched the reconstituted flesh of AE writhe in the grip of Zeus, the immortal rapist, who was ten times the size of a man and still made of stone.

Performing the sacrifice: three deceptively simple words that represented a world-changing undertaking.

And yet, it should have been easy. It should have gone smoothly, once Mithridates' mind was made up.

But it was not easy. It went far from smoothly. It went wrong at every turn, badly and slowly, and awry in every way.

Mithridates was beginning to wonder if Hell itself were not fighting him. Could Hell have a nature of its own? A will to survive? A drive toward "becoming," as did the human souls who inhabited it?

If so, was he about to commence his greatest slaughter ever? He'd paved his road to Hell with the bodies of his harem women, saying he was keeping them from his enemies. Would the results of this sacrifice be worse? If that were true, what did this mean to the continuance of his own immortal soul?

And if none of the above were true, why were his bowels like jelly and his teeth chattering? Was it merely the Persian superstitions he'd been born with that made him imagine a supernal hand in problems merely consequential?

Or was his slow hand correct in hesitating, his arrogant mind wrong in proceeding to force a sacrifice that none had made before?

Everything was fraught with trouble, that was inarguable: first the wood would not stay piled. His soldiers could not make a simple pyre. Every time they placed the logs crosswise at the top, one would tumble, dislodging others, and the whole lot would cascade down to lie in a heap, every log upon the pit's floor, not so much as one piled atop another.

Again and again, he made the soldiers pile the ceremonial logs in ancient fashion. Again and again, the piles came tumbling down.

Finally he called upon the centurion to oversee the moderns, and at last the god's woodpiles were well and truly made.

By this time, the pit-boss demons had come over, asking what was wrong, sniffing around and clapping Mithridates on the back and leaving lice on him when they shuffled away.

It was time to change shifts. The pit-boss demons whipped their charges up the hand-hewn rock and departed, one calling as he waved a clawed hand, "Man do job, or demon do! Man sorry then, you bet!"

Holding his breath, Mithridates watched the demon and the sorry souls of the silent work gang disappear beyond the pit's high rim.

Perchance without the onlookers, things would go better, he told himself. Perhaps the presence of the demons, or the thin souls of worn penitents slaving nearby, had hexed the venture.

Less had been blamed for more, in terms of oracular failure and the temper of the gods, when Mithridates had been alive.

But he was not alive. He was little better off than the wispy souls in the exhausted work gangs. If this sacrifice could not be performed, what did he have to look forward to then but an eternity of suffering?

Thinking of his risk in those terms strengthened him. What, truly, did he have to lose?

Satan might wish to challenge Heaven itself by raising Zeus, but that was the business of the Devil and the Greek Overmind, not Mithridates, who'd never been more than a king, and now was less than even a man—a limpid soul having trouble with a single, morbid ritual.

But no matter how he cheered himself, he could not change the way the ritual kept stalling, stumbling as if it were a balky mule or a sick old man.

The bullock, now, was rousing from his drugged state. The red-eared private couldn't hold the beast's head, let alone lead him to the head of Zeus. The bullock kicked and bit. His head came down; his horns threatened everything within their reach.

Mithridates couldn't afford the loss or damage of even one of the three soldiers he'd chosen for the sacrifice. They had to go whole into the flames.

This was why he'd picked the Roman. From the

Old Dead centurion, Mithridates would get whatever help he needed to sacrifice the modern soldiers. There would be no such qualms as Calley's sort displayed.

Mithridates was aware, as he yelled to the Roman to help the New Dead with the bullock, that his Calley-ness was wearing thin. He knew it by his feet, by the way they slipped in the boots he'd appropriated.

He knew it by the final warning that the pit-boss demon had given him, and the wall-eyed look on the demon's face.

But demons had trouble telling one damned soul from another. And Mithridates needed only a little more time.

The bullock was throwing his head and bellowing as the centurion urged it forward with the flat of his sword on its rump, yelling to the private, "Hold his head, fool! Hold his head up!"

Mithridates again met the bullock's eyes, above the rock dust kicked up by scrabbling, cloven hooves. Was there foreknowledge in the dumb beast's glare? Sadness? Madness? Or was it accusation he saw there?

He looked away, and when he did he saw once more the tent of mist over the colossal loins of Zeus.

All sounds had ceased from that direction. Once the workers had cleared the pit, an eerie quiet had descended that only the bellowing bullock dared to break.

The bullock, finally, stood between the two piles of wood. His head was high, held still by crossties on his halter. At the end of each crosstie was a New Dead fool, each holding his rope with all his might, each bracing himself on the bottom logs of the cypress piles.

"That's good," called the private, who was pouring the oil on the wooden piles as he'd been bid. "Hold him still!"

"Secure that bullock better," warned the centurion in a tired voice used to shouting over clashing armies. "Run those ropes between the bottommost logs. They'll hold. Use your heads, not just your muscle! When the first swordcut comes, he's going to pull your arms from their sockets if you're not prepared."

Simultaneously, the private kept pouring the oil, which was slow to coat the logs, slow to find the feet of the soldiers, slow to dribble on the rocky ground.

And meanwhile, Mithridates was worrying about the look in the pit-boss demon's eye. Damn Calley and his mindless rage. There'd been no need to kill the overseer demon, Zuzit. No need at all to mark Mithridates as a soul whose days were numbered. Only the paling of Calley's aspect, which once had disguised his person, might save him—and that for just a little while.

The bullock lunged backward, kicking out as he wheeled. His rear hoof caught one of the soldiers in the knee. The sound of crunching joint was sickening. The soldier lost his grip on the tether he'd been sliding through the logs. The rope came loose and whipped like a snake through the air as the bullock reared and plunged.

The second soldier, taken by surprise, was pulled from his feet by the bullock, who lunged for the far wall. The private atop the woodpile with his oil jug dropped it, overbalanced, and came careening down the pile, logs tumbling in his wake.

"Get that beast back here!" Mithridates shouted unnecessarily. The centurion, cursing vilely, was already thrusting the private to his feet and giving the necessary orders.

Everything was going wrong. Only Father Zeus could save him. . . .

The soldier with the broken kneecap was sitting on the pile, crying softly and rocking back and forth.

Mithridates cursed his Luck almost as completely as the centurion had, moments before.

He didn't watch the struggle to recapture the bullock: there was no place for the beast to run but in circles. Sometimes all of Hell seemed like this pit, with humanity's souls careening around in it as the screaming bullock did, in sight of his undoing, unable to escape, merely putting off the inevitable.

Was all this misadventure purely happenstance? Or was it a sign, one Mithridates should be heeding? Could he leave his oath to Zeus unfulfilled? Could he escape, somehow, what was coming to him for having let the Calley in him kill the demon? For mounting the coup that had lured so many souls to their deaths? For everything uncountable he'd done before?

Was there truly a list of each man's sins, somewhere? And who decided what was sin and what was not? Not Mithridates, that was certain.

The centurion was closing in upon the bullock now, a pistol in his hand.

"No!" Mithridates screamed, suddenly running as fast as he could. "Don't shoot him! I need him alive for the sacri—"

Bang! went the centurion's pistol. The bullock dropped to its knees.

Mithridates, puffing, reached the centurion's side and spun the man around, his fury uncontrollable. "All I've done, and you shoot the bullock! You'll take his place if he dies, I swear by—"

This close, the face under the transverse-crested helmet looked vaguely familiar. But all Romans were of a type to the Iranian eye. And centurions, like other elite corps of fighters, had a look to them in common. He couldn't know the man, though he'd known thousands of his sort. And yet the face was naggingly familiar. . . .

The thin mouth said, "The bull's just doped. This is an anesthetic gun. How'd you think I got it down here? Sir." The honorific was added grimly; the eyes of the centurion were as hard as the rock all around. The look in them seemed disparaging.

But there was no arguing with the efficiency of the centurion, or the proof of what he'd done. "Carry on, then," Mithridates said gruffly.

The soldier slapped the anesthetic gun into Mithridates' hand. "There's three more rounds left. They'll come in handy if you're up to what I think—and up to doing your own killing."

Now the gaze of the Roman was downright challenging, and the face under the helmet looked less Roman than it had before. It seemed to shiver as its owner fought for control over his own expression.

In Hell were many men who'd fought for Rome in ancient times. This one didn't matter, Mithridates told himself, not if he was a mongrelized outlander or one of Sulla's own mercenaries, or even a defecting

Persian. None of it mattered—so long as he did the job.

Competence was what the moment demanded. Competence and nothing more.

Mithridates closed his fingers on the butt of the pistol in his palm and said, "So be it."

He hadn't thought as far ahead as had this nameless centurion he'd drafted into his service. He must remember that this man had seen him shoot the Mick in cold blood.

But all blood was cold in Hell, and his own was running colder by the minute.

He met the bright eyes still fixed on him as if Mithridates were a target and said, "Get the bullock and the men into position. Then, when I say, light the fires."

"Sir," said the centurion again and turned his back without waiting for further orders.

A Roman through and through, Mithridates decided. Too bad Zeus had not wanted a man, rather than a woman, for his pleasure.

But Zeus had not wanted a man. Zeus had wanted AE. Mithridates had been steadfastly avoiding the curtain of mist over the loins of the colossus. Now he turned that way, rather than watch the soldiers with the bullock, or the pit's rim, over which he might see vengeful demons striding down to arrest him for killing one of their number.

Why did he feel hesitant to confront the reality of what he'd done with AE's head? Was it a trace of Calley, still within him? Was his mind yet tainted by Calley's, with its modern clash of rote morality and learned expediency and hard-wired instinct?

Calley was merely memories now, a pair of dogtags in the dirt. Maybe not even so much as that, for Calley was somewhere else: was wherever his body was—probably in New Hell, telling all to the Undertaker during resurrection's mandatory debriefing.

Or not in Hell at all, yet. Somewhere in purgatory, awaiting reassignment. Somewhere lost in time, or else how could mere dogtags contain so much of a man's soul?

Suddenly too much was wrong with this endeavor. If he'd still been at his desk in the Pentagram, Mithridates would have ordered Calley's 201-6666 file. . . . In his mind's eye, he did, and got back the terse computer error code: *Bad file name or soul not found. Ignore, Abort, Retry?*

"Soul not found in Hell," his dark fantasy whispered as if it were a presentiment, the gods' own truth. Calley's dogtags were in Hell, Mithridates could attest to that. But no more. For all he knew, Calley could have died a final time, found his judge here and used Mithridates' sweat to buy his way to Heaven. Or never really been in Hell at all. . . . Life; death; afterlife; its mockery of death and resurrection; purgatorial stays; salvation; even consciousness itself: what did man know of any of these?

The nature of being had eluded better minds than Mithridates' own. What had come to him from Calley's dogtags, if not the essence of the man, wherever that man's body dwelled? If essence could traverse time and space, exist without flesh, migrate to other flesh, then how could Mithridates prove that anything here was real, even whether he himself was real?

Mithridates reached blindly for support, shuffling

forward, and his outstretched hand touched the shoulder of stony Zeus.

Not even the feel of stone steadied his trembling limbs, his pounding heart. If Calley's fate was uncertain, what of his own? Had he died some final death in Tartaros, after all? Was he embedded in Calley's body, not the opposite? Had he imagined Calley's to be the face on the corpse he'd ordered set adrift in Phlegethon's currents of fire? No one recognized him as Mithridates, not in all this time.

"I suffer, therefore I am," he told himself aloud. The rest must be left to better men, to brighter men, to men with time to waste. He was not that clever. He had never been. He was a small man with great fears, a pretender to greatness, an emulator of methods that had worked for better men than he, without real understanding of those methods, only of their outward manifestations.

If he had a mirror, he could have peered into the face he wore and seen whose eyes looked back at him: his own, or crazy Calley's, or someone else's. But he had no mirror. He had only the colossus of Zeus to tell him what was real and what was not.

Zeus' stony flesh seemed to yield under his pressure as he leaned upon it. Mithridates' eyes snapped open to examine the arm of the colossus against which he leaned.

It looked like stone, still. It was pitted like stone. It must still be stone. And yet it was warm to the touch, and had a pinkish tinge he didn't remember.

He sank down there, his ears ringing with the sounds of the drugged bullock bellowing and the cursing soldiers dragging it to its appointed end between the piles of cypress.

Rock dust was everywhere, filling the air like the curtain of mist that had come into being around AE.

Despite the stinging dust, he blinked and blinked again, peering into the mist hovering over the giant's loins. He saw something there, moving as he'd seen shadows move in there before.

But what he saw was white and long and sylphlike, in no wise resembling the basalt head of AE.

What had he done? He didn't want to think about it. He'd slain his whole harem, all his wives. What was one boot-wearing modern woman to him?

He found himself down on his hands and knees like a slave from the work gang, squinting at the place where the colossus' giant form met the rock. Was Zeus well and truly chipped out of his sarcophagus of rock? Mithridates ran a finger there, where the ribs of the god met the bowels of Hell.

His nail slid unimpeded between the two.

It was too late to turn back, he was certain. "Father Zeus?" he said softly.

No god responded.

"Father Zeus," he said again, louder. "Confirm my righteous action in your cause! Speak to thy servant. Say my name, at least."

But only silence was his answer, although in the farthest reaches of his skull he imagined that he heard a grunt of pleasure, a howl of woe, or the rustling of the very fundament beneath his feet, as if a dragon were slithering, roused from sleep. Whatever transformation was under way, Zeus would not—or could not—speak to him until it was complete.

It was too late to turn back now, he told himself again, when the centurion called, "What are you doing there? Sir."

He scrambled to his feet, aware that he'd been caught with his rump in the air and his nose to the ground.

When he'd dusted himself off and wiped his stinging eyes, he saw that the bullock stood, head low, legs spread, nostrils distended and drooling, crosstied between the two woodpiles.

The broken-kneed soldier was sitting on the lowest of the cypress logs, one crosstie threaded through the pile and wrapped around his hand. Opposite him sat the second modern warrior, his jaw swelling visibly where he'd been kicked in the fray.

The private with the red ears was standing beside the centurion, who had one hand on his short-sword. "Sir. Shall we light the pyres?" the centurion asked Mithridates.

But his eyes asked, *Are you ready to shoot these men, point-blank, with the gun I gave you?*

"Yes," said Mithridates, to what was spoken and what was not.

The mist behind him had eaten AE; the doings behind him had eaten his alternatives; Hell itself had eaten all the rest of him as it had consumed all of Calley but his dogtags.

There was nothing left but to press on. Still, he hesitated. He had not answered the question weighing on his heart: once Hell was destroyed, where would the animate remains of Mithridates find a home?

Why did Satan want Zeus raised, when Hell's destruction surely must follow?

Mithridates found no answers to these questions in the brief time between when he gave the order and when the private with the big ears flicked his Zippo alight and bent to the oil-soaked pile of cypress on his right.

Light flared as flame leaped up the right-hand pyre, licking the very head of Zeus.

Mithridates had the anesthetic gun in his hand. He shot the private first. The red-eared youth fell atop the left-hand pyre, his lighter setting it instantly aflame with a roar that might have come from the belly of an angry god.

In quick succession, as the soldier holding the bullock's tether to the right-hand pyre said, "Hey!" Mithridates shot him, and then his broken-kneed companion on the left.

Then the flames roared high in hungry glee, and the bullock began to scream. Everything was awash in fire and smoke and blazing light, so that Mithridates could see nothing else: not the centurion, not the bullock, not the anesthetized soldiers burning where they lay.

Even the silent stone colossus of Zeus seemed to disappear in a wall of flame as the sacrifice began and Mithridates stood there mute, every word he was supposed to intone forgotten.

The flames seemed to be speaking to Mithridates, but he couldn't understand what they were saying. And the instructions that had been in Calley's orders, the words to intone to raise up Zeus—these too were gibberish in his mind.

He had forgotten the incantation. He couldn't remember how to raise the god, not even what Zeus had told him to do. He panicked. He couldn't think at all. He just stood there while the flames mounted. The fire blazed too fast, too hot, to last for long.

The moment of his salvation, of his revenge, of his primacy was fleeing from him as he huddled amid the waves of heat and noxious smoke, choking and coughing his lungs out.

Everything was lost, he was sure. His eyes were tearing. His flesh was weak. The place where AE had bitten him blazed as if it had caught fire. He clapped his hand upon the bite and went to his knees, wracked with a paroxysm of paralyzing pain and fear.

His knees wouldn't hold him. He couldn't breathe. The black smoke wound around his head and dragged him to the ground like a bullock on a tether. He crawled there, where the air was better. The bite was enflamed; where AE's basalt teeth had pierced his skin, the pain was unbearable. The bite's poison ran through his blood, setting his every vein afire. And his loins burned now, too. The green dribble he'd seen on his thigh became flames of green that consumed his scrotum and his penis. All his organs burned like hellfire.

He rolled onto his back, his hands between his legs, his knees drawn up. And there he writhed, coughing and screaming in the smoke.

"Zurvan!" he called out in his misery—not to Zeus, not to Mithra, but to the primordial Iranian god who predated both the heavens and the earth. "I'm sorry. Help me. Help me, God!"

Like all men before him, *in extremis*, he sought his blood's father, the progenitor of his kind. He repented then, caught between the fires of Hell and the wrath of Heaven, which Satan had thought to thwart and Zeus to overrun.

He called upon the mercy of the universe itself as the flames in his groin and the flames in his blood and the flames of the sacrifice around him all seemed to merge.

He was sorry. He was a child of unknowing evil. He was a sinner. He was a man. No more. No better. But no worse.

He begged for forgiveness, and he imputed mercy where there had been none, in his private universe of pain. And because the universe he called Zurvan had put man within itself, and mercy in mankind, forgiveness was there also.

It was there for the worst as much as for the best; it was there in Hell as it was in Heaven. It was there for Mithridates, fool of fools.

The fire in his loins subsided; he was able to straighten his legs. The fire in his veins subsided; he was able to get up on his knees.

But the fire he had started had not subsided. This blazed high, hungry flames eating up the wood and the oil and the screaming bullock and the drugged men, giving only black smoke to heaven in return.

Mithridates began crawling through the smoke, moans coming from between his blackened lips, crying out as he crawled but not knowing that he did. "AE!" he called. "AE! Forgive me, AE!"

He crawled toward the colossus, over hot and unyielding ground, weeping freely and sure that he was dying a final death, beyond which lay only nothingness.

All that awaited him was the fire he'd felt in his loins, the fire he'd felt in his veins, the fire he'd consigned unknowing soldiers to . . . then nothing.

If he could have doused the flames with his tears, he would have. If he could have saved everyone in Hell, he would have. Whatever the task, he would at that moment have undertaken it, if only he could save himself thereby.

"I have saved Heaven," he bleated miserably as he crawled and coughed and moaned and crawled some more, in the general direction of the stone Zeus. "I have saved Heaven by failing to perform the sacrifice. Have pity on me, Zurvan! Have pity!"

In his life, he'd turned a deaf ear to that final plea more times than he could remember. Yet there was a lessening of his torment when he said the words. He found he could raise his head. He managed to open his eyes.

But through those eyes he saw the crackling skin and the popping heads of the men he'd sacrificed to a ritual he'd failed, in the end, to perform.

And through those eyes he saw the centurion cutting, with sure swordstrokes, the crossties of the bullock.

Then he saw the bullock stagger, and shake his head, and fall to his knees, and finally lurch back on all four feet to run from between the bonfires of the god.

It was a shambling run, a drugged and damaged run. The bullock ran on trembling legs, a run that showed Mithridates the bullock's blistered hide, his singed tail, and his dribbling bowels as the bullock fled the burning bonfires to the edges of the pit.

Mithridates saw the bullock stop where the rock walls rose sheer and high, and heard the mournful bellow even above the roaring of the flames.

Not until then did he notice the centurion coming toward him through the smoke. The Roman short-sword was in the centurion's hand, and it gleamed with firelight, red as blood.

"No!" Mithridates screamed, for now he recognized the sword, if not the man. The sword had slashed him at Cabira, piercing his thigh with its exotic poison.

The centurion came on inexorably through the smoke. The soldier's strides were wide and bold.

Mithridates could barely crawl. But crawl he did, scrambling on his hands and knees, not looking where he was going, simply fleeing this soldier who was his special Reaper, his private Angel of Death, who had followed him through time and death and afterlife, for thousands of years.

The guard from Cabira would kill him again, this he knew. He knew that he'd failed the god Zeus beyond redemption, that he'd failed in the sacrifice beyond repair. Satan would chase him throughout the afterlife, forever, if the death that the centurion brought him was not his last.

But then he realized that Satan would not chase Mithridates, Great King, King of Pontus. Satan would chase Lieutenant Calley, who had failed to perform the sacrifice to raise Zeus, who had disobeyed his orders, and who had killed the demon overseer.

So he gathered his legs under him to sprint away

from the guard from Cabira, from the centurion coming toward him, slashing the air in short strokes of anticipation.

He would run from death, like any man. He stumbled forward: one step, two, in the dense and burning night of smoke.

He tripped on the stone colossus, obscured by the pall. He fell upon it.

His head pierced the veil of white that had so long hovered over the god's loins.

Zeus might be encased in a skin of stone, but Zeus he still and surely was: within the godly veil of white, no wisp of ashen smoke wafted.

Mithridates lay there, his head inside the veil and his torso sprawled across the chest of the silent god, forgetful of the centurion from Cabira at his heels.

He blinked his eyes to clear the tears from the smoke. He raised his hands to knuckle them, for he did not believe what they told him he saw.

There was AE, upon the god's loins, white and whole and human. There was AE, her face swollen with tears, naked and riven, bruised and broken from falling out of the sky in the lion-drawn chariot.

But alive. At least, alive in the way that any of them was, in Hell.

"AE," rasped Mithridates, stretching out his hand to her. "Do you forgive me? Please forgive me, AE. I didn't know. I didn't understand."

The woman turned her tear-stained face his way so that her cheek lay on the god's groin, and said, "Did you do Zeus' bidding? Did you free this travesty to ravage all of Hell?"

"No," he croaked desperately. "No, you must believe me. I did not. He's stuck in his trap of stony skin, forever. Please, AE, say you forgive me."

She closed her eyes. She seemed to shrink. Purple bruises stood out on her face.

For a moment Mithridates was afraid she'd died again, or fainted. "AE!" he begged. "AE! Please . . ."

Her eyelids fluttered. She opened them a crack, and new tears welled out. "I forgive you, Mithridates. It's not your fault. I'm going flying. Want to come?"

There was a sigh that issued from her lips, a sigh that seemed to slide down her nose, which seemed to empty her.

Mithridates had seen people die before. He knew that final settling for what it was. He stretched out his hand to touch her cheek, to say, "I'm sorry," once again.

But the centurion behind him plunged the short-sword into his back and it reached his heart and stopped it before he could get the words out.

Death was sweet in Pontus. Death was flowers and green grass and lamentations. Death was the clean flame and wafting on fertile breezes up to heaven.

Death in Hell was not like that.

Death in Hell was searing hot and icy cold and feeling the fingers of Fate in your vitals. Death in Hell was torment heaped upon torment, for thousands upon thousands of years.

So why was there no Undertaker prodding him? Why was there no milking of his memories? Why was there no pain beyond the pain?

Mithridates wasn't sure. He knew who he was, if

not where he was. And he knew that he'd done well. For once he'd done something right. He'd tricked the Trickster, Father Zeus. If he hadn't saved a life, he'd saved the afterlife. He'd saved Hell itself, and perhaps saved even Heaven.

He wasn't hot; he wasn't cold. He was only Mithridates. He floated in a place where nothing was, and he thought of AE, who'd forgiven him before he died.

Wherever he was, he wasn't frightened. Wherever he was, he no longer felt the fool. He had repented. He had begged the universe for mercy and received it. He had been forgiven for his sins by AE.

Though AE's forgiveness might not be the forgiveness of God Himself, it was the forgiveness of a woman who flew closer to God than he had ever been.

Even if he was doomed to float this way forever, he had cleansed himself of so much evil in those final moments that he did not even hate the centurion who'd murdered him again, after thousands of years.

Hell was a cycle, after all. Thanks to AE, and the guard from Cabira, and the dogtags of crazy Calley, and even thanks to Zuzit, the slain demon overseer, that cycle would continue.

For all the souls who'd not yet found it in their hearts to repent their evil, for all those who'd not yet found someone to forgive them, Hell was the place to be.

In the place where Mithridates floated, it seemed very pleasing to the universe that this was so.